REVENGE SERVED COLD

An Arizona Wine Country Mystery

BY

SUZANNE FLOYD

Lori
I hope you
enjoy this book.
Thank you
Suzanne
Floyd

www.SuzanneFloyd.com
Cover by Bella Media Management

I dedicate this book to my husband Paul and our daughters, Camala and Shannon and families. Thanks for all your support and encouragement.

Revenge Served Cold

When vandals first began plaguing Skylar Bishop's boutique winery in southeastern Arizona, she hoped it was just bored teenagers out for mischief. When it turned violent, she knew better. The middle of the night call confirmed her suspicions. Someone was going to take revenge on her father by ruining her. But who was he? Why had he waited thirty years to come after her father? She'd been building her winery in New Haven for five years, why had he waited until now to exact his scheme of revenge?

Finding the man doing this won't be easy; after all the authorities believe he's dead. Who will look for him or even know who to look for. He's managed to remake himself while staying under law enforcements' radar. As the revenge escalates and becomes more violent, Deputy Greg Wilkenson has to keep Skylar and others he cares about safe from the unknown maniac. Will they figure it out in time?

PROLOGUE

What's he doing here?

He stared out the window as the big man gathered the young woman in a bear hug. His daughter! With a name like that she had to be his daughter. Suddenly he wanted to head slap himself. Why hadn't he put it together before now? That last name, that business. Who else could it be? He'd shut that part of his life off so thoroughly it never dawned on him until this minute. His stomach churned. She was the exact opposite in looks from her old man. He's big and burly, she's petite. He's dark, she's light. It's no wonder he hadn't put them together until now.

When the bear of a man looked up, staring straight at the window where he stood, he felt his bowels loosen. It was irrational but it felt like he was staring right at him, seeing him through the mirrored glass. It was impossible to see into the building with the sun shining the way it was but he couldn't stop the feeling of being exposed. He took several cautious steps back just to be on the safe side.

CHAPTER ONE

"What's wrong, Dad?" He was frowning at the building across the street.

With a little laugh, he gave himself a shake and turned away. "Nothing, just felt like someone was watching us."

I laughed at him. "This is a small town. You know what that's like. Everybody has to know what everybody else is doing. You should be used to it. It's the same way at home."

"So it's still home?"

I smiled up at him. "Always will be, Daddy. This is just where I need to be for now. I'm making some good wine here. I'm even winning some awards."

He beamed with pride. "Of course you are. Chip off the old block." As we crossed the street I hugged his arm. When we came abreast of the window he'd been staring at he slowed down, looking at the window again. "So who's watching us? Maybe a jealous boyfriend?" He suggested hopefully.

I laughed again. This was a topic he visited frequently. "No boyfriend, jealous or otherwise. Sorry. Guys take up a lot of time and energy. I'm just too busy right now. You know how that goes. You have any prospects on the horizon?" I asked, turning the tables on him.

Pink tinted his cheeks, giving me some hope. "Okay, come clean. Who is she? Do I know her? Is she local?"

"Oh, don't you sound small town. What does it matter where someone comes from?"

"Don't change the subject." I scolded. "Who are you seeing?" He had me curious now.

"I just got to town. How about we have a nice lunch before we start the third degree?" If he's the one asking the questions, nothing stands in his way. Now he wants to avoid the inquisition. It could only mean one thing; he's serious for the first time since Mom died more than twenty years ago when I was only three years old.

We barely got seated in a booth at my favorite restaurant when Dad started with questions of his own. "So, Kitten, how are things really going? How's Joe doing? I worry about the two of you over here all by yourselves." As far back as I can remember Dad has called me Kitten as a term of endearment. My heart swelled with the memory.

"Well, let me see. Things are going great. I've released my second year of wine, the vines are healthy, and my trees are all flourishing. I'll have a bumper crop of grapes, peaches, apples and berries. My peach wine has received critical notice. I can barely keep it in stock. I'm about ready to release the blackberry and raspberry wines. Joe is doing great. I wanted him to come to town with me, but you know him. He'd rather stay at the vineyard and work. Town isn't for him." Dad and Joe have been best friends since they were teenagers. Now he's here with me getting my winery and vineyard up and running.

We only stopped talking long enough to give our order to the waitress. Then I looked at him. "Okay, you have all your questions answered. It's time for you to answer a few. You've met someone." It was a statement not a question. "Tell me all about her. Who is she, and how did you meet?" I waited to see if he'd give me a straight answer or dance around it like he always had in the past when there was something he didn't want to talk about.

He cleared his throat several times, stalling for time, and looking decidedly uncomfortable, but I waited him out. I wasn't going to miss this opportunity to get some information about his life for a change. He cleared his throat one last time, sighed and said, "Well, it's more like I finally noticed her. We've known her for years. Molly Peterson." That's all he said, and I waited again. He didn't need to think I was going to let it go at that. I nodded at him, and gave a little finger wave, like "come on." After our food was place in front of us, I had to wait again while he dug into his sizzling hot enchiladas. At last, he drew a breath, and slowed down. He'd been shoveling in the food like he hadn't eaten for a week, and was starving. Finally with a sigh, he picked up where he'd left off.

"At the Wine Association meeting last month we sat together, like always. She was up for an award for her latest reserve selection. When she won, as expected, I started to give her a kiss, like I usually do but..." He stopped, lost in a memory for a minute. Giving himself a shake, he continued. I suspect it wasn't just a peck on the cheek this time. "After the meeting, we went out for dinner to celebrate. We talked about everything and the next thing we knew..." He paused again, and I took a gulp of air. If he was going to tell me something about his sex life, I really didn't want to hear it. But since I asked, how could I stop him?

I should have known better. "When the wait staff started stacking chairs on the empty tables around us, we realized it was after midnight, and the place was closed. We hadn't even realized how late it was until then. I couldn't get the evening, and that simple kiss, out of my mind. Why hadn't I seen her before? Really seen her I mean. She's a wonderful woman, warm, caring, intelligent, funny. We've been seeing each other since. You don't mind awful much, do you, Kitten?"

He looked so worried, I had to laugh. "Oh, Daddy, how could I mind?" I reached across the table, taking his big calloused hand in mine. "You've been alone for a long time. I want you to be happy."

"Not alone, I've had you, and Joe, of course."

"That's not what either of us mean and you know it," I scolded. "When are you going to bring her over?"

"When are you going to come home?" he countered. "Besides, it's not like you haven't met her. We've been neighbors for years."

"Neighbors, yes, and I do like Molly. She's a sweet lady. But this is different. I can't come home right now though. Things are really getting busy. The festivals will be starting next weekend, and I need to be here. Those bring in a lot of tourists. I can't leave Joe here by himself. If he thought he was going to have to deal with people, he'd run away and hide." We both laughed. Joe was the best when it came to the vines, and taking care of the wine as it went through all the stages. He just isn't a people person. "Can you both come over sometime this summer?" I asked. We spent the rest of lunch discussing when Dad and Molly could get away from their wineries. Nothing was decided as we headed out to the cars.

Again, Dad looked over at the bank building, slowing down, trying to see in the blank windows. A shiver traveled up my spine, like someone walking on my grave. "What is it? What do you see?"

"Nothing, I guess that's the problem. Those windows look like eyes staring at me. You don't bank there, do you?"

I shook my head. "No, I do business with the other bank in town."

He gave a satisfied nod, and then turned away, opening the door to his rental. "I'll follow you out to the vineyard."

Dad only stayed overnight. The sole purpose for this quick visit had been to make sure I was all right with him seeing Molly Peterson. As I watched him drive off the next morning, I could only shake my head and chuckle. I'd never seen him that concerned about something this simple, which meant it was a big deal.

I'd followed Dad into town so I could pick up some supplies. We had lunch together again before he left for the airport in Tucson. Driving back through town, my gaze automatically strayed to the large building that had given Dad such an uneasy feeling. It didn't look malevolent in any way. Shrugging, I dismissed the building and all within, turning my thoughts to the business of the day.

The upcoming round of festivals would keep Joe and me busy along with our three full time employees. As yet, our small winery wasn't big enough to hold its own festival, but we benefited from the influx of traffic brought in by the others in the area. The peaches would be ripe in another month and harvest would begin. The people we'd used in the past were already lined up, and eager for the work. Most were either high school students looking to earn money for college or retirees wanting a little extra spending money. Either way the locals enjoyed working in all of the tasting rooms.

CHAPTER TWO

For a busy weekend kicking off the first festival of the season, we were dead. So far we hadn't even had one car stop by in the hour we'd been open. "Joe, take a run down to the road, see if you can find out what's going on." Our vineyard was along the road with the tasting room and house about a quarter of a mile from the main road setting among the soft rolling hills of southeastern Arizona. A sign is posted at the lane leading up to the house and tasting room. It had been there the day before when I'd gone in to town for supplies, but maybe something had happened to it overnight.

Fifteen minutes later, Joe was back, his usual somber expression more angry than somber. "Someone took the sign down, nearly buried it in the grasses at the side of the road." Before he finished speaking, three cars pulled into the yard, laughing people spilling out heading for the door.

"We almost missed you," one young woman giggled. "We drove down this road three times before we finally saw your sign. It's kind of hard to see." She'd obviously been to several tasting rooms already.

"Yeah, especially when someone takes it down," Joe mumbled, as he headed outside.

"Anyone the designated driver?" I asked. "We have soft drinks and bottled water in the refrigerator just for you." Things didn't slow down until the last customer left at five o'clock. Even starting an hour later than usual, we had a good day. My peach wines were gaining popularity and selling fast.

"What happened with the sign, Joe? Did someone hit it?" I asked when we were alone for the evening.

He shook his head solemnly. "Doubt it from the way it was buried. Someone deliberately took it down. I had to hunt for it."

I huffed and puffed for a minute. This was the first time we'd had any trouble since I opened the winery. Had I crossed someone, ruffled some feathers? Several of the other vintners hadn't been happy I was making fruit wines, but I didn't think anyone would try to sabotage my operation. Well, we'll just keep any eye on things; make sure there isn't any more trouble.

Before opening the next morning, Joe went down the lane to check on the sign. I really didn't expect it to be missing again. When he didn't come back immediately, nerves began to eat at me. It's only a quarter of a mile from the house to the main road. He could walk there and back in the length of time he'd been gone. Just as I decided to check on him, he stormed into the room.

"What took you so long? What's happened now?" His dark expression told me something wasn't right.

"The sign isn't just down, it's gone. I looked on both sides of the road, and that dad blame sign ain't anywhere." He stormed out, heading to the shed. "We need another sign." He spent the rest of the morning making certain this sign wouldn't come down easily. Whoever tried to take it now would have a battle. They might even be caught in the process.

Tourists swarmed through the area again, but we had no more problems. If this kept up, we would run out of our peach wine before the season was over. Even the non-alcoholic sparkler I'd been experimenting with was flying off the shelves. The designated drivers enjoyed having something to drink along with their wine tasting counterparts. I was tired but happy when we closed up for the night.

We had three days to get on with the business of making wine without worrying about customers. I spent my time topping off the barrels, replacing what is lost due to evaporation, and racking the barrels to remove the sediment that settled to the bottom. This needed to be done three times a year, and was hard work. Each empty barrel had to be put on the barrel washer before it could be used again. We recycled the water used in the winery, running hoses out to the vines making sure nothing goes to waste.

Joe is the vineyard manager, making certain the vines are well taken care of. With the success of my peach wine, I want to make sure nothing happens to the trees. Joe keeps a careful eye on them as well. My blackberry and raspberry wines will be ready for bottling soon. If they're as popular as the peach, I've got a couple more winners. I'll have to plant more trees to increase the crop output if this keeps up.

There was no more mischief for three days, and I began to relax. Maybe it was just some kids out to see what they could get away with. Being of a more suspicious nature, Joe continued to be on the alert. Our sign remained in place; he'd made certain of that. I doubt even a muscleman could uproot it now.

Thursday morning all seemed ready for another weekend onslaught of tourists when Joe slammed into the tasting room. "How many cases of glasses do you have in here?"

"Six, why?" He looked ready to bite someone's head off. "What happened?" My stomach was suddenly tied in knots.

"Four cases of glasses were smashed in the storage shed. I thought I had things secured better than that." He was taking these attacks personally. This winery is as much his as it is mine. I was the daughter he never had, and he was proud of anything I did, almost as proud as Dad.

Our signature glasses had "Sky Vineyards" and grape clusters resting on clouds above the rolling hills of the area etched in the glass. We had enough in the storage shed behind the winery to make it through the next several weeks, but I'd have to order more to replace what was broken. This wouldn't put us out of business by any means. The nuisance factor was maddening though.

"You took care of everything, this isn't your fault." I gave him a hug. "I'll talk with some of the other owners later to see if they've been having any trouble. Maybe it's not just us." He didn't look convinced.

"Did you call the sheriff? Maybe there will be fingerprints somewhere." He grumbled and nodded. He didn't like having to rely on anyone but himself and God. Besides, having a deputy's car on the property when the tourists showed up wasn't exactly ideal. Still we needed to report this before it went any further. Maybe the deputy would get here before anyone came, or at a time when we weren't busy.

I should have known better. The cruiser pulled in right behind the first carload of tourists, following them from the main road. They were probably having a heart attack about now, especially if they've already stopped at several tasting rooms. Fortunately, the deputy hadn't used his lights or siren.

As the car load of tourists came to a stop in front of the building, the deputy continued around back to the storage shed where Joe would meet him. Thankfully, he'd thought to tell the dispatcher where to have the deputy come. God bless him, he thinks of just about everything.

The group was laughing, slapping the driver on the back when they came into the tasting room. "Usually a police escort is in front instead of in back," one of the women laughed. "Do the cops keep a strict watch on the drivers around here?" They were still laughing, but there was an undercurrent of worry.

"They watch for speeders or anyone driving erratically, that's why several of us have started offering soft drinks or bottled water for anyone willing to be the designated driver. Anyone interested? There's a variety of soft drinks." I pointed to the small fridge in the corner. The driver gave me a grateful look, and went to retrieve a Coke while his friends lined up for tasting. "I also offer a non-alcoholic peach sparkler for tasting." The young driver was interested in that along with his Coke. Maybe a deputy hanging around would put my sparkler on the map along with my wines.

The deputy waited until the tasting room was empty before coming inside to talk to me. The economy of the town of New Haven and the surrounding area was largely dependent on the tourist trade at the many wineries. Everyone worked hard not to cause problems, at least until now. I left Becky, one of the women who helped out in the tasting room, to handle any customers who came in while I went in the winery to talk to the deputy.

"Mr. Barnes tells me this isn't the first trouble you've had." He'd introduced himself as Deputy Greg Wilkinson. "Why didn't you call after the first incident?" He scowled at me. Probably in his early thirties, he was over six feet tall with coal black hair and eyes the blue green color of the ocean. At five feet four inches, I had to look up to make eye contact.

"Until today, I thought the missing signs were the work of teenagers having a little fun at my expense. Breaking into the storage shed, and destroying the glasses puts a different spin on it." He gave a curt nod, apparently satisfied with my answer.

"I lifted some fingerprints. I'll need to take yours for elimination purposes." Until he finished with official business, he remained stoic, barely cracked a smile. As he packed his fingerprint kit away, he gave me a hand wipe to clean my fingers. A smile finally broke out on his rugged features. "My mom and sister really like your wine, especially the peach."

"Thanks! How about you? Do you like it?"

He looked a little embarrassed now, like he wished he'd kept his mouth shut. "It's a little sweet for me. I like a Shiraz or a good Cabernet."

"Well, you'll have to come back when you're off duty. I have a pretty good Shiraz, even if I do say so myself." I couldn't believe I was flirting, but it was fun. Even in high school, I'd been so intent on learning all I could from Dad and other vintners about the wine business; I hadn't taken time for the usual high school activities, dating included. Maybe it was time for a change.

"I just might do that." He winked at me, and turned to leave. "If you ever need help in the tasting room, my sister would love working for you." He winked again, disappearing out the back door.

I stood there for several long moments, fanning myself with my hand. That guy was definitely worth a second look, someone I could get serious about. I jerked upright. Where had that thought come from? I didn't even know him. He's good looking, sure, but looks aren't everything. Just because he's a cop doesn't mean he's a nice guy. My argument with myself did little to discourage my wayward thoughts.

The rest of the day was slow enough that I was able to get some work done checking the wines in the stainless steel vats or oak barrels while Becky handled the tasting room. Several different varietals and blends were about ready for bottling. I wanted to talk to the other owners in the area, but I needed to wait until the tasting rooms closed for the day. Talking about trouble in front of customers wasn't a good idea. My nearest neighbor was three miles away down a winding, rambling back road. Picking up the telephone would be easier, but I wanted to do this face to face. If someone was targeting my winery, I needed to know. If others were also having trouble, it wouldn't be good, but it would still be a relief. It'd mean I hadn't been singled out. Would the others admit they'd been the victim of vandalism? No one wanted to admit to being a victim. If I could talk to them face to face, I'd be able to tell if they denied having any problems. At least I hoped I could.

Being the only female owner/vintner in the area at the time, and making fruit wines, I had met with more than a little opposition when I first moved to New Haven five years ago. Some of the other owners had been interested in buying this property, but Dad had seen to it I got it instead.

I didn't think any of the other owners would try to sabotage my operation though.

Thoughts of Deputy Wilkinson crept into my mind throughout the day, his handsome face intruding when I least expected. I don't have time to get involved in a relationship right now, I reminded myself. Besides, he could be married or have a significant other. But why was he flirting with me then, hinting he'd be back to taste my Shiraz when he was off duty? I argued with myself. Each time he intruded, I had to draw my thoughts back to concentrate on the work at hand.

CHAPTER THREE

Chase Templeton, my nearest neighbor, and one of those who wanted this property, was my loudest critic when I first started here. He said fruit wines were an embarrassment to the industry. He tried to get me to quit or move away. Was it possible he was behind this? Would he cause trouble for me, and then pretend to come to my rescue just to look like the white knight riding in to save the damsel in distress? Just to impress my dad? The answer to that was a resounding yes! The guy was a little slimy.

"You sure you want to go over there?" Joe asked. "That guy ain't what I'd call up front and honest." I was getting ready to go over to Templeton Vineyards to talk to Chase.

"No, but I still need to find out if any other wineries are having trouble. I don't want to be the only one." Thinking about that possibility made my stomach hurt.

"You think he'd tell you the truth? If he thought it would get him on your dad's good side, he'd probably do or say just about anything."

"I know, but I need to know what we're up against. If the others are having the same trouble, maybe the law will pay a little more attention than if it's just us."

"I'll go with you then. He won't pull some of his slimy tricks if I'm around."

I had to laugh. His low opinion of Chase Templeton mirrored mine, even his description. But I shook my head. "I'm not sure he'd say anything if you're around. You've made your feelings very clear where he's concerned. You aren't on the top of his best liked list either. I'll stay out of his reach." He wasn't happy about me going on my own, but he didn't argue further.

Once Chase realized who Dad is, he'd come on strong, flirting, asking me out, offering advice. He'd even made a pass or two. Rebuffing him hadn't cooled his attentions in the least. It wasn't until he tried taking his advances further, that things got a little dicey. I was alone in the winery once when he came over for some innocuous reason. He tried to kiss me just as Joe walked in. Seeing me push Chase away, Joe just about lost it, and Chase ended up with a black eye. He'd threatened to call the sheriff, and have Joe arrested for assault, but I countered with a threat of my own. I'd have him charged with sexual assault. Even if I couldn't make it stick, his reputation would be tarnished. Ever since, the two men have danced around each other with barely concealed dislike, edging towards hatred.

I found Chase working in his winery. Being alone with him in the big space caused my stomach to churn, but I forged ahead. I didn't think he would be so dumb as to try anything again. But to be on the safe side, I kept my cell phone in plain sight. I had 9-1-1 on speed dial. With the cooling evening air, the light breeze had me wishing for a sweater instead of just the light weight T-shirt I had on.

The wide double doors were open. I stopped just inside to survey the scene. It was the first time I'd been in this part of Templeton Vineyards' operation. As I was setting up, I'd visited all the wineries in the state, sampling their wines, checking out the competition. But I hadn't been any further than Chase's tasting room. He kept his operation very close to the vest. We all make wine using the same basic method; just the small nuances and blending make the difference. Templeton Vineyards is a bigger operation than mine, and I've never understood why he guards what he does so closely.

"Spying on me, Skylar?" Lost in thought, I hadn't noticed Chase move behind me until he spoke, causing me to jump in surprise, and maybe a little guilt.

Spinning around, I held my hand over my heart, hoping to calm the thumping. "Oh, hi. No, I'm not spying." I gave a nervous laugh. "I came over to see you." That was the wrong thing to say, and typically Chase took it the wrong way.

"Well, I'm always glad to see you, Skylar." He invaded my personal space, stopping within inches of me. "Why don't we go up to the house? I have a nice Cabernet sitting out. We can share the bottle." He took hold of my arm to lead me off.

Digging in my heels, I remained in one place. If he tried to make me move, it would definitely look like he was dragging me away. Not an image he'd want his employees, who were now aware of our presence, to take notice of. "This isn't a social call. I need to ask you something."

"Ask away. Then we can have some wine and relax." His smile was so smarmy, I wanted to throw up.

"That's not going to happen. I've told you before I came here to open my own winery, not find romance."

"Nothing says you can't do both," he leered. "You've got your winery up and running. Relax and have some fun."

"Is that how you do business, the way you look at your winery?" I cocked my head at him. "Doesn't seem like a very sound business strategy to me. When I find time for romance in my life, I'll look for a man who is interested in me; not someone who is more impressed with who my father is." He had the grace to blush.

"I came over to ask if you've been having trouble here; any vandalism?" I watched his face carefully, trying to judge if he'd tell me the truth.

He frowned, giving his head a shake. "No. Why? What's going on?" Suddenly he was all business.

I hesitated before answering. Was I over reacting? No, I didn't think so. Something told me this could get serious. Huffing out a deep breath, I told him about the three incidents. When I finished he didn't look very worried. "So, am I over reacting?" I asked with a frown.

He took his time before saying anything, considering the possibilities. He finally shook his head. "Something happens to one of us, we all need to take notice. I don't think anyone in the area would attack the wineries. We've added to the overall economy. A lot of people have part time jobs at the different wineries." He was talking more to himself than to me. Looking at me again, a big smile spread across his face. "Well, I'm not sure what's going on, but I'll definitely keep my eyes open. I wouldn't want anything happening to my favorite neighbor." He tried to drape his arm around my shoulders.

Okay, so either he was behind my troubles so he could ride to my rescue, which I'd suspected, or he saw this as the perfect opportunity to do just that. I ducked beneath his arm, heading for the door. "Thanks, Chase, but we'll take care of ourselves. It's good to know things are okay here." I wasn't feeling as cavalier as I sounded.

A shudder of revulsion passed through me as I drove away. Chase was oilier each time I encountered him. His vineyard and winery were nearly twice the size of mine, and I never understood why he felt threatened by my small operation and my fruit wines.

Before heading home I stopped at two other wineries with the same results. No one else was having any trouble. Everyone seemed to think it was teenagers from out of town looking to have some fun at someone else's expense. It felt very personal to me.

Joe was pacing in front of the house when I pulled in, causing my heart to sink. Had something happened while I was gone? Instead of driving around back to park my truck in the garage, I stopped beside him and jumped out. Before I could say anything, he stomped up to me. "What took you so long? Did that bum try something?" His weathered face was creased with worry. He held me away from him, looking for any bruises or signs of violence.

"I'm fine." I patted his hand. "Chase was...well his usual self. Hopefully I've gotten my point across at last."

"What took you so long then? I expected you back over an hour ago."

I looked at my watch, surprised at the time. I'd been gone over two hours, much longer than I expected. "I'm sorry. I stopped at a couple of other wineries to see if they'd had any trouble. Cyndi McMahan and I got to talking. I forgot about the time. I didn't mean to worry you." I told him the general consensus, drawing a deep breath, and letting it out slowly. "I'm not sure I agree."

He nodded, "Feels personal. Don't know why, just does. How you want to handle it?" Joe was never long on conversation, cutting out unnecessary words.

"I'll put the truck away. We can discuss our next move while we eat."

Hoping for a game of catch, Cody, our Golden Retriever, ran beside the truck as I drove around back.. He's our official greeter at the tasting room, and the gentlest dog I've ever had. As a watch dog he leaves a lot to be desired. If anyone broke into the house, he'd lick them to death before they could make away with any valuables. Maybe that's not such a bad thing though.

Joe opened a bottle of the Mead I've been experimenting with while I finished making the pasta salad I'd started earlier. On busy days in the tasting room we don't get much chance to stop for lunch. Today hadn't been like that, and we'd stopped to eat during a lull. That had been hours ago, and we were both hungry now. This was fast, easy and filling; which made it perfect all around.

Sitting down within minutes, Joe forked up his first bite, savoring the mixed flavors of the different pastas and vegetables. "What do you suggest we do first?" I asked.

"The wild animals roaming around would make motion sensor alarms and lights useless. We can alarm the buildings in case we have more trouble there. You going to call Clay?" He didn't look at me when he asked.

"No! This is our winery. We need to take care of things ourselves. I can't go running to Dad every time some little thing crops up."

A lopsided grin curved his lips making them disappear into his bushy mustache. He patted my hand as if to say, "That's my girl."

"Was that a trick question? What did you expect me to say?"

"Just asking. He probably won't like it if we don't tell him."

"As long as we put a stop to it right now, there's no reason for him to ever find out. Besides, he's busy romancing Molly Peterson." I chuckled at the thought. "No sense causing worry when it's not necessary. How do you like the Mead?" I changed the subject. "Is it worth adding more bee hives?" Mead is the original wine from medieval days, made from honey. The hives I'd put out were as much for pollination as they were for making honey for mead. So far I'd only made one batch just to test it out. I'd need a great deal more honey than I currently have if I wanted to go into full production.

He took another sip, and nodded his head. "It's good, but don't go off in too many directions. Concentrate on getting the rest of your fruit wines going. You're doing a dang good job. In another year you'll be ready to take on something else. You can try your hand at the Mead then."

I stared at him for a moment. "Wow." I finally breathed. I didn't know which surprised me more his high praise or the length of his speech. That was the most I've heard him say at one time in all the years I'd known him.

He smiled at me. "Been saving that up for a few years." That's all he said, just went back to eating.

~~~

I didn't sleep well that night; every little noise had me looking out the window, jumping at shadows. I dreaded facing the day with the possibility of more vandalism, but there was little choice. Friday was a busy day for all the wineries, especially when a festival was scheduled for the weekend. At Joe's relaxed expression as he came in for breakfast after checking everything out I sagged against the counter with a sigh of relief. "No problems?" I asked hopefully.

"I haven't been to the vineyard or orchard yet, but close to the house everything is okay."

"Maybe the others were right, and it was just out-of-towners doing some mischief."
~~~

“Maybe.” He didn’t sound convinced, but didn’t argue either.

As expected, the tasting room stayed busy the entire day. We had repeat customers almost every weekend, and I was beginning to recognize a few of them. Dad always kept a video of the customers that came through his tasting room, reviewing it later to memorize faces. People liked to be remembered; it was good customer relations. My customers enjoyed knowing I remembered them, too. Could we use a video outside to find out who was vandalizing us? I wondered. Of course, if we had no more problems, it was a moot question.

“No trouble in here today?” Joe came in through the winery behind the tasting room after the last car load of tourists drove off.

I shook my head. “Everything was fine. How about with you?” During the time we were open to the public we had divided the areas, his and hers. Joe would have a heart attack just thinking about running the tasting room.

“So far, so good.” He was back to short answers, and I had to smile at him.

“But you don’t think we’re out of the woods yet.” It wasn’t a question.

He mulled over his answer, finally giving his head a shake. “Still think something else is going on. Don’t know what, just a feeling.”

This wasn’t reassuring, but I understood what he was saying. If teenagers were just having fun vandalizing things, why would they stop after three days? Why had they picked only our place? I guess time would tell.

Saturday was busy enough that I called in reinforcements. Becky Daniels and I stayed busy all morning, leaving no time for conversation. Mid-afternoon, a young couple joined the crowd at the walnut bar in front of me. “Welcome to Sky Vineyards. Are you both joining us for a tasting, or is one of you the designated driver? We have soft drinks or bottle water." I began my standard speech without really taking notice of them.

"Both tasting." That voice sent a small shiver down my spine. When I looked at him, he gave me a crooked smile, and my stomach did a crazy flip flop, something that had never happened before. But this was no ordinary customer. This was Deputy Wilkinson!

Slightly off balance, I pulled out two glasses, setting them down along with the list of available wines. Trying to remain professional and casual wasn't easy with those ocean blue eyes watching me. "It's six tastings for eight dollars, and you keep the souvenir glass. If you have a glass from another winery, it's five dollars. Do you prefer dry or sweet?" I was talking too fast, way off my usual smooth delivery, but I couldn't keep my brain on track. He was beyond disturbing.

Shifting my focus, I looked at his companion, hoping to be able to concentrate. He was openly flirting with me, so she couldn't be his wife or girlfriend, I told myself. She didn't seem upset by his flirting either. Maybe this is the sister who likes my peach wine. But what difference did that make to me?

"I want your peach. I love it." The pretty blonde was close to bouncing in her exuberance.

"Welcome." I handed back her identification. Pattiann Douglas, different last name; that could mean many different things. Why was I obsessing over this? I tried to drag my wandering thoughts back in line. "What can I get for you?" I looked up at Deputy Wilkinson.

"How about some of that great Shiraz you said you had?"

"Shiraz it is, Deputy Wilkinson." I wanted him to know I remembered him.

"I knew she'd remember you." Pattiann beamed up at him, then turned back to me with her infectious smile. "My big brother is pretty unforgettable." I silently agreed. Trying to remain aloof wasn't easy with him watching me so closely.

I'd learned in Dad's tasting room there's a fine line between allowing the customers to enjoy their selections, and keeping up a careful line of friendly chatter. I left them to their first tasting while I took care of the next couple. When they finished and had a chance to discuss their next choice, I walked back over. "So how was the Shiraz?"

"Every bit as good as promised." I couldn't stop the stupid little grin at his praise. "How about trying that Cab you mentioned next?" By some miracle the crowd had thinned enough for Becky to handle the remaining few, allowing me the opportunity to flirt a little.

As they each made their remaining choices Deputy Wilkinson barely sipped his. My stomach twisted. "Not to your liking?" I really wanted him to like my wines.

"Oh, they're all good," he paused, looking around the room.

Before he could continue, Pattiann leaned across the bar, speaking in a stage whisper. "It wouldn't be good if he was stopped for drunk driving, since he's a deputy." She was no more than five years younger than me, but seemed like a happy-go-lucky kid. I envied her exuberance.

Her brother jokingly jabbed her in the ribs with his elbow. "Next time we go wine tasting you're my designated driver."

"No way! Mom's been to all the wineries. She already knows what she likes. She'll be home tonight, and can drive us around tomorrow." She looked at me expectantly. "You are open tomorrow, aren't you?"

"Sure am. I'll look forward to seeing you both again."

"Especially..." Pattiann started, but her brother poked her in the ribs again, this time not so playfully.

Just then more tourists opened the door, Cody leading them into the room. We all looked at the newcomers, and Pattiann gave a little squeal before moving behind her brother. Cody stopped, looking at her with his big head tilted to one side as if he was asking what her problem was.

With a shake of his head, he turned away, flopping down in the corner with a resigned sigh.

"It's okay that he came in, isn't it?" the forty-ish woman asked nervously. She looked at me then Pattiann.

"It's fine. He comes in and out." I turned to Pattiann. "I can send him outside if you'd rather. He's really very gentle. He won't come near you unless you want him to." She was shaking slightly, clinging to Greg's arm. "Cody, go find Joe." I didn't wait for her to answer, I felt terrible for scaring her. Cody stood up, his tail between his legs, like he'd done something wrong. "Go find Joe." I repeated, trying to sound cheerful so he wouldn't think he was being punished. He obediently padded out the back door.

"He doesn't need to leave." she touched my hand. I'm just being a baby," she whispered. "He's just so...so big! He startled me, that's all. Let's finish our tastings." Her face was pink with embarrassment as she turned away; watching the door Cody had disappeared through.

They left a few minutes later. I wasn't sure they'd be back the next day since they just split a case of wine between them. Giving myself a mental shake, I turned back to the new customers waiting to be served.

Deputy Wilkinson remained in my mind the rest of the day. Why hadn't I seen him until this week? I hadn't had any contact with law enforcement until now, but wouldn't I have seen him around town in the five years I'd lived in New Haven? I'd never seen Pattiann before today either.

~~~

In our small community with nearly everyone depending on the tourist trade, churches in the area held early services so the business owners who were open on Sunday could attend, and later services for those who wanted to sleep in. Joe and I were among the early attendees. I usually fixed a breakfast casserole on Saturday evening, letting it bake while we were gone Sunday morning. We ate as soon as we got home. That would tide us over until the last customer left at the end of the day.
~~~

We'd gone three days without any trouble. I was beginning to believe it had been teenagers looking for thrills like the other owners suggested. If I said it often enough, maybe it would be true.

Joe slammed on the brakes at the end of the lane. "Dag nab it!" For a crusty old man he puts himself out to be, this was as close as I've ever heard him get to cussing. He was staring at our sign beside the road. Someone had spray painted it black. They couldn't tear it down, so they painted over the words. So much for teenagers looking for thrills.

"Take the truck, and go to church," he grumbled. "I'll get another sign put up before it's time to open. At this rate we're going to run out of signs." He started to open the truck door, but I stopped him.

"We can both go to church. We'll be home in plenty of time to fix the sign. We'll need to call the sheriff again, but I don't know what they can do." I was afraid things would escalate to something worse though. I didn't want anyone getting hurt.

At church I asked for special prayers for safety at the winery. Something we didn't understand was going on, and we were going to need all the help we could get. Joe had trouble sitting through the service which was unusual for him. I knew his mind was occupied with what was going on at home.

I was surprised to see Pattiann sitting three rows in front of us, a woman with stylish blonde hair and a rose colored sun dress sitting beside her. Probably her mom, I thought. I couldn't see her face so I didn't know if she'd been to the tasting room before. I wondered where her brother was. Maybe he'd been called in to work. In that case, he definitely wouldn't be coming to the tasting room. I also hoped his absence wasn't an indication he didn't attend church. The ruggedly handsome deputy had managed to instill himself in my thoughts far too often. I didn't have the time or energy right now for anything but the vineyard and winery. I tried in vain to dismiss thoughts of him, and concentrate on what Pastor Rick was saying.

Joe was in a hurry to get home once the service was over. As soon as the benediction was given, he stood up, not waiting for the pastor to proceed down the aisle. He was worried he wouldn't be able to get the new sign up before we opened, and we'd lose business on the last day of this festival weekend.

"You need to change clothes, and get something to eat. There's still plenty of time before we open up."

"I had coffee and a piece of toast before we left. That'll tide me over until I get the sign fixed." He stomped into his end of the house to change. Cody started to follow him, but sensing Joe's mood he turned to follow me instead. Sometimes I think the dog has more intuition and common sense than most humans.

I kept the casserole warm for Joe, and he came in just before I opened the tasting room. "You want me to keep Cody with me today?" he asked. "The deputy's sister was scared of him yesterday."

"He can stay out front. They bought a case so they probably won't be back today." I wasn't sure how he knew they were planning on coming back.

"Saw that young deputy before they left. Said he'd see me today so I figure he'll be here." For the first time since we found the blacked out sign, he gave me a knowing smile that had me blushing.

I turned away. Maybe Cody wasn't the only one who was intuitive around here. Or maybe my feelings were too easily read. "Whatever you think is best. I'll get the door unlocked." I disappeared before my face got any redder.

The last day of any festival is always busy. People want to get their wine before heading home. I didn't have time to think about the good looking deputy for the next three hours. Cody was curled up in his corner when the door opened again. He'd had a busy morning also, greeting everyone, and enjoying all the attention lavished on him. He looked up to see who was coming in. Instead of getting up to greet them, he turned his back, tucking his head down like he didn't want to get in trouble again.

"Oh, Cody, come say hi! He's really a nice boy, Pattiann. He won't hurt you." My heart bounced once or twice before settling down to its normal steady rhythm. Cody's tail thumped against the floor, but he didn't move.

So this was Pattiann and Greg's mom. She'd been in many times, and I knew she liked my peach wine. "Hi, Dora." I tried not to make eye contact with Deputy Wilkinson, unsure whether I had my emotions under control.

"They conned me into being their driver today," she said as she went to the small refrigerator for a Diet Coke. "Greg wanted to be able to drink, and not worry about getting picked up." She reached up, giving his cheek a pat. "He's such a good boy." Now he turned bright red and I laughed.

"Enough, Mom. Drink your soda, have a cracker." He picked one up, stuffing it in her mouth before turning to me, "I want to try that Cabernet again. I only took a sip yesterday."

"You didn't open the bottle last night?" I teased. "What were you waiting for?"

"I opened the Shiraz." It was close to closing time, and they were the only customers left in the room. Most of the other tourists had already headed back to Tucson, Phoenix, or wherever they were from.

When it was obvious there wouldn't be any more customers, I locked the door, but Dora and her family stayed, visiting and enjoying a full glass of wine. Joe joined us, taking out a glass, and pouring some of the raspberry wine I hadn't been serving

"Hi, Joe," Dora's bright smile lit up her pretty face.

He dipped his head in acknowledgment. "Afternoon, Dora. These two belong to you?" My mouth dropped open for a second before I recovered from my surprise. He even knew her name. He usually didn't mix with the customers. What's up with that? I wondered.

"What's that you're drinking?" Dora asked when he held up his glass, examining the rich color. She hadn't taken her eyes off him.

"Raspberry. Not selling it yet.

"Raspberry!" Both Dora and Pattiann exclaimed. "That sounds great." Pattiann added. "Can we try it?"

Joe looked at me for approval. I knew he wanted to pour them each a glass, otherwise why would he have chosen a wine we don't have for sale yet. Hm, was he showing off? This was an interesting turn of events.

Dora looked at her son, "One glass won't hurt, will it?"

He heaved a sigh, like he was so put upon. "A small one," he finally agreed. "But you have to drive extra careful going home. I don't want to end this great day in a heap alongside the highway." He looked at me as he said the last. There was a lot of flirting going on here.

Joe poured everyone a glass of raspberry wine, handing one to me as well. "Wow!" Pattiann exclaimed. "I don't know which I like better, this or the peach. When are you going to start selling it?"

"Not for another month or so. We're waiting for final label approval from the state." The consensus was we had another winner, and they each wanted a bottle once we started selling it. Even Greg liked it.

My heart did the little flutter thing that had been plaguing me lately when Greg suggested we join them for dinner. His sea blue eyes watched me. At the mention of food, my stomach rumbled loud enough for everyone to hear. "I guess that's answer enough," Greg chuckled. "Lock up and let's go. I'm starving."

I thought Joe would decline, but he was as eager as the others to go. Maybe he's more than a little interested in Dora.

The pleasant evening stretched out, and it was after eleven when Joe and I got home. We'd had a wonderful time, but suddenly exhaustion was catching up with me.

Making sure Cody had plenty of food and water, giving Joe good night kiss; I fell into bed, and was asleep before my head hit the pillow.

CHAPTER FOUR

Cody beat me up the next morning, whining at the door to go out. There was no sign of Joe yet which was unusual. When we bought the property, we'd added apartments, giving us our own space, using the original house as the tasting room. Even though we had our own kitchen, we usually ate together for company and convenience. It also gave us time to discuss business.

I followed Cody through the tasting room to see if Joe had started breakfast before I put on a pot of coffee. Cody stopped at the outside door. His urgent barking had me following him down the row of vines to a crumpled body. My stomach clenched. "Someone help. God, please let him be alive." I sent up a whispered prayer. By the time I reached him I was screaming for help, reaching in my pocket for my phone. Dialing 9-1-1, I pulled Joe's bloody head and shoulders into my lap. He let out a low moan as I moved him.

"Nine, one, one, what is your emergency?" The operator's calm voice helped me control my rising panic.

"Send an ambulance to Sky Vineyards."

"What's your name, Miss?"

"Skylar Bishop. Please hurry." She remained calm in the face of my frantic pleading. Joe continued to moan, but at least he was alive.

"What's his name, Skylar? Do you know what happened to him?"

"His name is Joe Barnes, and it looks like someone beat him up." Tears were streaming down my face, and I was praying at the same time I was talking to the operator.

"The ambulance is on the way. A deputy will be there within minutes."

I hadn't even thought of that, now I wanted Greg here. "Which deputy? Send Gre....Uh.. Deputy Wilkinson. He's been here before." I could hear sirens in the distance. The ambulance pulled into the lane in the next minute with a deputy's cruiser right behind. "They're here," I said into the phone. "Thank you." Without waiting for a reply, I closed my phone, turning to the EMT's. "Please hurry. He's hurt."

When Greg stepped out of his cruiser relief flooded through me. "What happened?" He came over, taking my hand.

I told him how Cody had found Joe laying in the field. "You had any more trouble since I was here before?"

"Joe had to replace the sign yesterday."

"What did the deputy say when you called?"

"Well," I hesitated, "we didn't call. It was just a sign."

He scowled at me. "You still should have called."

"Nothing would've been done," I argued. "Would they even send out a deputy, or just take a report over the phone?" He had the grace to blush slightly at my accurate statement. "This is different. They hurt Joe," I said.

"Why didn't you say something last night? We were together all evening but neither of you said anything."

I gave a small shrug. "I guess we both forgot about it." I kept watching the paramedics as they worked on Joe, praying he was going to be all right.

"Tell me what happened here. Do you know when this happened?"

I shook my head. "When we got home last night I went straight to bed. I thought Joe did too. He didn't come in for breakfast as usual, and Cody was going nuts." Tears blurred my vision. Joe pretended to be a crusty old guy, but he's as gentle as a lamb. "Why would someone do this?" I whispered. "Please, God, let him be okay."

I didn't realize I'd spoken out loud until Greg took my hand. "They'll do everything possible for him. At least the nights aren't too cold if he's been out here all night." Little comfort, but it was something.

The paramedics lifted Joe onto a gurney, and moved towards the ambulance. "Is he going to be okay?"

The younger of the two nodded at me. “Some cuts and bruises, and probably a concussion. Do you know how long he was out here?”

I shook my head. They moved the gurney into the ambulance, starting to close the doors. “I’m going with him.” I didn’t give them a chance to argue as I stepped up beside Joe.

The small hospital in New Haven is considered one of the best rural hospitals in Arizona. This time of day there were few emergencies, and the ER was empty. I stood in the corner of the small cubical as the doctor worked on Joe. When he moaned and moved away from the nurse cleaning several of the deeper cuts, my knees nearly buckled with relief. This was the first sign of consciousness he’d shown other than the few moans at the vineyard.

He opened his eyes looking around wildly, trying to sit up. The doctor pushed his shoulders back down. “Take it easy, Mr. Barnes, you have a concussion. Just rest there.”

“Skylar, where is she? Was she hurt?” He didn’t move his head again like he knew it would hurt.

“I’m right here, Joe.” I stepped up beside his bed, taking his hand. “I’m not hurt.”

“Hi, Joe.” I hadn’t been aware Greg was standing outside the examining room until he pushed the curtain aside. He looked at the doctor for the okay to question Joe. At the doctor’s nod, Greg continued into the room. “You feeling up to answering a few questions?”

Joe’s tight grip on my hand was almost painful, but I didn’t care. He was alive, that’s all that mattered. Before answering, he cut his eyes to me without moving his head. “You sure you aren’t hurt?”

“I’m fine. I didn’t know anything happened until Cody starting going nuts. What happened?”

Greg stepped up beside the bed, giving me a look described on every cop show on television as his ‘cop face.’ He wasn’t my friend now, he was all business. “What can you tell me about the attack? When did it happen?”

Joe closed his eyes for a minute, and I panicked thinking he'd passed out or worse. When he opened his eyes again, I sagged against the bed in relief. He looked at me before answering Greg. "Don't go worrying about me, kiddo. I was just trying to get this old brain wrapped around the facts." Looking back at Greg, he explained. "I came outside just before sun up to see if anything happened during the night. Got down the first row of vines and smelled smoke."

My stomach clenched. Someone was trying to burn down my vineyard! "We had some heavy dew during the night," he went on. "Everything was still damp enough the grass just smoldered. Whoever did this doesn't know squat about starting a fire."

Smart enough to get you away from the house, and beat you to a pulp. I kept that thought to myself.

"Kicked the small mound of leaves apart. That's when someone hit me from behind. Knocked me down, and started kicking me."

"Could..." Greg silenced me with a look.

"Did you see who it was? Was there more than one person?"

"Don't know who it was. Dark as the ace of spades that time of morning. My flashlight rolled into the vines. Got the impression there was just one guy though. Couldn't be very big 'cause he couldn't kick very hard." Hard enough to give you a concussion, I wanted to say, but again I kept the thought to myself.

"You think it might have been a teenager?" Greg asked.

Again Joe closed his eyes, going over the events in his mind. "Don't think so," he answered. "That's just a guess though."

"Could it have been illegal aliens, and you came out at the wrong time? Did he say anything?" This close to the Mexican border, we've had our share of problems with illegals coming through the area. Joe started to shake his head, only to wince at the pain and stopped moving. "Just a couple of grunted words I couldn't make out as he kicked me, but I didn't get any accent. This seemed more personal." Greg continued to ask questions long after I ran out of things to ask. I guess that's why he's a cop, and I'm a vintner.

The doctor wanted to keep him overnight for observation, but Joe wouldn't hear to it. "I can rest at home just as good and it won't cost me a dime," he grumbled. When I promised not to let him out of his easy chair, the doctor finally agreed to discharge him.

Since I came in the ambulance with Joe, Greg drove us back to the winery. Joe balked at being stuck inside all day, and I finally relented. "You can sit on the porch, but you're not working the rest of the week." He started to protest the directive, but I held up my hand. "Don't argue. I thought I'd lost you this morning." My throat clogged with tears, and I had to stop talking for a minute. This man meant so much to me. The thought of losing him was almost as unbearable as the thought of losing Dad.

"The tasting room isn't open again until Thursday. What needs to be done anywhere else, Juan and I can handle." Juan Garcia came to work for us shortly after we bought the place when he was just fifteen.

His parents were here illegally, but Juan was born in Arizona. Last year his folks went back to Mexico hoping to eventually make it here legally. I admire them for that move. Unlike so many others here illegally, they didn't expect special treatment just because they've been here for years, and have children who are citizens. If the opportunity comes up, I'll sponsor them so they can come back legally this time. Juan has been soaking up as much knowledge about wine making as he could, hoping someday to be a vintner himself.

"Cody will keep you company," I told Joe now.

"Least he won't talk my ear off," Joe grumbled in his usual fashion.

Word travels fast in our small community, and it wasn't long before people started dropping by to check on Joe, especially the older single women who saw Joe as an eligible bachelor. When Juan and I stopped for lunch, Joe was still sitting in his chair on the porch where I left him. He wasn't any happier than when he first sat down, but now he had something new to grumble about.

"Blame fool women," he groused. "Think just because a man's got a bump on his head, he can't see past their casseroles, cakes and pies to know what they're up to."

"What are you talking about?" I sat down on the porch railing, swinging my foot.

"Go take a look in my kitchen," he directed. "We're not going to have to cook for a month if this keeps up." He followed me inside. I gasped at the number of dishes and pans sitting on the counter. "Look in the refrigerator," he said.

It was just as full, and I had to laugh. "You didn't know you were so popular, did you?" Red crept up his neck, and he turned away hoping I wouldn't see.

"Blame fool women," he grumbled again. "You're gonna have to put some of this stuff in the freezer so it don't go bad." I heated up one of the casseroles, and Juan joined us while I told Joe all we'd done in the short time we'd been home from the hospital.

He still wasn't happy about being stuck on the porch, but didn't argue this time when I headed out. I'd called Dad after I got Joe settled the first time. He wasn't happy about that either, but Dad needed to know. He was ready to get on the first plane and come over, but I forestalled him. There was nothing he could do here. He wasn't happy we hadn't told him about the earlier trouble either. Again there was nothing he could've done. At the time, I wasn't certain this was anything more than bored teenagers looking for some excitement. Now I knew better.

By six o'clock, Juan and I finished in the winery, and were ready to call it a day. Days were long this time of year. Joe usually spent his time in the vineyard, pruning the vines, and checking soil samples. Today, Juan had worked alone.

While I'd been at the hospital with Joe in the early hours of the morning, Juan had been looking after the vineyard. I asked if he wanted to share another casserole with us, but he was off to see his girlfriend. At twenty, he wasn't much younger than me, but he had a ton more energy than I had today.

There were even more casseroles, cakes and pies tonight than there'd been at noon. I shook my head in wonder. After leading a relatively solitary life for the last five years, suddenly we were Grand Central Station. Who knew Joe was such a chick magnet. I laughed at the image.

After putting a casserole in the oven to heat, I sat down with Joe on the porch to enjoy the early evening breeze. A car I recognized pulled into our lane. "Uh oh, another one of those 'blame fool women.' Maybe I should go tell her to take her casserole or cake home. Like you said, we have enough food to last a month." I had to work hard to keep a straight face.

"Don't be rude! You were raised better than that." His sun-weathered face had suddenly taken on a pink tinge as Dora stepped out of her car, holding the obligatory casserole dish.

"I heard what happened, but I couldn't get away. Are you all right?" She hurried up the steps to the porch, ignoring me. Belatedly, she caught herself, smiling sheepishly. "How are you doing, Skylar? You weren't hurt?"

"No, I'm fine, Dora." It was hard not to laugh at these two. I don't know how long they'd known each other, but there was definitely chemistry brewing between them.

She handed me the dish. "Just a little something so neither of you has to worry about cooking, at least not tonight."

Joe's warning glance spoke volumes. He didn't want Dora to know she wasn't the only one bringing food, and certainly not the first. The dish was still warm. "Would you like to stay?" I asked. "It looks like there's plenty."

"If you're sure it wouldn't be too much for Joe." The question was directed at me, but she didn't take her eyes off him.

"It'll be good for him to have someone to talk to besides me." I excused myself and went inside. I had one casserole to take out of the oven, and another to put in to keep warm while I tossed a salad and set the table. To my surprise, there was a salad in the fridge, thanks to one of those 'blame fool women.' I chuckled to myself. It looks like their efforts were in vain. Joe's affections were otherwise spoken for.

When I came back outside, we had another visitor. We were going to need another place at the table. "Hi, Greg."

He shot to his feet as I came out on the porch. "Hi. How'd it go today? Have any more trouble?"

"I think we've had our share for the entire year. Did you find out who did this?"

He shook his head. "There were plenty of footprints, but nothing to lead us to a suspect. Other than that and the pile of leaves, there was nothing."

Another dead end, I told myself with a sigh. Whoever was doing this certainly knew how to fly below the radar. It was time to change the subject. "Where's Pattiann?" She was the only one missing from last night's group.

"At the hospital," Dora answered, sounding like it was routine, but my stomach churned uneasily. "She wanted to come over to check on Joe, but her shift isn't over until eleven."

"Shift?"

"She's a nurse." The simple explanation brought my heart rate back down. After what happened to Joe, I didn't want anyone else dragged into this, whatever 'this' was.

"I think everything's ready to eat. You staying?" I cocked my head at Greg. "There's plenty."

In my entire life, I'd never seen Joe so animated during dinner. A concussion can bring on some personality changes, but I didn't think it would happen this fast.

Besides, all his attention was focused on Dora. It brought a smile to my heart. It was about time he found someone to love.

Dora offered to help clean up when we finished, but I sent her outside with Joe. Whatever was brewing between them, I was willing to help foster it along. Besides, Greg stayed inside to help me. His offer of help I didn't decline.

Settled back on the porch a few minutes later with chilled glasses of raspberry wine, I groaned when Chase Templeton's truck came roaring down the lane. Joe grumbled, but stayed put instead of taking off at the first sign of Chase the way he usually did. Beside me, Cody's grumble echoed Joe's. Who knew a dog could grumble.

"Not someone you want to see?" Greg lifted an eyebrow at me.

"Just an insufferable neighbor."

"Insufferable fool," Joe amended, "wouldn't give us the time of day until he discovered who her daddy is."

I wanted to kick him. Why did he have to become so chatty now?

Chase jumped out of his truck, running up the steps sliding to a stop at the sight of Greg sitting casually beside me, holding a wine glass. Eyeing Greg's uniform, Chase looked at me. "Did something else happen today? I heard what happened to Joe."

"I'm fine," Joe growled. "A bump on the head and a few cuts isn't going to stop me." It came out like a challenge. It was his opinion Chase would do just about anything to get his hands on my land, and keep me from making my 'froufrou' wines. I didn't think Chase would go so far as to assault someone though. He'd rather date the land owner; maybe even marry her to get access to the land and her father.

"This is Deputy Wilkinson and his mom, Dora. They're friends. They came by to check on Joe. Chase Templeton, our neighbor." I made the introductions, wishing Chase would leave, but he settled down on the top step like he was here to stay.

"And friend," Chase added pointedly. "I came as soon as I could get away. You weren't hurt, were you, Skylar?"

"As you can see, I'm fine." I didn't know what else to say. Conversation lagged for several awkward moments.

"Did you catch the perp who did this?" Chase asked, breaking the drawn out silence. Perp? There are entirely too many cop shows on TV.

Greg took his time answering, slowly sipping his wine. "Still working on it. Her place is going to be under surveillance to make sure it doesn't happen again." Was that a warning?

"I live next door; I'll keep an eye out. I don't want anything happening to Skylar." I bristled at his possessive tone but kept quiet. There's time enough later to tell him to back off.

Joe didn't bother to wait. "Your house is three miles away. What do you think you could see?" I suspected Greg's sudden coughing fit was more to cover up a laugh than a real need to clear his throat.

Silence stretched out again, and again Chase was the one to break it. Nodding to the glass in Greg's hand, Chase looked at me and asked, "One of your wines?"

"We only serve our wines here," Joe answered for me. It was my turn to cough, covering up a laugh.

"I'd offer you a glass, Chase, but I know how you feel about my fruit wines. Sorry, it's all I have open tonight." Fortunately that was the truth. The partial bottles left over yesterday I'd sent home with Dora and Pattiann. His cheeks turned pink enough for all to see even in the dim porch light.

"That's okay. I wouldn't want to drive after I had anything to drink." His superior attitude was obviously to impress Greg, who was still in uniform and holding a glass of wine.

"I'm off duty," Greg stated, like that made a difference.

The silence stretched out again. Dora and Greg weren't in any hurry to leave. It was up to Chase to do us the honor and take off. After several long minutes with no one saying anything, Chase seemed to get the message and stood up. "Well, Joe, I'm glad you're doing okay. Skylar, if you have any trouble in the night, I'm only a phone call away. I can be here in minutes." The implication clearly stating it would take law enforcement a lot longer.

"Thanks. It's nice of you to offer. And thanks for stopping by." It was such an awkward moment. I sort of felt sorry for him; but not enough to encourage him to stay.

"That was embarrassing." Dora said what we were all thinking once Chase drove off. "Who is that guy?"

"A big bag of wind who thinks he's a lot more important than he really is," Joe stated.

I patted his arm. "He owns Templeton Vineyards," I said to prevent Joe from saying anything really nasty. "You haven't lived in New Haven very long, have you?" It was time for a change of subject.

So far, Greg hadn't said much since Chase first arrived, but I could feel his watchful gaze on me. "I started working for Santa Cruz County about eight months ago," he finally spoke up. "Mom and Pattiann moved here after that, so we could all be close."

"After burying two husbands," Dora said, picking up the story, "I didn't think I'd ever want to go through that again, so it's been just the three of us for a long time. I've begun to rethink that though." She looked at Joe whose face was bright red. She gave a self-conscious laugh, before continuing, "While Greg was at Northern Arizona University, we lived in Flagstaff. By the time he graduated and started working for the Coconino County Sheriff's Department, Pattiann was at NAU, so we were all still together. When he came down here, Pattiann had her nursing degree. It didn't feel right for him down here by himself and us in Flagstaff, so we found jobs here. This is a beautiful area, and we're enjoying the small town atmosphere."

"Where do you work?" Something told me none of this was news to Joe.

"At National Bank. I'm a loan officer." The bank that freaked Dad out when he was here last week, I thought. I still didn't know what that had all been about.

Greg set down his empty wine glass and stood up. "I guess we'd better be getting home, Mom, and let them get some rest. Thanks for dinner and the wine. Both were good."

"Thank your mom for dinner," I laughed. "She brought it over. Thanks for that, Dora. I'll get your dish back to you."

"There's no hurry, Honey" she assured me. "I'll probably see you this weekend." She looked at Joe as if for confirmation. I was going to have to grill him. He was keeping secrets from me.

Greg stepped close to me, his voice low. "Now that you've heard my life history, it's your turn to tell a little of yours. I look forward to hearing it." He winked at me, heading down the steps to his truck, whistling a little tune.

I released the breath I hadn't been aware I was holding until that instant. For just a minute, I thought he was going to kiss me. I wasn't really sure how I felt about that. I kept telling everyone, including myself I didn't have time for a relationship. Was that just an excuse not to get involved? That was something I'd have to examine at a later date.

As soon as they pulled out of the lane, Joe stood up. "Well, I'm calling it a night. I'm a little tired. It's been a hard day. Everything all buttoned up around here?"

"Not so fast." I took his arm. "How long have you known Dora? And why didn't you tell me about her?"

"There's nothing to tell." My disbelieving look and his red face put the lie to that statement. "She's been to the tasting room some," he stated the obvious. "She was out looking at the vineyard once, and asked a few questions about wine making. I gave her a tour."

"You gave her a tour?" I couldn't believe what I was hearing. He had never voluntarily interacted with any of the customers before.

"You saying I don't know enough to give a tour?"

"Don't go changing the subject. You know enough about this winery and making wine in general, to open and operate one of your own. This place is as much yours as it is mine and you know it. We're talking about you giving a tour to a stranger. You like her, don't you." I didn't give him a chance to deny it.

His normally ruddy cheeks got even redder, and he dipped his head to avoid looking at me. "Guess I'm a little old for something like that."

I put my arms around him, squeezing him tight. "You're never too old for romance. I think it's wonderful."

He hugged me back, quickly stepped away. He isn't one for showing his emotions. "Time to turn in." He quickly turned away, but not before I saw the smile on his face.

I chuckled all the way inside, a warm glow filling me. Dora is a nice lady, and if Joe likes her, so much the better. It was high time he found someone.

CHAPTER FIVE

When I came out the next morning, everything was as it should be. Thankfully there hadn't been any more trouble. Unbeknownst to me, Joe had arranged with Juan and another employee to have them patrol the vineyard and orchard overnight. I guess that was one of the reasons he was so anxious for me to go inside last night. He didn't want me to know and be worried.

There was no keeping Joe on the porch again. As soon as he finished breakfast, he headed outside. "Not waiting around for more blame fool women to come around plying me with food again today," he grumbled, letting the screen door slam shut behind him.

I laughed out loud. There was one 'blame fool woman' who could bring food every day and he wouldn't complain. I felt sorry for all those other women. Their efforts had been wasted.

It was a beautiful spring morning, the temperature crisp with the promise of a sunny day. Drawing in a breath of the fragrant air, I expelled it on a sigh. Chase pulled into the lane stopping my enjoyment of the morning. Joe didn't want the women hanging around, and I didn't want Chase here.

He stepped up on the porch beside me. "No trouble last night? I had a few of my men keeping watch."

I bristled at the presumption that I needed his protection. "That's not necessary. Joe and I can look out for ourselves."

"Joe didn't do very well the other night. Where is he? Still taking it easy?" He looked around. "Your dad coming over to check on things?" he asked hopefully.

I ignored his question about Dad. "Joe's out back." A niggling doubt pricked at my mind. Was Joe right? Did

Chase have something to do with our trouble? I didn't want to believe he'd do something so underhanded, but he was awfully anxious to impress Dad. If he thought coming to my rescue would do the trick, he was sadly mistaken. "Don't bother having your men watch our place. We're taking care of everything." There was nothing he could find out about our operation that he could or would use, but I didn't want him or his employees around when we weren't here. It felt too much like spying.

"Does your deputy friend have any suspects?" His tone dripped sarcasm.

"They're still investigating. Can you think of anyone who would do something like this?" I raised an eyebrow questioningly.

"No, of course not! Why would you think that?"

"Just asking," I shrugged. "You know more people than I do. I thought maybe you heard someone wanted me gone bad enough to try something like this." He hadn't hidden his view on my choice of wines early on.

"I don't know anyone who would hurt Joe."

Me thinks thou doth protest too much, I thought, quoting Shakespeare. If it meant getting his hands on my land without alienating Dad, I figured he'd give it a try. "The sheriff's department is keeping an eye out for anyone who shouldn't be here. I wouldn't want anyone to get in trouble." I hoped he got the message.

"I was just trying to be a good neighbor," he pouted.

"Of course you were and I appreciate it. I just don't want any of your employees getting into trouble for being a Good Samaritan." The biblical reference seemed to fly over his head, but he was slightly mollified. I let the silence stretch out like I had the night before. I didn't have more to say.

Finally taking the hint, he turned to go. "I need to get back. I just wanted to make sure everything was okay here. See you." I watched him go, still suspicious of his motives.

As Chase turned onto the road, a big car I didn't recognize turned into our lane. The tasting room wasn't open today so it wasn't a customer. When the man stepped out of the passenger side I realized the town mayor was paying me a visit. The man driving the car stayed behind the wheel.

"Good morning, Miss Bishop." The man had a pompous air about him. At least six feet tall with a broad chest and a flat stomach that suggested he stuck to a heavy workout regime. His light brown eyes were solemn like he was here to impart sad news. He had a bushy crop of snowy white hair that was never out of place.

He'd been the mayor of New Haven since before Joe and I moved here. Although I'd seen him in town many times, this was the first time he'd spoken to me. I wondered what the occasion was. It wasn't an election year.

"Good morning, Mayor Brady. How are you this morning?"

"Please, call me Roland; there is no need for formality in our little town. Do you mind if I call you Skylar? It's such a pretty name." His smile was rather oily. Before I could answer, he continued. "I heard about the attack here yesterday, and I wanted to stop by to see how Joe's doing. I don't like any of my citizens being attacked like that." He joined me on the porch, sitting down in one of the wicker chairs without waiting for an invitation.

"He's doing fine, Sir...er Roland. Thank you for asking." We aren't citizens of New Haven, and we can't vote for him, so why is he here, I wondered.

"Well, I am glad to hear that. I was shocked when I heard he had been hurt. I understand this is not the first trouble you've had." Again he didn't wait for me to comment before going on. "I had a little talk with Sheriff Stevens about this. I will not stand for crimes being perpetrated against the citizens of my town. He is going to make this a top priority." He had a precise way of speaking that was very distinctive.

"Ah, thank you." I wasn't comfortable with his sudden familiarity. "I'm sure Sheriff Stevens takes this seriously also." I didn't want to point out that we weren't citizens of 'his' town.

"Well, I won't take up any more of your time." He stood up. "I just wanted you to know that even though you don't technically live within the town limits of New Haven, I consider you and Joe one of us." He marched down the steps, and the two men drove away without another word. Watching, I could see the broad smile on the mayor's face as his driver reversed and drove off. How does the mayor of a town as small as New Haven warrant having a driver?

"What did that pompous fool want?" Joe came around the corner of the house in time to see the tail lights from the mayor's fancy car disappear down the lane.

I shook my head, not really sure. "He said he'd heard what happened to you, and wanted to make sure you're all right. He won't stand for 'crimes against the citizens of his town'." I made air quotes emphasizing the mayor's words.

Joe laughed. "He must be getting ready to run for reelection. Can't think of any other reason he'd come here."

"But we can't vote for him," I objected. "We can't help him at all."

Joe shrugged, dismissing the man. "He thinks it will make him look good to those who can vote for him."

~~~

There was no more trouble, but Joe kept a close eye on everything. On Thursday morning he checked to make sure no one had tampered with our signs. With the tasting room open, we both wanted to make sure people could find us.

Greg and Pattiann were our first customers. She'd stopped by each day before going to work, checking Joe's progress, and making sure he wasn't over doing it. I hadn't seen Greg since the night of the attack when Chase dropped by. I hope he hadn't gotten the impression there was anything between Chase and me.

"You checking up on Joe?" Greg wasn't in uniform so maybe he had the day off.
~~~

"Our days off don't always coincide, but they do today," Pattiann confirmed for both of them. "We just came to visit before you got too busy. How is Joe doing? Mom would never forgive me if I didn't check." She smiled happily. I hadn't been sure how they felt about their mom and Joe keeping company, but it looked like they were okay with it. At least Pattiann was. Greg still hadn't said anything.

"He's doing fine. I can't keep him down. He says he's too hardheaded for a little bump to do any damage. At least the hardheaded part I believe," I added with a laugh. "You want to try anything? I think there a few wines you haven't tried yet."

Greg shook his head. "Can't. I have court this afternoon."

I frowned. "I thought this was your day off."

"The court doesn't care if it's your day off. You just show up when you're scheduled. No more trouble here?"

"Nothing so far. I've seen the patrol cars passing several times. I really appreciate it." I smiled at him, hoping to warm up his attitude. He didn't seem as friendly today as he'd been earlier.

"No problem; got to keep our citizens safe." My heart took a dive. If that's all it was, his flirting hadn't meant anything.

Two could play his game. "As one of the citizens in question, I appreciate the effort." My tone was as cool and impersonal as his. Had the mayor's little talk with the sheriff cooled Greg's interest in me?

From the look Pattiann gave the two of us, she was as confused as I felt until Greg winked at me. My heart skipped a beat, then caught up with itself. I didn't know him well enough to know when he was teasing, but that wink was definitely playful.

Cody followed customers into the room, stopping when he noticed Pattiann standing at the bar. With what would be called a resigned sigh from any human, he turned heading back outside.

"I'm sorry, I thought he was allowed inside," the young woman said. "Shouldn't I have let him in?"

Pattiann looked embarrassed. "He can come in. It's just me." Her voice held a slight quiver. "He can come in," she said again. "We need to get going anyway." Looking back at me, she asked, "Is it okay if we come by tonight? I know Mom wants to come over to make sure Joe's doing okay."

"Of course it's okay. Why don't the three of you come for supper? Ah... If you don't have other plans, that is," I quickly qualified.

Greg winked again. "I can't speak for Mom and Pattiann, but I'll be here. See you then." Just like that, the man I'd flirted with over the weekend was back. I don't know if he's just moody, or if he was teasing me.

For the next week Dora was either at our house in the evening, or Joe went to hers. I couldn't quite wrap my mind around the change in him. First Dad finds love with Molly Peterson, now Joe seems to have found love with Dora. Things always go in threes. I wondered if I was next. Butterflies took up residence in my stomach. Greg hadn't been over as often as Dora because of his job, but when he could, he stopped by even if only for a few minutes. So far he hadn't asked me out. Maybe it was because our jobs kept both of us busy, usually at opposing times. At least I was hoping that was the reason.

Friday night Joe was only gone a half hour when his truck came roaring down the lane, gravel spraying from under the tires when he stopped in front of the porch instead of driving around back to the garage. My heart sunk. Did they have a fight? I wanted him to find happiness.

Getting out of the truck, he slammed the door, and stormed up the steps. "Templeton's spreading rumors about the two of you."

"What do you mean 'rumors about us'? There is no us!"

"He was telling people at the bank he's dating someone, 'accidentally' letting it slip that it's you."

"What?!" I came out of my chair like it was suddenly on fire "That wouldn't be the bank where Dora works, would it?" At his curt nod, I stomped down the steps. "I hope Dora didn't believe him." My stomach was churning. From the look on Joe's face, she probably had some doubts about me now. I held out my hand for his keys.

"Need some company?" He smiled for the first time since he got home.

"You're welcome to come with me, but this is my show."

Chase was sitting on his porch much as I'd been when Joe came home from Dora's. "Skylar, Joe. What a nice surprise. Sit down and join me in a glass of wine."

"This isn't a social visit."

"No?"

"No." I just stared at him to see if he had any idea how mad I was.

"Was there more trouble at your place today? I hope no one else got hurt." He stood up, a look of concern on his face.

"Trouble of a different kind. Someone is spreading rumors."

"What kind of rumor?" His words were innocent enough, but he shifted from one foot to the other, his eyes looking anywhere but at me.

"Did you tell people at the bank today that we're dating?"

His face got red and scrunched up. "Noooo." He drew the word out like in a cartoon.

Joe took a step forward, but I put my hand on his arm to keep him from saying or doing anything. It couldn't be any more obvious that Chase was lying. I wanted to see how far he'd go to get out of this. "That's not what I heard. Would you like to explain it to me?"

"No." He was still having a hard time keeping his face still.

"So you're not going to defend your actions."

"I can't defend against something I don't know anything about." He sounded so sincere and superior.

For just a moment, I had second thoughts about who started the rumor. Was someone else behind this? But Chase worked his mouth back and forth, his eyes still looking anywhere but at me. No, he was lying through his teeth. "I have it on good authority that you were telling people we're dating."

"That's not what I sa...uh. No, I didn't say that."

"What exactly you did say? I'd like to hear it for myself."

"Uh, well, I don't remember exactly what I said. I was just talking to some of my friends. I wasn't talking to the employees." He knew precisely who had overheard him.

I could imagine how he was talking. Everything about Chase was overblown, including his voice, loud. The truth stretched to the breaking point. Even people in the back room probably heard what he said. "Just give me a brief idea of what you said about us."

"Well, I might have said something about us being friends. I can't help it if people took it the wrong way. I can't control what others think."

"If you weren't talking about me, no one would have misunderstood you. We're neighbors with competing vineyards. That's all. You could have cost us some friends."

"That deputy?" he asked scornfully. "He isn't even in the business. What does he know about anything?" Joe took another step towards him, his fists clenched at his sides.

"Dora and her family are friends of ours. What difference does it make if they aren't in the wine industry? If I hear any more about us dating, you're going to find yourself in more than a little hot water."

"This is still a free country. I can say anything I want." His chin jutted out defiantly. He put me in mind of a little boy stomping his foot when he didn't get his own way.

"Not when it's a lie!"

He clamped his lips into a straight line, and didn't say any more.

I spun around, and stomped back to the truck. It hadn't been a very satisfactory confrontation. He still thought he had the right to say anything he wanted, even if it was a blatant lie. Protesting it in public would only cement the thought in the minds of others. I didn't care about the rest of the town, but I didn't want Dora and her family to think I was seeing Chase; or anyone else for that matter.

I wasn't sure if anything might develop between Greg and me, but there was definitely something brewing between Joe and Dora. I didn't want something said about me to reflect poorly on him.

"Where does Dora live?" I needed to explain that Chase had lied.

"You really didn't need to come over and explain, Skylar," Dora said when we showed up on her doorstep a few minutes later. "Joe said it was a lie and I believe him." She smiled at him, reaching out to take his hand. A blush crept up his neck, but he accepted her hand in his.

"I'm glad, but I wanted you to hear it from me also. Chase is nothing short of a big bag of wind."

"Not exactly what I'd call him," Joe muttered, causing both of us to laugh, breaking the tension I was feeling.

We didn't realize how late it was getting until Pattiann came in the back door. She was surprised to see me, but not Joe. He was becoming a steady fixture at their house like Dora was at ours. I couldn't believe I'd only known them a few weeks. I wasn't sure how long the flirtation had been going on between Dora and Joe.

CHAPTER SIX

The train whistle from my cell phone ring tone startled me out of a sound sleep, my heart pounded in my chest. Reaching for the phone, I looked at the clock. Two o'clock in the morning! This wasn't a time for social calls. It had to be an emergency. My only thought was something had happened to Dad.

"Hello? Dad, is everything okay?" In my rush to answer the phone, I didn't look at caller ID.

A harsh laugh grated on my nerves. "Not hardly, Skylar. I wanted to let you know you can thank your old man for all the troubles you've been having lately. It's time he paid for what he did to me." The voice was gravelly, not one I remembered hearing before. He was trying to disguise it.

"Who is this?"

"Wouldn't you like to know?" He gave another harsh laugh. "Don't worry about who this is. Just know I'm watching you. Your troubles have just begun."

"I don't know what you're talking about. Dad never hurt anyone. Go sleep it off." I pushed the end button on my cell phone. I wasn't going to listen to some drunken nut ball in the middle of the night. Before I could look up the number the call came from, my phone rang again. This time I checked caller ID, "Blocked number." Of course, it wouldn't be any fun if I knew who was calling. Did I dare ignore it? It kept ringing, and finally I answered it. "What do you...?"

"Don't you ever hang up on me again," he interrupted, his voice raised in a rage. "You listen to me! Your old man ruined my life, now I'm going to ruin yours. Everything you've worked for is going away, and you can thank your old man for that. If there was real justice in this world, it would be your old man who ended up with nothing." Each time he said 'old man' there was a sneer in his voice.

"What did my dad do that you hate him so much?"

"He ruined my life," he screamed. "If it weren't for your old man I'd be a millionaire by now instead of..." He caught himself before saying too much.

"Instead of...? What?" I asked, hoping he'd fill in the blank.

"Never mind!" he snapped. "Just know that he ruined my life."

"How? When?"

He drew a ragged breath, and I could hear him swallow hard several times before finally answering. "Thirty years ago I started my own bank in Central City. Your old man accused me of embezzling from him and several other clients."

"Did you do it?"

"That's beside the point," he ranted.

"No, that is the point." I tried to keep my voice calm, hoping he'd say something that would tell me who he was, and where he was calling from.

"Shut up! I'm doing the talking here. Your old man told me to give everyone back their money, or he'd turn me over to the cops. It bankrupted me. It took me years to make myself over. Now it's your turn to have what you've worked so hard for taken away from you."

"I haven't done anything wrong. Just what do you think you can do to me?"

"I can do plenty. Barnes isn't the only one who can get hurt," he sneered, chuckling when I gasped. He was enjoying the little game he was playing. "That's right; I'm the one behind all your troubles. But this is just a taste of what's to come. You'll never know when I'm going to strike next, or who will be my next victim."

"You've just admitted to assault. What's to stop me from calling the sheriff?"

"Well, you don't know who to tell the sheriff I am," he sneered.

"All I have to do is ask Dad about what you're saying. I'm sure he'll remember your name, and what you look like."

His harsh laugh was just as grating as it had been the first time I heard it. "Oh, that guy was dead and buried a long time ago, so that's not going to help you in the least. I told you I had to make myself over, and I did, from the ground up, so to speak."

"You're the one who broke the law. It seems to me Dad cut you a break. If you hadn't committed a crime, you wouldn't have lost everything."

"I said to shut up!" he shouted. "You listen to me. I'm just letting you know what you have to look forward to. Enjoy what you have for now, because it won't be yours for long. Before I'm through with you even your friends will be gone." He slammed the phone down causing me to pull mine away from my ear.

My hands were shaking so hard I had trouble finding the night stand to put the phone down. Was this guy serious? Oh, yeah, I silently answered my own question. He was dead serious. Somehow I had to figure out who he was and stop him. One thing was certain though, I wasn't going to stand around, and let him ruin the winery, and hurt my friends. Joe and I would protect what was ours.

I had to call Dad, I had to tell Joe. Looking at the clock, I collapsed on the bed only to get back up to pace across the room. The phone call had lasted only five minutes. It felt like he had raged at me for hours.

By the time it was late enough to call Dad, I was dressed, and on my third cup of coffee. I could hear the panic in his voice as he answered the phone. I guess it wasn't that late after all. "Kitten, are you all right? Is Joe okay? What happened?" Since the incident with Joe, he'd called every day to make sure we were both okay.

"We're fine. I just need to ask you about something." I'd gone over several different ways to tell him about the call, but they were all gone from my head, and I just blurted out. "Do you remember an incident about thirty years ago when some guy embezzled from you?"

He was quiet for a moment, as though dredging it up from his memory banks. "Sure, but how did you hear about it? Did Joe tell you?"

"No, he's here in New Haven."

"Who's there?"

"The guy who embezzled from you."

"Huh?" He sounded confused.

"Here, Dad, in New Haven." I repeated.

"That not possible. He's dead."

"So that's what he meant." I wasn't aware I'd spoken out loud, my mind going over the conversation. Finally Dad's words penetrated my thoughts.

"What who meant? What's going on?"

I dragged my thoughts back to the present, recounting the middle of the night call. "That's what he meant when he said 'that guy was dead and buried'; that he made himself over from the ground up," I finished. "But how did he make people believe he was dead?"

"After he left town, word got back to Central City that he'd died in a car fire," Dad explained. "His body was burned beyond recognition. There was some kind of evidence that made the police believe it was him. This was before DNA testing."

"Then someone else died in his place." My voice was flat. This guy was dangerous.

"You've got to tell that deputy friend of yours." His voice held the same urgency I was feeling. "They have to check this out. If it's really him, he's dangerous." He echoed my thoughts. "I'm coming over."

"There's nothing you can do, and you're needed at the winery."

"I can help find him. I know what he looks like," he argued.

"That won't help, Dad. He said he made himself over. He doesn't look like you remember him. He probably had plastic surgery or something."

Dad huffed and puffed with frustration and worry. "Okay," he finally said. "I'll stay here. For now. But you have any more trouble, I'm coming over. I don't know what I can do, but I have to be there." He overrode any argument I started to make. If the situation was reversed, I'd want to be there with him.

"Do you remember his name?" I asked. I don't know what good it would do to know his name, but I asked anyway.

Again Dad was silent before answering, thinking back all those years. "Ah, yeah, it was... Simpson, Edward Simpson. No, Edward Simmons."

Joe walked into my kitchen handing me a steaming cup of coffee. I mouthed "Thank you," and continued talking to Dad. Joe settled against the cupboard, listening to my side of the conversation.

"Be sure to tell Joe to be on the lookout. He knew the guy, too. And talk to that young man of yours."

"Joe is here now. And Greg's not my young man," I protested. Greg and I were a long way from anything like that.

"It doesn't matter, you tell him about this." We talked for a few more minutes then hung up.

Joe cocked an eyebrow at me as I ended the call. "Let's eat while you tell me what's going on." We headed back through the tasting room to his kitchen. We were still eating food the women had brought after he was attacked. It was nice not to have to worry about cooking, but I'll still be glad when all reminders of that day are out of the house.

Telling him about the phone call, I asked, "Do you remember the incident?"

He nodded. "Clay's right, that guy was dangerous. He took money from a lot of people, and was mad when he got caught. He didn't see anything wrong with what he did. Give Greg a call. Don't know exactly what the sheriff can do at this point, but they need to be aware someone is out to cause us more trouble."

By the time I'd repeated the phone call to Greg then again to another deputy, I was getting very tired of the situation. As expected, there was nothing the sheriff could do until we could identify the man. Even the possible murder of an unknown man thirty years ago couldn't be tied to anyone here. No one knew who the man was or what he looked like now.

~~~

He chuckled as he put the phone down. "Oh, this is going to be fun. As the old saying, 'pay back's bitch.' And for the Bishop's it's going to be a real bitch." His laugh was more maniacal now. "Revenge is best served cold," he went on, talking to the empty room. "And this is thirty years cold." Again he laughed at his own joke.

~~~

For the next week, we lived on pins and needles waiting for the other shoe to drop. I wasn't sure what he was going to do next, but I was certain whatever he did, I wasn't going to like it. My nerves were stretched to the breaking point. There'd been no more calls, and no more vandalism. I didn't know what to think. Had he been bluffing? Was he just a drunk who found out who my father was, and decided to play a sick game? It didn't feel like a game to me.

Dora and Pattiann were staying away for their own safety. I took his threat against my friends seriously. Greg came over under the guise of official business. The silence from Chase was almost deafening. Several times I'd seen him in his vineyard, but neither of us acknowledged the other. I felt like I was back in junior high where petty grievances were blown all out of proportion.

Friday we were still alive and in business. To the best of my knowledge no one else had been having trouble, but I wasn't going to let my guard down just yet. "I guess the ball is in his court," I told Joe and Greg. We were in the tasting room just before opening for the day.

"Do we just wait for him to attack? He could take his time until I relax, then strike again. Or he could go after my friends first; then come after me." They had no more answers than I did.

While we had customers in the tasting room, Joe stayed out front with Cody. Even though Cody was a lover not a fighter, his size might discourage someone from trying something. Juan and our other employees kept watch in the vineyard and buildings. But the worst thing that could happen was to have this nut case attack innocent people.

When the train whistle ring tone on my cell phone went off at two in the morning again, I woke with a start, my stomach already tied in a knot. No use looking at caller ID, the number would be blocked like before. Picking up my phone I didn't say anything before I heard his crazy cackling laugh.

"You feeling pretty smug about now?" he asked. "Nothing more has happened? Remember, I said you weren't going to be the only one to pay the price. It's your boyfriend's turn. I wonder how he's going to feel about you now." His voice held a sneer.

"I don't have a boyfriend. What did you do?" My first thought was of Greg. Did he know of the growing feelings we shared?

"Don't lie to me!" he snarled. "I know everything about you. I'm going to make you suffer like your old man made me suffer." The phone went dead.

Before I was even out of bed, Cody started barking; someone was pounding on the door. I could hear Chase yelling for me to open up. Grabbing my robe, I headed for the kitchen. "I know you're in there, Skylar, so open this damn door or I'll break it down."

I was shocked by his disheveled appearance when I opened the door. In the five years I've known him, he has always been a snappy dresser, never going anywhere unless perfectly groomed. Now his clothes were splotched with red wine, his hair sticking up in different directions. His face was so red with anger I thought he was going to have a stroke right on my doorstep. "What happe..."

"How could you do this to me?" he cut me off, his voice raised in a shout. He pushed his way past me just as Joe came through the tasting room. He stood quietly behind me making sure Chase didn't try anything. "I haven't said anything to anyone about you," Chase continued. "I haven't even been in town for the last week. Why did you have to do this?" For a minute I thought he was going to cry.

"Chase, tell me what happened?"

"You know damn well what happened." He took a step towards me, stopping when Joe and Cody each gave out a low rumbling warning. "I told the sheriff you threatened me," he finally said. "Even your boyfriend can't get you out of this. I have video surveillance in all my buildings and it'll prove what you did."

"What exactly are you accusing her of, Templeton?" Joe's low voice sliced through Chase's ranting.

"Maybe you're the one behind this." Chase turned on Joe, his fists clenched ready to take a swing.

"What happened, Chase?" I kept my voice calm.

"Stop playing dumb with me!" he shouted. "You trashed my tasting room, destroyed I don't know how many cases of wine." I gasped, and he sneered at me. "Your fake shock isn't going to fool me. You threatened me. Now you've carried out that threat. Well, I've turned over the videos to the sheriff. It won't take them long to place one or both of you at my place just a few hours ago. Even your lap dog deputy won't be able to keep you out of trouble."

I flinched at his derogatory description of Greg, but now wasn't the time to argue that point. "Joe and I have been here all night, Chase, but maybe the video will show who did break in to your place. Why would either of us do something like that?"

"I don't know why you would do it, but you're the only one who's threatened me."

"Edward Simmons?" Joe asked quietly.

I nodded. "He called just a few minutes ago. He said it was my boyfriend's turn to pay for what Dad did. He thinks Chase is my boyfriend. He's going after people he thinks I care about."

"What are you talking about?" Chase demanded. "You did this to me!"

"No, I didn't." I paced across the room. How could I protect those I care about when I don't even know who he is? There were a lot of people he could go after, Dora, Pattiann, Greg, my employees, my customers. Tears clogged my throat, but I refused to let them fall. "How do I stop him? I don't even know who he is." I turned to Joe.

"The sheriff's department will figure it out. This isn't your fault." I knew he was right, but it felt like it was my fault. I didn't want anyone else getting hurt because of me.

"What the hell are you two talking about? You aren't making any sense."

Turning back to Chase, I asked, "Who else did you tell that we're dating?"

He huffed indignantly, "I didn't tell anyone that."

"Chase, I know you did. Now, who else did you tell? This is very important."

"Don't try to turn the focus away from what you did," he snapped. "You broke into my winery, threw a lot of my best wine on the floor. You're not going to get out of this."

I wanted to scream at him, shake him until his teeth rattled, do something to make him understand how much danger he could be in. "I didn't do that! But someone is trying to hurt me by hurting people I care about." That was probably not the best way to say that because he instantly smiled at me. Okay, how do I get myself out of this? "Who else did you tell, Chase?" I tried to keep my voice calm when I wanted nothing more than to shake the living day lights out of him.

"I didn't exactly tell people we were dating," he hedged, "just that we'd been spending a lot of time together."

"Why would you do that? It isn't the truth. There's never been anything between us."

"Not for the lack of trying on my part," he stated hotly. "I always thought we'd make a great couple, combine our wineries. Have a bigger operation"

"The two of you or you and Clay?" Joe asked pointedly.

Chase colored slightly, but just shrugged, ignoring the question. "So if you didn't break into my winery, who did?" How do I explain a dead man seeking revenge on my dad by going after me and my friends? And how do I make this mad man understand Chase isn't my boyfriend?

"You need to call the sheriff," Joe told me calmly, ignoring Chase's question, "Maybe the call can be traced."

"What are you talking about? What does a phone call have to do with what happened to my tasting room?" He was beginning to get angry again.

"Someone has a grudge against Dad," I finally explained in simple terms, "He thinks he can hurt Dad by hurting me, and in a roundabout way by hurting my friends. I guess that includes you since you're telling people we're dating."

"So you're saying this is my fault?" He raised his voice again.

"No!" I said in exasperation. "It's this crazy guy's fault, but you opened yourself up by linking your name with mine right now."

"That doesn't make sense. Why doesn't your dad just tell the police who he is? They can arrest him, and be done with it."

I heaved a sigh. "It's not that simple. Until a week ago everyone thought the guy was dead."

"This story just keeps getting better," he said sarcastically. "I don't believe any of it. I just want my winery fixed, and someone to pay for all the wine that's been ruined." He glared at me. Obviously he thought I was the one to pay. "Whoever did this got caught on video." He sent Joe a meaningful glare, still wanting to place the blame on Joe or me. "The sheriff will be able to identify the culprit in no time." He turned, stalking out, and slamming the door behind him.

"What a way to start the morning," I muttered. "I need coffee. We aren't going to get any more sleep tonight." Right on cue, someone else knocked on the door. Greg and two other deputies were standing there looking very official. I opened the door wide, letting them in. "Can you put on some coffee, Joe, while I get dressed? It looks like we aren't the only ones who need it." I didn't want to be questioned in my pajamas.

It took more than an hour and two pots of coffee to explain and sort through everything. The video had been taken to the station. Hopefully, it'd prove neither Joe nor I had broken in to Chase's winery. Since Greg rotated shifts, he was on night duty right now. He hadn't been able to do more than drive by, and couldn't verify we didn't leave here any time during the night. Our only proof could turn out being the video Chase had turned over.

Greg waited until the other deputies left. Pink was just beginning to paint the sky with dawn. He took my hand, bringing it to his lips, kissing my fingers. "We're going to figure this out. I checked out Edward Simmons. Officially, he's dead. He can't hide forever though. We'll get him."

"Before he hurts someone else? I don't know how to stop him." I gripped his hand, thankful for his support. "He said he lost everything, and he wants me to feel the same loss. Should I close down the winery? Move back to California? At least for a little while until you catch him?"

"Closing the winery isn't going to help, Sky, and right now you can't leave. While the investigation is still on going, you have to be here. Chase is going to be telling anyone who will listen that you or Joe did this. If you leave now, it will just make you look guilty."

"Great! How do I keep him from hurting anyone else?"

Greg put his finger over my lips. "The one at fault is still out there, and we're going to find him." He leaned down, placing his lips where his finger had been. The kiss was like butterfly wings against my skin, yet it sent my heart rate off the chart, and I leaned in for more. Greg willingly obliged, pulling me to him, deepening the kiss. When he lifted his head, he rested his forehead against mine. “Wow! I’ve wanted to do that since that first day. Maybe I can get an encore later?”

As much as I wanted that, I had to shake my head. “It could be dangerous just being seen with me. I don’t want anyone else hurt, especially you or your mom or Pattiann.”

“I’ve taken precautions for them, and I can take care of myself. In case you haven’t noticed, I carry a gun.” That didn’t make him invincible, but I didn’t argue.

I stayed outside watching him drive off before going back inside. I hoped whoever this nut job was hadn’t been watching us. It wouldn’t take a rocket scientist to know he’d picked on the wrong man when he went after Chase.

Joe was waiting for me inside with fresh coffee and breakfast. The man was a real life saver. “Time to call Clay,” he said, “can’t put it off.”

“What’s going on?” As early as it was, Dad was wake and clear headed. “More trouble?” I’ve never been able to hide anything from him.

“He called again, flaunting the fact that he’s going after my friends. He broke into Templeton Vineyards.” I gave him the short version of the early morning events, leaving out Chase’s accusations. The phone was on speaker, so Joe and I could both talk to Dad.

“Deputies will be calling you about this guy, Clay. Told them what I know, but I didn’t have all the details. It was a long time ago.”

Dad sighed. “I thought I was finished with all that thirty years ago. It’s a good thing I kept all the information in my files. I think there’s even an old picture or two in there.” He was quiet for a heartbeat, blowing out a breath. “I’ll bring the file over.”

“Dad, you don’t have to come over. You’re in the middle of spring pruning just like the rest of us.”

"I have to see you're all right, Kitten. I'll just come over for a day."

When I started to argue, Joe touched my arm, shaking his head, and the argument died on my lips. "Okay, let us know when you'll be here." We talked for a few more minutes before hanging up.

As if the day wasn't bad enough, that afternoon the owner and sole reporter for our small weekly newspaper paid me a visit. "Hello, Skylar. How are you doing?" Her sympathetic look didn't fool me for a minute. The paper was more of a gossip rag then a real newspaper, and she was here looking for gossip.

"I'm just fine," I said carefully. I'd learned early on you never told Betty Richards of any troubles unless you wanted them splashed over the front page of the next edition, and embellished to such an extent even you didn't recognize them. "How are you doing on this beautiful afternoon?"

"Why, I'm fine, and thank you for asking. I just came over to see if there's anything I can do for you after, you know." Her voice dropped to a whisper. So much for friendly chit chat, I thought.

I didn't have to try really hard to look confused. I didn't know what she was talking about. "No, I don't know," I whispered back. "Why don't you tell me?"

"I was just wondering if the rumors around town were true."

Playing her game took a lot of time and concentration, but if you weren't careful you could fall into her trap, saying something you didn't want printed. "I haven't been in town for a while, so just tell me what you're talking about."

"A rumor has been floating around about a possible...merger of sorts between Sky Vineyards and Templeton Vineyards. I just wondered if the little incident last night would put a stop to that. Chase is pretty upset."

For a second my vision blurred, and I saw red. How could Chase be so stupid to even hint to Betty something so untrue? I gave a brittle laugh, trying to downplay even the suggestion of such a thing. "I don't know where you hear these rumors, Betty, but there's no truth to this one. No merger of any sort is going on around here." Don't overdo it, I reminded myself. If she thinks there's a shred of truth, she'll run with it.

She eyed me sharply for a long moment. "Well, I just wanted to make sure. Everything else going all right?" She was on a fishing expedition now.

"Yes, business is good. People seem to love my peach wine." Her eyes glazed over when I started talking about my wines, which she wasn't interested in.

"I'll let you get back to work. You have a good day." She hustled out to her car, in a hurry to get back to town.

Joe came out of the storage shed where he'd most likely been hiding. At one time, she had set her cap for him, pursuing him unmercifully. "What'd the gossip queen want this time?"

Relating her 'merger of sorts' rumor, Joe shook his head. "That fool doesn't know when to keep his mouth shut. Looks like it came back to bite him this time." He turned back to his work. I didn't understand why Betty had waited this long to come out to investigate her rumor. Or was she waiting for it to heat up so she'd have more gossip to print?

Sunday morning came early after the long day and short night yesterday. I debated whether it was safe to go to church, not for me, but the other people in the congregation. Finally I rolled out of bed. Hibernating wasn't the answer. Besides, I knew Joe would be up and ready to go. Dora and Pattiann were always at the early service now, and that was the one place Joe felt it was safe to see them.

Sitting in the last row instead of our usual seats, I was hoping to avoid contact with others. I couldn't live with myself if being friendly with someone got them hurt. When Greg and Dora came in, they stepped around Joe on the aisle, motioning for me to scoot over to make room between us. I looked around to see where Pattiann was. She was always with Dora when she came to church. When I didn't see her, butterflies attacked my stomach. "Where's Pattiann?" I leaned across Greg, whispering to Dora. "Is she okay?"

"Someone called in sick so she's working an extra shift. She's fine." Dora patted my hand that was already shaking. I released a pent up breath, trying to relax against the seat, and calm my frayed nerves.

Dad was flying in this afternoon, bringing the file from thirty years ago for Sheriff Stevens. Hopefully there'd be something in it to help identify the person behind all our troubles. He had to leave again Monday afternoon. I know he's worried about Joe and me, I just hope nothing happens while he's here.

By the time we closed for the day, delicious aromas were coming from Joe's kitchen. On the days we were open Joe and I usually ate something simple because we didn't have a lot of time to prepare an elaborate meal. I wondered what was different today. Maybe because Dad would be here in another hour, Joe had decided to make something special.

Entering Joe's kitchen, I was surprised to find Dora standing at the stove, an apron tied around her slim waist. "Hello, Sky honey, I hope you don't mind that I'm fixing dinner for everyone."

"Mind?" I gave her a hug. "I was going to order a pizza or something, and have it delivered when Dad gets here. Whatever you're fixing smells so much better. Thank you."

"You're welcome, Honey. I know how hard things have been lately. Besides, we all wanted to meet your dad."

"All?" I looked around the otherwise empty room. "Who else is here?"

"Joe's showing Greg and Pattiann around the winery. I've already had a tour." She gave me a beaming smile.

"Joe told me he gave you a tour on one of your first visits. It's amazing. He's never given anyone a tour in the five years we've been open. I think you've made a conquest." I smiled at her. Over fifty years old and Joe was finally coming out of his shell.

"You don't mind, do you?" She looked a little worried, until I laughed.

"As long as you make each other happy, I'm happy. He's the only uncle I have. The only thing I've ever wanted for him is to be happy." It looks like both of the men who had a hand in raising me have finally found romance. The thought put a genuine smile on my face, the first one of the day.

Dad came in a few minutes later, wrapping me in a bear hug. It always felt like coming home. "How you holding up, Kitten?" he whispered in my ear.

"I'm doing fine, Dad." I introduced him to Dora just as Joe came in with Greg and Pattiann. "Have you met Dora's kids, Greg and Pattiann?"

"Joe did the honors outside," Dad answered. He eyed Greg carefully, seeming to take his measure. He'd always known when there was someone I had a special interest in, even though there'd only been a few of those.

Within minutes we were eating the delicious meal Dora had prepared. Conversation was light throughout dinner; everyone was ignoring the elephant in the room.

"That was a wonderful meal, Dora. Thank you for doing that, you're a great cook." Dad smiled at her.

"You're welcome. Joe seems to think so." A warm glow spread across her cheeks as she smiled at Joe.

"Is that so?" He raised an eyebrow at his longtime friend whose cheeks were now bright red. Dad might be able to pick up on any special feelings I have for someone, but he'd completely missed with Joe.

He winked at me, then changed the subject to what was foremost on his mind, giving Joe a break. "Has anything new happened?"

I shook my head, "No, thank God, but right now it's like waiting for the second shoe to drop. I know he's going to do something else." Just speaking the words out loud made my stomach hurt.

"The video from Templeton Vineyards showed a person in dark clothes, a baseball cap pulled low over his forehead," Greg said, directing his comment to Dad. "The techs estimate he's at least four or five inches shorter than Joe's six feet four inches. He's smaller built, and it looks like he's got the beginnings of a beer belly. He's also taller and stockier than Skylar. If he was trying to make himself look like either of them, he didn't do a very good job. Most likely, he wasn't aware of the video surveillance since Templeton doesn't have it posted. This information hasn't been released to anyone," he cautioned, "including Templeton. The man can't seem to keep his own council. As long as this guy thinks Skylar is our main suspect, we're hoping he won't do anything else."

Jim Stevens arrived early the next morning to interview Dad, and go over the information from thirty years ago. Greg had looked over the file last night, but wasn't sure there was much to help us now. We all knew the few pictures Dad had wouldn't be helpful. Even if the man hadn't had extensive plastic surgery, he was considerably older now. Sheriff Stevens agreed with Greg's assessment, but said he'd do some checking.

As Dad was getting into the rental car to go back to the Tucson airport that afternoon, I stopped him. "You haven't said anything about Molly. Is everything okay with the two of you?" With everything that's been going on here, I hadn't had time to ask him.

The soft expression in his eyes was enough of an answer, but he told me anyway. "She's just fine. She said to tell you we're praying for you. When things slow down for both of us, we'll come over, and spend a few days. You know her, but I want to make sure you're okay with us as a couple." I understood what he was saying. I needed to see them together to know they would be good for each other.

"Speaking of couples," he continued, with a gleam now in his dark eyes. "I like Greg, and the rest of his family. I think you picked a good one."

"Wait a minute, Dad," I interrupted him. "You're getting way ahead of yourself. Greg and I aren't exactly what you could call a couple. We haven't even gone out on a date unless you count the five of us going out to dinner as a date." If his kiss was any indication though, there would be more of them in the future.

"The way that man looks at you, I don't think you need to worry about a date. He's truly smitten." I laughed at his old fashioned word. "As long as we're talking about smitten," he went on. "That bug seems to be going around here at your winery. I've never seen Joe quite like he was last night. You think he's happy?"

"You wouldn't believe how happy, Dad. Dora has brought him out of his shell. He even gives a winery tour every now and then."

"Joe?" His mouth dropped open, as surprised as I'd been. "Wow! That's quite a change. I'm glad. He's been alone too long." I couldn't agree more, for Joe and for Dad. With a final hug, he reluctantly got into the rental car, waving out the window until he turned onto the road. I stayed outside until his car was out of sight. With a heavy heart, I went back inside where Joe was waiting for me.

"You'll see, Kiddo, things will work themselves out. God and Greg aren't going to let anything happen to you and neither am I." He gave me a brisk hug. "Now let's see what didn't get done today."

CHAPTER SEVEN

With Dad's visit, I forgot about Betty until the paper came out three days later. It was a busy day for a Thursday, and there were several couples in the tasting room when my cell phone rang with its loud train whistle ring tone, startling everyone, including me. Laughing, I pulled it from my pocket, "Sorry," I apologized. "It has to be loud so I can hear it over all the noise when I'm working out back." I dismissed the call without checking caller ID. Almost immediately, it rang again. Becky was helping me, and she nodded indicating she could handle things out front. Calling back so fast it could be an emergency.

Stepping into the back room, I pulled the phone from my pocket. My heart climbed into my throat, cutting off my breath when I looked at caller ID, "Blocked number." It could be a lot of different people, even an advertisement. But I was willing to bet it wasn't.

The instant I clicked on to answer, he snarled at me. "I guess what happened to Templeton didn't discourage him any. Merging with him isn't going to keep him or you safe; it just put a bigger bull's-eye on his back."

"What are you talking about? I'm not merging with anyone." Chase wasn't even speaking to me, why would this nut think we were merging?

"Do you think I'm stupid? I read the paper! I thought trashing your boyfriend's tasting room would put an end to the two of you. Now I find out there's more going on than I thought. I don't want you merging with someone, and getting bigger, I'm putting you out of business."

I gasped, remembering Betty's mention of a 'merger of sorts'. "Whatever Betty put in the paper is gossip not gospel! If you've lived in New Haven very long, you should know that." Panic gripped me by the throat. What would he do since he believed Betty's lies? How could she keep printing things she knew weren't true. "You can't hurt people just because you believe a pack of lies."

"I can do anything I damn well please," he growled. "I told you I was going to take away everything dear to you. If that means taking down everyone you're close to, I don't mind in the least. You might as well accept that you're finished here in Arizona."

"After what you did at Templeton Vineyards, the sheriff won't let me leave until he's through investigating," I argued. "Chase told him I did it." Even though I wasn't actually under investigation, I knew Sheriff Stevens didn't want me leaving town. Apparently Betty had missed that piece of information.

He was quiet for so long I thought he'd hung up, until he started laughing. "Oh, this is so much better than I'd planned." He was quiet again as though considering something. When he spoke again, laughter rang in his voice. "Yes, I think I want you to stay right here where I can keep an eye on you. You can keep your stupid little winery for now." With a maniacal laugh the phone went dead.

I sagged against the wall. What was he going to do now? His evil laugh filled my mind long after he was gone. He didn't want to just put me out of business any longer. He wanted me in trouble with the law. He was going to do something else, something worse than what he did at Templeton Vineyards. The question was what and to whom?

He keeps calling Sky Vineyards a 'stupid little winery.' Could he have something to do with one of the other wineries? He'd been in banking in California, but that didn't mean he still was. He could be doing anything now.

Before going back to the tasting room I called Greg. The sheriff needed to know my mystery caller was still in business, and looking for more victims. Greg picked up on the second ring sounding like he just woke up. "Are you okay, Skylar? Has something happened?"

"I'm sorry; I forgot you're working nights. Go back to sleep, I'll talk to you later." I was so wrapped up in my own problems I forgot other people had their own lives to live.

"It's okay, Babe. What happened?" He swore softly when I finished telling him about Betty's article and my latest call. "I don't understand how that woman stays in business. Her rag is nothing short of slander. The only thing in it is gossip, recipes, and whatever news she can reprint from the big city papers. I've lived here just short of a year, and I know that. Maybe he hasn't been in town long, and hasn't figured that out yet."

He was quiet for a minute before going on, "We don't have that many people moving here all the time. That may be a way to figure out who he is." He offered to come over to make sure we were safe, but I told him to go back to sleep. I didn't think we were the target at the moment. This maniac was going to hurt someone else, and try to make it look like I did it.

My next call was to Pastor Rick Bennett. I needed to talk to someone not connected to any of this, who could give me a different perspective. "Could I come over to talk to you this evening? I hate to bother you at night, but I can't get away right now."

"It's no bother, Skylar. Does seven sound okay? Do you want to come to the church or the parsonage?" The man was a blessing to the church, and the community. He always had time to listen to anyone, even if they weren't part of his congregation. Right now his calm presence was just what I needed.

For the rest of the day I wasn't much use around the tasting room, and I finally left it in Becky's capable hands. Maybe I could lose myself working outside. "I'm glad you're going to talk to the pastor," Joe said when I told him about my latest call. "We're too close to the situation to see any way around this guy. Pastor Rick will have some good advice." I wasn't sure how much advice anyone could give me, but I had to talk this out with someone not involved.

~~~
~~~

I showed up at the parsonage a few minutes early, and sat in my truck until seven. Arriving early for an appointment is almost as bad as showing up late. Beverly, Pastor Rick's wife, opened the door with a smile and a hug. "I'm sorry to interrupt your evening, Beverly." I tried to apologize, but she brushed my worry aside.

"You aren't interrupting anything, but some boring reruns on television. Go on in to Rick's office, I'll bring some coffee, decaf of course." She laughed. "You both need to be able to sleep tonight." Rick was waiting for me with another hug, and ushered me to a comfortable chair. After Beverly deposited a tray with a thermal coffee carafe, two mugs and all the fixings on Rick's desk, she left us alone, closing the door behind her.

"You look upset," Pastor Rick said, handing me a warm mug. "Tell me what's going on." The entire town knew about the attack on Joe, and Chase was making certain everyone knew what happened at his winery and blaming me.

I didn't know exactly where, or how to begin. Finally I just blurted out, "Some mad man is going to hurt someone because of me." Not exactly a clear statement, but it was a start. Taking a deep breath, I started over from the beginning, thirty years ago.

He listened quietly, interrupting only to ask questions to clarify a point. When I ended with the latest call today, he was silent for a minute, digesting everything I'd said. "Was the information your dad brought over helpful to the sheriff?"

"I don't think so," I sighed. "It was just information about the embezzlement, who he stole from, things like that. There wasn't any real evidence that could be used now. Sheriff Stevens said he'd check with the county officials in California to see if they still have any evidence from the accident. After thirty years I don't know how much help it'll be.

"I don't know exactly how plastic surgery works to change a person's appearance, but time alone would change how he looks now. He wants to put me out of business, and hurt the people I care about." I gave a humorless laugh. "Even someone I don't really care about. He thinks I'm involved with Chase."

"The way I see it, your father did this man a favor by not turning him over to the police, and he squandered it. Compounding his sin, he killed another man so he could disappear. It appears to me this Edward Simmons is a narcissist, and probably a sociopath. As long as it's good for him, he doesn't see that it's wrong."

"If he's lived a crime-free life since his original crimes, why is he willing to ruin that now by drawing attention to himself again?" It didn't make sense.

"Until we know who he is, we won't know if his life has been crime-free in the last thirty years. So far the only consequences he's suffered from his original crimes is losing the bank he started. If he killed an innocent man to fake his own death, I doubt he'd stop at anything to get what he wants. Whatever he does, he feels it's his right to do it. The only consequences that interest him are the ones benefiting him."

"What if he kills someone? It'll be my fault." That was my biggest worry.

"Whatever he does, it isn't your fault," Pastor Rick stated firmly. "Somehow the community needs to be warned, but you can't be the one to do it. That would make him even angrier at you." For a long moment he was quiet, thinking over the options. He smiled. "It's too bad we don't have a real newspaper in town. People wouldn't have to rely on the grapevine, gossip and misinformation to learn what's happening in town. In the ten years Beverly and I have been in New Haven, I don't think Betty Richards has ever printed anything of her own even resembling actual news."

"Or the truth," I added. We both laughed, but an idea began to germinate in my mind. For now though, I put it aside to examine at a later time.

When I left an hour later, I was feeling better than I had in days. Thinking over what Pastor Rick said about newspapers being a good source of actual news, I wondered if we could somehow get Betty to print a warning. If we could plant the suggestion that someone was out to hurt the town, she just might print it.

Dora and Joe were sitting on the porch when I returned from Pastor Rick's. Like Pastor Rick, Joe thought it was too risky trusting Betty to print anything helpful. But Dora was all for it. "It just might work if we can make it sound like gossip. That woman stalks around town eavesdropping on any conversation she can, trying to pick up something she can embellish and run with. She's in the bank nearly every day just standing around. That's probably where she heard Chase telling about a "merger" between the two of you. I guess we don't have enough crime in our little town to satisfy her thirst for salacious things to print."

"The woman wouldn't know the truth if it jumped up and bit her," Joe grumbled. "When Sky first opened up here, the article she wrote had more holes in it than Swiss cheese. She said we were from back east somewhere, and I was her father here to help her open her winery." He shook his head.

"I hadn't even sold my first bottle of wine when she decided to critique them," I added. "She'd never heard of fruit wines, and thought I was using fruit juice from the grocery store to make them. She puts herself out as an expert on everything, but she really doesn't know much about anything."

"A good reason not to rely on her to pass along a warning," Joe stated calmly, giving me a stern look.

I didn't argue, but I didn't give up on the idea. I also decided to do a little detecting of my own. Until now Joe and I had been so busy building our winery I hadn't taken the time to get to know many people beyond the other vineyard owners, my regular customers, and employees. The wine district in Arizona was expanding, and our area was becoming a popular location for new vintners to start out. Each year since Joe and I moved to Arizona, at least one new winery and vineyard opened up.

Greg's suggestion that my tormentor was relatively new to the area stuck in my mind. Why else was he just starting to harass me? I'd been here five years with no problems beyond Betty's jokes about 'fruit juice' wine, or derision from some of the other vintners. No one had tried to ruin me until now.

At two in the morning I gave up trying to sleep, and pulled on my robe. It was still a little chilly outside, but being cooped up in the house was beginning to feel a little like jail. Taking the small area telephone book with me, I sat down in the porch swing. Cody padded along beside me, unsure what I was doing, but not wanting to be left behind. If I could check off the names of the people I knew, or knew of who had lived in the area at least as long as us, it might help me figure out who were relative newcomers.

My heart started racing when a truck slowed on the road in front of the house, turning into the lane leading right to my front porch. Is Edward Simmons watching everything I do? Until this moment, I hadn't even thought about how exposed I was sitting under the porch light. My muscles froze, like a deer caught in the headlights of an oncoming car just waiting to get run over.

My breath escaped in a rush when the door opened, and the cab light came on. Greg sat there scowling at me for several seconds before stepping out. Cody's tail thumped on the wooden porch. I should have known it was someone he knew. If it had been a stranger, Cody would be standing there waiting to greet someone new.

"What the hell are you doing out here in the middle of the night for any and all to see?" He was angry.

"Keep your voice down. You don't need to wake Joe."

"Maybe I should wake him." He stomped up the steps. "Someone should put some sense into that head of yours."

"You thinking you could and should be the one to do it?" His angry words sparked my own temper. I'd had it with people trying to tell me what to do.

He paced the length of the porch and back, his boots echoing on the wooden boards in the still night. "Damn it, Skylar, there's some crazy guy out there threatening you, beating people up, and you sit out here, an easy target for anyone to take a potshot at." He threw himself onto the swing beside me, sending us rocking.

He probably isn't going to like my plan to figure out who'd moved to town recently, I thought, or the one to get Betty to write about the maniac terrorizing the wineries. The fact that Chase and I were the only ones to have trouble so far wouldn't stop her from making it sound like a band of terrorists had descended on our little town.

"Can we go inside," Greg asked quietly, "or at least turn out the light?" His voice was calmer, but still a little ragged around the edges. "We don't need to advertise the fact that we're sitting out here."

I got up, flipping the light switch off, throwing the porch into total darkness. There wasn't even a moon to illuminate my way back to the swing. I waited a minute for my eyes to adjust to the dark when I felt Greg reached out, taking my hand, pulling me towards him. I plopped down ungracefully beside him, and his arm came around my shoulders. I could feel his warm breath as he nuzzled my hair.

"I'm sorry, Sky. When I saw you sitting out here, my imagination conjured up all sorts of crime scenes, all of them bloody with no good outcome." He kissed the top of my head, his arms tightening around me for a minute. "There's no telling what this lunatic is capable of. If he killed someone thirty years ago to cover up his crimes, I doubt he'd hesitate to do it again. I don't want you getting hurt." His lips claimed mine in a gentle, exploring kiss.

When my arms circled his neck, my fingers sifting through the soft hair at the nape of his neck, pulling him closer, he deepened the kiss. Somehow I ended up sitting on his lap, cradled against his hard chest. My heart was beating wildly against his. His hands ran up and down my back, massaging the muscles until I felt like melted butter flowing into him.

After several minutes, he lifted his head, resting his forehead against mine, and then moved me off his lap. “I think we’d better call a halt for now before I get completely carried away. We both need to get some sleep. Tomorrow’s my day off. How about I come over when I wake up, and see what I can do around here? Then we can go out for dinner after you close. Mom will be here or Joe will be at her house. I wouldn’t want you to have to eat all by yourself.” His sexy grin brought my heart rate up several beats.

“Tomorrow is Pattiann’s day off,” I laughed. “She’s going to be working here in the tasting room.”

“Arrrg,” he gave a playful growl.

“You’re the one who suggested I give her a job. Remember?” I poked him in the ribs.

“Think we can find her a boyfriend by tomorrow night? Then she won’t have to eat by herself either.” We laughed and joked for a few more minutes before he stood up. “It’s time to get some sleep. Go in, and lock that door.” He pulled me to my feet, giving me another heart stopping kiss, before opening the door and pushing me inside. “Lock the door.”

“Yes sir.” I gave him a mock salute, laughing at him as I shut the door, turning the dead bolt. “It’s locked,” I said through the door. “Now go home, and get some sleep. See you sometime tomorrow.”

“Today,” he said as he walked down the steps.

CHAPTER EIGHT

It was a short night. The enticing aroma of coffee and bacon brought me out of a sound sleep just a few hours after I crawled into bed. "It can't be time to get up," I mumbled to Cody as I rolled over to look at the clock. "Seven-thirty! Yikes!" I jumped out of bed, and ran for the bathroom.

Fifteen minutes later I stumbled into the kitchen. Joe had brought breakfast to my side of the house today, probably to make sure I woke up since I didn't come to him. "You have trouble sleeping last night, too?" he asked. "A lot of noise out there."

My face got hot, and I knew from experience it was turning bright red. "Sorry about that. We didn't mean to wake you up."

"What were you doing out there at that time of the morning? With the light on no less."

"Okay, it was a dumb move," I admitted. "Greg already pointed that out. Rather loudly."

"Then it got kinda quiet after a few minutes." A smile played around his lips, tugging the corners into his mustache. "What was that all about?"

I hadn't gotten over the first blush, and now my face started to burn again. "We made up." I muttered. "He's coming over today to help out. He has the day off."

"And just who's he going to be helping? You won't get much work done if he's in the tasting room."

"He can work with you and Juan. Pattiann will be with me. That should keep everyone above board, don't you think? At least until Dora gets here." I raised an eyebrow at him. It was my turn to laugh at him when his face turned red. In all my life, I'd never seen Joe blush the way he had since meeting Dora. The man was really and truly in love. I gave him a hug, and picked up the mug of coffee he poured for me.

A few hours later Becky and Pattiann walked in together; joking and laughing about something. I'd been afraid Becky would be upset about having to share her space with Pattiann. I should've known better. They were getting along famously. At fifty-something, Becky and her husband had retired to New Haven several years ago. Jim had been in the military for thirty years, and now enjoyed staying in one spot instead of moving around every few years. He worked part time for Cyndi McMahan's husband at their vineyard. "Just enough so's I don't make a nuisance of myself to Becky," he told everyone. Their grown children were scattered across the country, and Becky had taken to mothering me every now and then in their stead. It looked like she was doing the same with Pattiann now.

While they shared the tasting room, I racked more barrels, cleaning sediment and putting the empty ones on the barrel washer. It was a long process, something that needed to be done several times a year. While I worked, I tried to think of people who had moved to the area over the last couple of years. Using the phone book had seemed like a good idea at two in the morning, now I wasn't so sure. There had to be an easier way. I just didn't know what that was at the moment.

I didn't know how Greg was going to take to the idea of his mom feeding Betty information, even indirectly. The next paper didn't come out until Thursday, almost a week from now. I don't know how long it takes her to make up her articles, but it seemed there was plenty of time for her to hear something. I don't think she ever printed something told directly to her, unless of course it was particularly juicy. In her case, gossip was grist for her mill.

Joe and Greg came in the back door just minutes after Dora came in the front. Becky only works half a day the four days we're open, sharing duties with several other women who enjoy earning a little extra money. Greg looked tired probably from a lack of sleep last night. Guilt then embarrassment brought a flush to my face remembering how we'd spent a few wonderful minutes on the porch in the early morning hours.

He draped his arm across my shoulders, kissing my temple. "Who would have thought making great wine was such hard work? I'm going need a shower before we go to dinner."

"We're going out?" Pattiann looked at us expectantly.

"No, Sky and I are going out." He tweaked her nose. "You can keep Mom and Joe company."

She made a pretense of pouting. "But it's my day off. I want to do something fun." She had a hard time keeping a straight face.

Being an only child, I'd missed out on the fun, and maybe a little frustration, of having siblings. This bickering seemed to be a normal occurrence between these two. But I couldn't tell if they were just playing around, or they were really getting mad at each other.

"Well, if you weren't so picky about boyfriends, you'd have one by now, and could be having your own fun," Greg said casually.

"Me picky?" she shot back. "Who just about ran off the last three guys I dated?"

"Who asked me to?" Greg countered.

Dora sighed loudly. "Give it a rest, you two. Joe and Skylar aren't interested in your make believe squabbles." She turned to me. "Any time she gets tired of a boyfriend, she gets Greg to act the overprotective big brother, and the guy is quickly a thing of the past. Then she blames him when she doesn't have a date. I'm not always sure either one of them is playacting all the time."

Pattiann decided to call some friends from the hospital, and have a "hen party" she said. "It'll be more fun than hanging out with my brother," she teased, then gave him a kiss before she hurried out the door. Dora and Joe were going to get something to eat and watch television. With a clear conscience, Greg and I went to dinner in town.

Friday is a popular night to go out to eat everywhere, and New Haven is no exception. By the time Greg and I made it to town, Manuel's was crowded with a number of names on a waiting list. For a small town, the restaurants manage to do a brisk business especially on the weekends. The wineries have proven to be a boon for most small towns in southeastern Arizona.

It occurred to me this was the perfect opportunity to check people out, trying to pick out those who'd moved here in the past few years. This psycho didn't strike me as a family man so I ignored the tables with children. I couldn't picture him as a loving husband or boyfriend either, but he would probably want to give the impression of being a normal man. There was a table of four men at the back of the room. I'd seen a couple of them around town on several occasions, but the others I'd never seen before. Unfortunately, I knew very little about most people here, or in New Haven in general. I've been so busy getting the vineyard and winery started that I didn't get out much.

"Earth to Skylar, Earth to Skylar." I became aware of Greg's hand passing in front of my face, his head tilted close to mine.

My eyes and mind focused on him again, and I could feel my face turning red. "I'm sorry, Greg. I guess I was lost in thought."

"Thought? Honey, you were concentrating so hard on the people in the room, you didn't even know I existed. What's going on? Do you see someone you know?" His sea blue gaze swept the room.

I shook my head, "No, just the opposite. I've lived here five years, and just about the only people I know are the people from the other wineries and my own employees. I probably see more of the tourists than I do the people in town. You, your mom and, sister are the first non-wine people I've gotten to know. That's pretty sad, isn't it?"

He wrapped me in a big embrace, and whispered into my hair. "Well, I'm glad you decided to come out of your business fog to get to know us."

As the hostess led us to a table, I could feel eyes following us, or maybe I was getting paranoid. Looking around the room as we sat down, no one seemed to be paying any particular attention to us. Paranoid, I thought again. All the same, I still had the eerie feeling of being watched. I couldn't stop myself from checking every few minutes to see if anyone was looking at us. At the same time it gave me the opportunity to check out the other diners.

"Okay, Skylar, what's going on? You're mind isn't here tonight." Greg touched my hand across the table causing me to jump in surprise, proving his statement.

"Nothing's going on. I'm just looking at the people." I could feel my face getting red at my lie.

Greg let it go for a minute, but when my attention started to wander again, he cleared his throat drawing me back to him. He raised an eyebrow questioningly, and I sagged in defeat. "Okay, okay," I sighed. "I don't know many people in town. I'm trying to figure out who is relatively new here."

He frowned in confusion. "Why? What difference does it make?"

"Well, it was your suggestion," I said accusingly. His blank look forced me to explain further. "When you said if Edward Simmons had been here very long, he'd know Betty's articles can't be trusted as truth; it got me thinking. I've been here for five years, and haven't had any trouble with anyone until recently."

I gave a small laugh. "Unless you count Chase. He wanted to buy my land, but I think he had trouble coming up with the money, and Dad got it first. Then he tried to discourage me on the idea of fruit wines. Once he discovered Dad owns one of the premiere wineries in Central California, he tried to cozy up to me. Anyway, if someone was out to get revenge on Dad, why did they wait five years to start their attack?"

"So you think you can figure out who's doing this by finding all the newcomers?" Greg relaxed against the booth cushion.

"It's a start. If I can figure out who Edward Simmons is now, maybe we can stop him."

"You do realize it's my job to figure that out, right? I'm in law enforcement, you're not?" Again that dark brow rose slightly, looking sort of like a question mark.

"Of course I realize that, but I can help, can't I? I'm not going to go out and apprehend anyone, or question them. But if I can help..."

One of the men I'd noticed earlier, walked up to our booth interrupting our conversation. What I assumed to be a smile spread across his too smooth, tanned face. "I'm sorry to interrupt your evening, but I wanted to introduce myself. I'm James Burke, the manager of National Bank here in town. You're Skylar Bishop, correct?" He offered his hand to me.

I nodded, reluctantly placing my hand in his. Almost immediately, I tried to pull my hand away, but he held on just a little too tight. So far he hadn't acknowledged Greg, and he continued to ignore him until I made the introduction. "This is Greg Wilkinson." Still, gripping my hand, his gray eyes slid over to Greg giving the briefest of nods. While his attention was diverted for that split second, I managed to pull my hand from his, just barely stopping myself from rubbing my hand on the napkin in my lap.

"I haven't had the pleasure of visiting your winery. Maybe sometime you could give me a personal tour."

"I'm sorry. Right now we're very busy. We aren't giving tours. The tasting room is open four days a week. Feel free to come on any of those days for a tasting. Someone will be glad to help you."

"You don't work in the tasting room?" He looked disappointed.

"That's what I have employees for," I hedged. "I'm the vintner; I spend a great deal of my time actually making the wine." There was more than a little sarcasm in my voice, but he didn't seem to notice. So far nothing I'd said was a lie. I just hadn't told the complete story. For some reason this man was freaking me out.

The waitress stopped at our table right then to take our order. I wanted to jump up and kiss her when Mr. Burke excused himself, going back to his table. As soon as she left us again, I took a small bottle of hand sanitizer out of my purse, squirting a generous portion into my hand. Greg watched as I kept scrubbing my hands. "Are you okay?" Maybe I was acting like a fool, but my hand felt dirty after the way Mr. Burke had gripped it.

"Who was that guy?" I asked. "Have you seen him before?"

"I know he's Mom's boss. I haven't met him before though."

"How long has he been in town?"

Greg frowned. "I'm not sure. He was at the bank when Mom started there about six months ago. What difference does it make?" he asked again.

"Like I said before we were interrupted, there's been no trouble until recently. Why would Edward Simmons wait five years to take his revenge on Dad? Why did he wait thirty years?"

"Maybe he didn't know who your dad is until recently. You said you haven't exactly advertised the fact. Who else knows?"

"Chase of course, and a few of the other vintners, but they've all been here longer than me."

"Is your dad's name on the winery?

I shook my head, "Just on the corporation papers. I don't exactly share those with anyone."

"People at your bank would have a copy," he said thoughtfully. "But I can't see anyone at any bank suddenly looking at your corporate papers unless they were checking up on you. Do you bank at National Bank?" When I shook my head, he was quiet for a minute before asking, "How often does your dad come over to visit? Maybe this guy saw him some time when he was here and figured it out."

My mind flashed back to Dad's visit when he thought someone was watching us. Telling Greg about that incident, I said, "Usually Dad just drives through town when he comes over. That time we ate here." I looked around the restaurant wondering if someone here was behind our troubles. Giving myself a mental shake, I dismissed that idea. "I need to find out how long James Burke has been in New Haven." I spoke more to myself than Greg.

"Okay, let me play devil's advocate for a minute. Whoever this guy is, he's probably close to your dad's age, right?" I nodded, and he went on. "So, Burke looks like he's at least ten years younger than your dad and Joe."

I sagged against the booth. I hadn't thought about that. "I see your point," I admitted. "Then the guy is just freaking me out, and I'm overreacting." I could still feel his eyes on me from across the room.

Greg reached across the table, taking my hand in his. "Whoever this guy is, he has you spooked, and you're seeing bad guys everywhere. That's understandable. And Burke came on a little strong."

"Ya think?"

He laughed. "Okay, way too strong, but he isn't the guy we're looking for. He just isn't old enough. For tonight, can we relax? I'm not going to let anything happen to you, tonight or any other time." He brought my hand up to his lips. I wasn't especially worried anymore that Edward Simmons was going to harm me. Now he was looking to hurt someone else, and put the blame on me.

I tried really hard to ignore Burke, but it wasn't easy as long as he was across the room. I could feel his eyes on me, but when I looked at him, the frown on his too smooth face instantly turned upside down into a lopsided sneer. There was something about his face, whether he was frowning or grinning, that was off. I couldn't place what though.

I was relieved when the four men finally stood up to leave. James Burke deliberately wove his way through the tables, walking slowly past our booth. He didn't say anything, just smiled and nodded, sending shivers through me.

"Can you relax now?" Greg asked, squeezing my hand. I hadn't been aware I was so obvious, and I could feel my face heat up yet again.

"It was freaky the way he kept staring at me," I said. "I know he's too young to be the man Dad knew back when, but there is something about him." I shrugged, unable to put into words exactly what I was feeling. I made a conscious effort to rid myself of the creepy feeling, and for the rest of the evening I did a good job of trying to forget about James Burke and Edward Simmons. Until I was home alone, that is.

Joe's side of the house was dark. He was either already asleep or still with Dora. I spent the next twenty minutes checking and rechecking every window, door, and closet. Everything was locked tight and empty just the way it was supposed to be.

~~~

For the first time since I opened the tasting room, I was dreading working there Saturday morning. I'm not sure what I expected James Burke to do to me, or anyone else, I just knew I didn't want to see him. Every time the door opened, my stomach churned only to settle back down when it was someone I didn't know. By the end of the day I was exhausted from the nervous tension. My shoulders ached, and I wanted nothing more than to soak in a hot bubble bath and go to bed.

At the same time, I was looking forward to seeing Greg. After the rather inauspicious beginning to our evening, thanks to James Burke, the remainder of last night had been wonderful. Night life is nearly non-existent in most small towns, and New Haven is no exception. Fortunately, there's one enterprising person who has taken advantage of the influx of tourists who come to the wineries and stay overnight. A large empty store had recently been converted
~~~

into a combination bar, restaurant, and night club where you could get burgers and sandwiches, drinks, play pool, or dance to a small local band on weekends. We had a great time listening to the music and dancing, or just talking, and I was ready to pick up where we'd left off last night.

In the few weeks I'd known them, Dora, Greg, and Pattiann had become an important part of our lives. On the evenings when they were all free, they had dinner with Joe and me, and it was no different tonight. I also wanted to find out if Dora had seen Betty this week, if she'd been able to drop some hints about our mystery man. I wasn't sure if she'd told Greg about our little plan to plant something about this guy's intentions in Betty's gossip rag, or what he thought about it. My guess is he won't approve. It'd also be a good time to ask her about James Burke, find out what she knows about him. There was just something off about the man.

Dora and Pattiann had dinner started when I walked into Joe's kitchen shortly after closing the tasting room. It was nice not to have to cook after spending most of the day on my feet. "You're both a wonderful addition around here," I said as I gave them each a hug. "Pattiann helps out in the tasting room, and you cook for us, Dora. And to top that off, you're great friends. What more could Joe and I ask for?

"Sit down, and put your feet up," Pattiann said as she poured me a glass of wine. "Mom has things well in hand. Now, tell us what's had you on edge all day. Has something else happened that we don't know about?"

I guess I'm not as good at hiding my emotions as I thought. Trying to explain my reaction to James Burke, I felt a little ridiculous. "I guess I overreacted to him. He just seemed a little strange."

Dora laughed, "He has that effect on most people. We try to keep him in his office as much as possible at the bank. He either has no expression on his face, or he's sneering. I think that's his idea of a smile. My guess is he's had too many Botox treatments. His facial muscles don't work quite right. One side of his face doesn't work like it should, the muscles kind of lag behind the other side. For a while I wondered if he'd had a slight stroke." She shrugged. "It can be really creepy, but I wouldn't worry about him too much. I doubt he's dangerous. He was probably trying to get your business. He has lousy timing."

I laughed with her, and could feel myself relax. If what she said was true, I had entirely misread him last night. Now I could dismiss him, and concentrate on the other crazy man in my life. "Have you seen Betty this week?"

"Why would anyone deliberately want to see that woman?" Pattiann asked disgust obvious in her tone. "I don't know how she avoids being sued."

"I wondered that when we first moved here, and she wrote those articles about us," I said. "She hides behind the First Amendment even when she's spouting lies. I guess no one has challenged that notion. It would have caused me more trouble than she's worth to try and get a retraction. As long as she doesn't name names, she feels pretty safe. Innuendos without names can't be proven as slander."

Pattiann shook her head. "I've seen her around the hospital. She spends a lot of time in the different waiting rooms hoping to pick up on anything she can print. The patients and their families have complained about her to the administration. So far they haven't been able to keep her out. All the nurses avoid her like the plague. So why do you want to talk to her, Mom?"

Dora made sure the men were engrossed in some television show before answering. Joe didn't think it was a good idea to have anything to do with her. I'm not sure if he thought I'd given up on the idea though. But we were pretty sure Greg wouldn't approve, him being law enforcement and all.

"We're hoping to plant the idea that someone is causing trouble in town. Maybe she'll actually warn people to watch out for themselves," she explained. "She's in the bank just about every day, but I didn't want anything coming directly from me. She's sure to know we're friends since she knows every little thing that goes on in and around town.

"Of course, everyone knows what happened to Joe, and at Templeton Vineyards," she went on. "I just made sure no one forgot about it, and said anyone could be the next target. It doesn't have to be a winery. Later, I heard some of the tellers talking about it, wondering what was going on in our small community. There's no telling what it will sound like by the time Betty gets it into her rag. Or if it will even makes it there."

Pattiann nodded. "I still don't understand how she's avoided being sued. Just leaving off names shouldn't keep her safe. She always insinuates enough so everyone knows who she's talking about."

Without us realizing it, Greg had come into the kitchen, catching Pattiann's comment. "Several people have tried to muzzle that woman, including Sheriff Stevens and Mayor Brady." We all swung around to face him, guilt written all over our faces. "Would you like to tell me what's perking behind those guilty looks?" he asked.

"Nothing for you to worry about, Dear." Dora patted his cheek. "Men shouldn't sneak up on women for fear of hearing us talk about women stuff." She walked over to the stove, stirring something with a heavenly aroma. "Now, why don't you and Joe get washed up? We're just about ready to sit down."

He didn't look at all convinced, but he didn't argue. For now. "So, Joe, do you know what these women have been cooking up behind our backs?" he asked with feigned innocence when we were finished eating, sitting around the table enjoying a glass of wine.

Joe looked at the food on the table. "It looks to me like they fixed chicken and cheese enchiladas, fried rice and some kind of pudding." He managed to say this with a straight face.

"Not exactly what I was talking about."

"Then speak your mind plain, Son," Joe said. "I don't speak in riddles." I kept my hand over my mouth to hide my smile.

Greg sighed. "Okay, plain and simple. These three are up to something. I was just wondering if you knew about it."

"Probably trying to trick the town gossip into saying something useful in that rag of hers," Joe said, proving he knew I hadn't given up on the idea. "I'd like to see someone turn the tables on her for a change."

"And just what is it you're trying to trick her into printing?" He glared at each of us in turn, his cop face firmly in place.

"Why shouldn't she print something useful for a change?" I asked. My tone was more than a little defensive.

"What useful tidbit are you trying to get her to print?" he pressed.

I looked at Dora for help, but it was Pattiann who stepped in. "Cut it out, Greg," she snapped. "Skylar doesn't know you well enough to understand you try to intimidate people with that cop stare of yours. If you want to put it to use, why don't you see if you can intimidate Betty? She tells lies about most everyone in town. So why shouldn't she do some good for a change?"

"What is it you're trying to get her to print?" he asked again, his tone didn't leave much doubt to his current mood.

"If she can warn people that someone is causing trouble, wouldn't that be a good thing?" I asked. "People need to be watchful. There's no telling where Edward Simmons will strike next."

"I haven't been in town all that long, but it seems to me she never prints anything helpful. If she could hint at a particular guilty party, that would be a different matter. She'd jump on that like bees on flowers. Something general like you're saying," he shrugged, "not so much."

"Crap!" I slumped against my chair. I knew he was right. Betty didn't like to be helpful. "I don't want anyone else getting hurt. If I could figure out why he's starting now, maybe I could figure out who he is."

"You don't need to figure anything out, Skylar. It isn't your job." His tone was stern, like he was talking to a disobedient child. "You need to stay out of it, and let us do our job."

"Stay out of it?" I asked with a raised voice. "It looks to me like I'm right in the middle of it, whatever 'it' is. So don't pat me on the head, and tell me to sit back like a good little girl, and let the big brave men take care of everything." I gave my chair a shove and stalked out.

"I think you've stepped in it now, Son," I heard Joe say with a chuckle before the door slammed shut.

Greg followed me outside. "Aw, Babe, I didn't mean it the way it came out. Come back inside. Let's all sit down and talk." He rested his hands on my shoulders.

My first instinct was to shrug him off, but for once I resisted cutting off my nose to spite my face. "I just need a few minutes alone. Go back inside." I tried to keep the anger out of my voice, hoping he'd do as I asked, and not press the issue. Luckily, he just kissed the top of my head, melting most of my anger before going back inside like I asked.

Dora and Pattiann had cleaned the kitchen, and the dishwasher was running when I went back inside fifteen minutes later. Now I really felt guilty. They were guests in our home, and I'd been letting them do all the work. I found them all sitting on the front porch. "Ah," I stumbled for a way to start. "I'm sor..."

"Stop." Greg held up his hand as he stood up. "I'm the one who needs to apologize. I know this guy's been hounding you. You need to be able to feel some sense of control over the situation, and I was taking that away from you. Can you forgive me?"

I nodded. "Only if you all can forgive me." I looked at the four people who were very precious to me. Greg wrapped me in a hug, giving me his answer while the others denied the need to forgive me.

"I thought you'd agreed trying anything with that woman wasn't such a good idea, "Joe said quietly a few minutes later.

"No," I contradicted. "I just didn't argue. I still thought anything was worth a try." He shook his head, giving me the fish eye. I knew full well what that meant without him saying it out loud. "Stubborn girl."

"So you think she'll print a warning just because you want her to?" Greg asked.

"No, because it's the right thing to do," I finally answered.

Both Joe and Greg chuckled at my comment. Until right then, I didn't realize just how naive it really was. "Why would she care?" Greg asked. "Hasn't she been hurting people with what she puts in her rag for years? Seems to me, she's happiest when someone else is hurting. Otherwise she wouldn't write the things she does. Take that article she wrote about you and Templeton. She pointed out how he was blaming you for what happened at his winery, and wondered, in her fine way, if it would stop any merger between the two of you."

I hadn't read the article. Now I wished I had. I'd given up caring what she wrote about me five years ago. Maybe I should start paying attention, especially since this mad man was paying such close attention.

"I still don't understand why he's just now trying to take his revenge on Dad." Coming up with no good solution to the subject of Betty, I switched topics. "Either he's relatively new in town, or he just recently found out who my dad is. Either way, it might help if we had a list of the people who moved here in the last couple of years. How do we go about that?" I looked at the others expectantly.

Greg shook his head. "Jim Stevens said he'd look into it, but going around accusing all the newcomers without some kind of proof would put us in the same boat as Betty Richards." I knew he was right; I just didn't like it. "Just because they moved to New Haven recently," he finished, "doesn't mean they're guilty of something."

"The first time we had trouble was just a few days after Clay came to visit," Joe said into the stillness. "Did anything unusual happen when he was here?" He looked at me across the porch in the approaching darkness.

I thought about the way Dad had acted while we were standing across from the bank. I didn't know what it had to do with anything, but it was unusual. After he left town the next day, I forgot about the incident, and didn't mention it to Joe. "That's one of the reasons why James Burke freaked me out, I guess. I thought he might be the one doing this," I said, after explaining how Dad thought someone in the bank was watching us. "The first time he called, he said Dad had ruined him, but Burke isn't old enough, so it can't be him."

"Did either you or your dad tell the sheriff about that incident?"

I shook my head. "I didn't. I don't know if Dad did, but I doubt it. Neither of us connected the two things. I still don't see how they could be connected."

Greg turned to Dora. "Are there any other people relatively new to town working there?"

She shook her head. "I'm the newest one there; everyone else has been here for several years at least. Most of them are locals."

"There are other businesses in that building," Greg stated. "Maybe it was someone from one of those offices watching you."

It was a thought worth looking in to, but I didn't even know what other businesses were there. Once again, I'd been so immersed in my own life for the past five years; I hadn't paid attention to what was going on around me.

I sighed in frustration. Every time I thought we were making progress, we ended up at a dead end.

CHAPTER NINE

Joe looked at me the next morning as we drove to church. “You need to tell Pastor Rick you went ahead, and tried to plant something in that gossip rag.”

I knew he was right, but I still didn’t want to. Besides, I didn’t know what difference it made. He hadn’t suggested it, and no one said he had. There was no way Betty would connect Pastor Rick with the hint. After the service, I stayed around until he was finished greeting everyone then asked to speak to him for a minute.

“Have you had more problems?” he asked as we sat down in his office. “I haven’t heard about anything more.”

“No,” I shook my head. “Remember when we talked about newspapers being a good source of information for the community?” He nodded and I went on. “I decided to try, and get Betty to print some sort of a warning in her paper.”

“Didn’t we decide it wasn’t such a good idea?” he asked. “She’s a loose cannon, and there’s no telling what she’d do.”

My face heated up, and I couldn’t meet his eyes. “I don’t know if she’ll print any kind of a warning or not, but I thought it was worth a try.”

Pastor Rick chuckled, giving my hand a pat. “If she prints something, it can only be a good thing. If she doesn’t think it fits in with her normal gossip, well,” he shrugged, “no harm, no foul.”

I sagged against the chair in relief. “I thought you were going to be mad at me.”

“No, you were just trying to protect people. That can’t be a bad thing. We just need to pray she does the right thing for once, and prints something useful.”

I half expected James Burke to come to the tasting room, so far he was a no show. I don't know what I expected him to do if he came in, other than creep me out. Why is he having Botox treatments if he's only in his forties? As men age, wrinkles and lines are considered to add character to their faces, not age them as they do women. I guess men could be as vain as women, not wanting anything to reveal their age. But something seemed to have gone wrong with the Botox. His facial muscles didn't work quite right. Dora said most of the time his face was a blank slate.

Dora and Pattiann had agreed not to try anymore gossip attempts with Betty. If she thought someone was trying to plant the information, most likely she'd turn it around, and print just the opposite which wouldn't help anyone. I hadn't seen her since the day she came looking for verification that something was going on between Chase and me. As for Chase, he hadn't been around either. I guess he's was still upset with me. Not that he'd been a fixture at Sky Vineyards before.

On Thursday I couldn't decide if I wanted to know if Betty had been helpful or not. I hated putting out money for her rag; it only encouraged her to write more of the same when people paid good money for her stupid paper. The occasional recipes she printed were said to be good, but I didn't think they were worth the money spent on the entire paper. I was hoping someone I knew had seen it, and would call me.

When my phone rang at mid-morning, I slipped into the back room to answer.

"What do you think you're doing?" I recognized the raspy voice even before I had the phone up to my ear.

"Ah, I was working until you interrupted me. What did you think I'd be doing?"

"Don't be a smart ass," he snapped. "Why did you have to go blabbing to that nosy bitch?"

"Huh? What are you talking about?"

"Why did you tell her I'm out to hurt people?"

"Well, aren't you?" I asked as calmly as possible. By now my heart was pounding so loud I was afraid he could hear it through the phone. Obviously Betty had written something about him. Maybe I should have spent the money to see what it was. "You beat up Joe, tried to set my vineyard on fire, you damaged the tasting room at Templeton Vineyards. So it looks to me like you are hurting people."

"Stop saying that," he screamed. "Your old man ruined me. Now I'm going to ruin you."

"How is it going to ruin me if you hurt other people? You aren't making sense, Edward Simmons." I was hoping he'd correct me with the name he's currently using, but all I heard was dead air; I couldn't even hear him breathing. I thought he'd hung up until he laughed.

"Nice try, Skylar, but Edward Simmons is dead. Ask your old man, he'll confirm that. Even that was his fault."

"No, it was your fault. If you hadn't been embezzling, none of this would've happened to you. You'd still have your bank in Central City. You need to take responsibility for your own actions." I could hear his ragged breathing now as his temper escalated again. Maybe by poking at him he'd slip up, giving some hint to his current identity.

"How did it hurt my dad or me for that matter, when you wrecked Chase Templeton's tasting room? Dad doesn't even know Chase beyond saying hi. And he's just my neighbor, nothing more." I was hoping he'd get the message that Chase wasn't my boyfriend, but his next statement proved he wasn't listening to anything I said.

"Templeton isn't going to want to merge with you now, is he? He isn't even going to want to be your boy toy," he sneered. "You're going to have to find someone else to play house with." Before I could set him straight on those issues, he cut the connection. I hoped the sheriff had put a trace on my phone like he'd suggested. We needed to catch a break; maybe this would be it.

That wasn't to be though.

"Unfortunately, Miss Bishop, your cell phone company isn't being very cooperative. They want a warrant. So far I haven't been able to obtain one." He seemed a lot more formal than he had when I first met him. He actually sounded upset with me for some reason. His next comment explained why.

"Deputy Wilkinson told me of your idea to have Betty Richards print a warning to the community. I wish you'd mentioned it to me first. Baiting a person like Edward Simmons isn't a smart idea. You never know what a psychopath will do, and I really believe that's what we're dealing with here. Making him mad isn't going to accomplish what you want. It could come back and bite you. This latest call should prove that. Please stay out of it, and let law enforcement handle things." Was this where Greg got his attitude? Or was this how all law enforcement acted?

It was obvious he'd seen Betty's column, and he wasn't happy with it or me at this point. I needed to find out what she wrote. Becky was working in the tasting room, but there were no customers when I went back inside. "Did you read Betty's paper today?" I asked.

"I wouldn't waste my money on her drivel," she snorted. "I don't know how she gets anyone to buy it, or how she stays in business. I didn't think you read it either." Surprise lifted her voice.

"I don't, but I need to see something in there." Since we still weren't busy, I slipped out to call Dora. I was sure she'd bought a paper just to see what Betty wrote.

"That woman is a wonder," she said when I reached her. "Just when I think she's totally worthless, she really lays it on thick. The woman should take up writing fiction."

"She definitely got his attention, and that of the sheriff," I said with a sigh. "Neither of them is happy with me right now." I told her about both of my calls.

"I thought Sheriff Stevens was smarter than that," she huffed. "He always seemed like a reasonable man, but I guess that's asking too much. If Betty's article draws this nut case out, that can only be a good thing to my way of thinking."

"I guess all of us civilians should just sit back, and let the big, brave law enforcement officers do all the work." She didn't miss the sarcasm in my voice and laughed, easing the tension building up in me. Drawing a deep breath, and releasing it slowly, I finally asked, "What did she write that has these wonderful men so upset?"

"I'll read it to you. "We have a mystery happening right here in our little town," she began. "It seems someone is out to ruin our economy. After attacking a prominent member of our wine community, and trying to set his vineyard on fire, this mystery man then attempted to destroy another of our citizens by ruining his business. Is this person a teetotaler, wanting to rid us of demon wine, or is something more sinister going on? Is our sheriff too sick to do the job the taxpayers of this county pay him to do? What about our illustrious mayor? Shouldn't he be concerned about all of the citizens, not just the ones who can vote for him? After all, the winery owners have boosted the economy of this town for years. Until these two men become concerned enough to do something about the crime wave hitting our small county, we all need to be on the lookout for anyone willing to hurt our neighbors. Be assured, I will be on top of it myself, and report any new attacks. Be sure to check this reporter's column next week to see what our sheriff and mayor are doing about this."

"Wow!" I breathed. "It's no wonder Edward Simmons and the sheriff are both boiling mad. I'm surprised the mayor hasn't weighed in on this article. Maybe he doesn't know I'm the one who instigated it."

"She did lay it on rather thick," Dora agreed with a laugh, "but for once I think she did everyone a good service. People need to know what's going on around here."

"Did you know the sheriff is sick?" I asked. "Has Greg said anything to you?"

"Not a word, but he doesn't say much about work."

"I wonder how Betty found out."

Dora gave a humorless laugh. "Most likely, she could find out things about the president the real media doesn't know. I wonder what she meant about checking back next week to see how the sheriff and mayor are doing. Is she planning on some sort of exposé? Why is she going after the mayor? He has nothing to do with finding the guy."

"I can't even pretend to know what she might do next," I sighed in frustration. "I just know Edward Simmons is really upset with her article. Until now, he's been operating below the radar, and he wanted to keep it that way. Maybe she needs to watch her back. He might go after her next."

Those words turned out to be prophetic.

~~~

Before seven o'clock Saturday morning George Davidson, the beekeeper I'd hired to look after the two hives I kept at the back of the property, came speeding down the lane, screeching to a halt in front of the winery. "We've got trouble at the hives. Call an ambulance and the sheriff!"

I was outside enjoying a few minutes of fresh air before we opened. Instantly my stomach knotted up. His face was pasty white, his hands shaking uncontrollably. "What happened, George?" I took hold of his arm, and led him over to a chair by the back door. "Can I get you something to drink?"

"Make it a strong one." His attempt at humor fell flat. "It's that gossip lady," he finally said after taking several deep breaths. "She's been hurt; the hives were pulled over on top of her. I don't know how bad she is."

Joe called 9-1-1 as we climbed into the truck with George. We needed to see if there was something we could do for Betty. As we drew near where the hives stood, I could see they were toppled over. Even from a distance, I could tell the ambulance wasn't going to help her. One of the hives lay across her legs, the bees nearly covering her body, angry their home had been destroyed.
~~~

Because we could hear the sirens, we stayed in the truck. There was no help for her now. If this was a crime scene, I didn't want to mess things up. I hoped those sirens meant it was Greg heading this way and not the sheriff. He was mad enough at me already. He'd probably see this as a result of the article, and blame me for what happened to her. I breathed a sigh of relief when I saw Greg through the windshield. His cop face was firmly in place.

George stepped out of the truck, and went around the back for his gear. "Let me fog them bees," he said. "Then you can see to her. If we can right those hives, they should settle down some." The angry bees weren't going to allow anyone near Betty, or their destroyed hives without the help of the fogger. With his beekeeper suit on, George lit the fogger, sending a layer of smoke over the bees. While they were temporarily subdued, the two men managed to upright the hives, then Greg radioed for the crime scene investigators and the coroner.

I was hoping the sheriff was in another part of the county. After his lecture the other day, I wasn't looking forward to seeing him anytime soon. But that wasn't to be. He pulled in right behind the coroner's wagon. With a glare in my direction that clearly said 'see what you've done,' he stomped over to Greg conferring with him in hushed tones.

Watching them, I couldn't help but notice what I'd ignored before. Sheriff Stevens was definitely sick, even Betty would have been able to know without any insider information. His complexion was gray, and he was slump-shouldered, his uniform hung loosely on his emaciated frame. Whatever was wrong with him, it had gotten worse since Dad's visit just a few days ago. I hadn't asked Greg about the sheriff's health, or Betty's mention of it in her article. That was a sore point between us at the moment, and I didn't need to add to it.

"What's he doing here?" I whispered to Joe as Mayor Brady's shiny Town Car pulled up beside the coroner's wagon. Ignoring the few onlookers, the mayor marched up to Sheriff Stevens and Greg demanding to know what was going on. His tanned face was now almost burgundy with anger; his loud voice carried across the field. Greg took charge, and a few minutes later, Mayor Brady got back in his car, sending up a cloud of dust as he drove off. But not before he glared through the windshield at me. Again I was struck with the fact that he had someone driving him. It crossed my mind that maybe there is a medical reason he can't drive himself. I couldn't believe he thought he was so important he hired a chauffeur.

Sheriff Stevens ignored the interruption, and walked over to where Joe and I were leaning against George's truck, a frown fixed firmly on his grayish face. "Morning, Miss Bishop. What can you tell me about this?" He nodded at Joe in acknowledgment of his presence.

"George Davidson is my beekeeper," I said, "he found Betty, and came to get us."

"And you don't know when this happened?" He probably already knew anything I could add, but he asked anyway. A deep scowl drew his eyebrows into a straight line above pale eyes. I shook my head, but didn't say anything. "When was the last time you checked on the hives?"

"I don't check on them. I hired George to do that for me. I don't know anything about keeping bees."

Sheriff Stevens heaved an impatient sigh. "So why do you keep bees if you don't know anything about them?"

It was my turn to sigh impatiently. Why was he asking me all these questions about bees? "The bees pollinate the vines and trees. I collect the honey to make mead. What does this have to do with Betty Richards' death?"

"Someone went to a lot of trouble to make it look like she was killed here, on your property by your bees. Maybe to make it look like you did this?" he asked, making it sound like a question. "I think we both know who that someone is. He's out to get you, Miss Bishop. That's why it's never a good idea to poke a stick at an angry animal. They always strike back."

"Are you saying this is my fault?" I asked indignantly, unable to believe what he was saying.

He heaved another heavy sigh. He was doing a lot of that. "No, that's not what I'm saying. The one who's at fault is the person who killed her. But by getting Miss Richards to provoke him, shall we say challenge him, in her article; he took up that challenge with deadly results. This is why civilians should never get involved in police work. Go back to your house now, I'll send someone up to question you as soon as we're done here." He turned away, leaving me to sputter in frustration.

"Of all the nerve!" I stomped off, heading across the field. By walking back to the house maybe I could walk off some of my temper; then again, maybe not. Instead, each step fueled my anger and remorse.

Joe walked beside me, keeping pace with my angry stride, but not saying a word. Once back at the house the full impact of what happened hit me. Tears flooded my eyes, clogging my throat, and making it difficult to breath. "Betty's really dead, Joe, and it's my fault."

He gave me a little shake. "You just cut that out right now. You didn't kill her, and you aren't to blame for what some crazy guy did. I don't care what the sheriff said."

"But if I hadn't come up with the scheme to get her to print a warning to the community, she'd still be alive."

"You don't know that. She might have printed the same thing on her own. She knew what was going on; she just chose to ignore it until she couldn't any longer. Every now and then she had to have a good thought."

"I still feel responsible."

"Well, stop it," Joe said sternly. "It's Edward Simmons' fault! He killed her. It's all on him." He pulled me into a big hug for just a moment. Because Joe isn't normally demonstrative, it meant all the more to me.

"He keeps saying he has to make Dad pay for what he did to him. But how does he figure killing Betty is going to hurt Dad. He never even met her."

"Thirty years ago Simmons did what he considered good for himself. It looks like he's still doing it. If he felt threatened by her article, if she was getting too close to the truth, I'm sure he felt justified in killing her. Right now he's trying to salvage what he has here."

"Did you know Sheriff Stevens was sick? He looked okay when he was here to see Dad." He didn't look okay today though.

Joe nodded. "There's been talk between some of the other winery owners. It's just been a rumor. I didn't pay much attention. Now it looks like the rumors are true."

I've had my head stuck so far in the sand for so long I hadn't even heard the rumors. What does that say about me? I wondered. "Is he going to have to resign, or will he keep working?" I asked. "Who will replace him if he resigns?"

Joe shrugged. "Maybe Greg can shed some light on the matter, but I don't think he wants to talk about it. Jim Stevens is his friend."

Minutes before we were ready to open, Greg pulled into the yard, driving around to the winery to keep the public from seeing the cruiser. Becky was working in the tasting room today, and Dora came over as soon as she heard what happened. The grapevine in any small town passed information faster than any news broadcast on television.

Becky and Dora followed me outside as Greg stepped out of his cruiser. He pulled me into a warm embrace unmindful of the others standing around waiting for information. "I'm sorry about the way Jim acted. He's under a lot of pressure right now." He kissed the top of my head.

"How sick is he?" Before he could say anything, I held up my hand. "Never mind, it's none of my business. What happens now?"

"We'll continue investigating. If Betty knew something about what's going on, she probably left information somewhere. We'll find it, and then we'll know who this guy is."

"But what if she was bluffing like she always did just innuendo and no substance? What then? Is he going to continue harassing everyone I know, maybe killing more people?"

"No matter what, we'll keep investigating. He can't hide forever." Greg sounded sure of himself, but I wasn't so confident. Edward Simmons had gotten away with murder for thirty years, what made anyone think he'd get caught now?

"Did she die from the bee stings? The bees were all over her." That many bee stings had to be terribly painful. Shivers crept up my spine.

He was wearing his cop face now. "We have to wait for the autopsy results. I can't say anything more than that." I'd seen enough cop shows on television to know the coroner could give an educated guess if there were obvious signs on the body. Maybe there weren't any outward signs other than the bee stings. What I'd seen of her legs, they were extremely swollen from the numerous stings. I was hoping she'd been unconscious at least before the bees were dumped on her.

"This happened on my property, Greg. I have the right to know."

"It was made to look like it happened on your property." Translation; someone brought her here, and dumped the hives on her, making it look like I had something to do with her death. This was probably more than he should have said, but I was grateful for it just the same.

~~~

I was never so glad to see a day end as I was now. Throughout the day, as tourists came in the tasting room, some of them had heard the talk of Betty's death. Not many were aware it had happened on my property though. I wasn't sure how this would affect my business, or that of the other wineries. Curiosity seekers might spill into the
~~~

area, or it could make the tourists stay away, afraid of what might happen to them. Only time would tell.

Pastor Rick was waiting for me when Joe and I entered the church Sunday morning, giving me a brief hug, and shaking Joe's hand. "Don't try to blame yourself for this, Skylar" he said before I had a chance to say anything. "Guilt is the devil's work. He takes great delight when we feel guilty for something that isn't our fault. Betty had been skating dangerously close to the edge for years with all of her lies. Several pastors in town tried to get her to change her ways, but she always claimed the Constitution gave her the right to say anything. It's a shame the one time she tells the truth, she has to pay with her life though."

During the service, he mentioned her passing, but made no comment of the details. Although she had lived in New Haven for a number of years, few people knew anything about her extended family, and no one would speculate about a memorial service. She'd been universally avoided by most of the people in town hoping to stay out of her paper.

A few reporters from Tucson and Phoenix descended on our small town; the novelty of someone dying from bee stings brought out the morbid. Somehow Greg and the sheriff kept the exact location where she was found, and the fact that the hives were deliberately dumped on her, out of the news. The locals knew the few details bantered about on the gossip grapevine, but no one was willing to say anything to strangers. They didn't want to give our town a bad name, and possibly harm the wineries and eventually the area's economy.

The fact that I hadn't heard from Edward Simmons again puzzled me. So far, when he did something, he was right there in my face, pointing out it was my fault. I didn't know if his silence had any significance or not. Who else would benefit from Betty's death? I didn't even know how this would benefit Edward Simmons unless he hoped to put the blame on me. It would definitely hurt Dad if I was charged with her murder.

With all this going on I had completely forgotten about James Burke. Until he came into the tasting room late that afternoon, that is. My stomach turned over as he stepped up to the long serving bar. With his crooked smile, he leered at me. "How are you doing today, Miss Bishop? I hope all this trouble doesn't reflect negatively on you."

"I'm doing fine. I'm sure the sheriff will have this figured out in no time." I was just grateful he was the only customer right then. Dora said he had poor timing and poor social skills which his current statement certainly proves. "What would you like to sample today?" I changed the subject, hoping he'd take the hint.

Unfortunately, he lingered over his choices, pontificating on each selection like he was a wine critic. For once, I was grateful we were slow, and no other customers came in while he was spouting off. Finally he chose two different wines and left, but not before promising to come again. "With just six tastings, I wasn't able to sample your entire line. I'll certainly be back." With that parting shot, the door closed behind him.

I sagged against the walnut bar. I hope he doesn't come back any time soon, I thought. Picking up a squirt bottle from the shelf behind me, I began spraying everything he touched. The man simply made my skin crawl.

~~~

What the hell do I do now? This wasn't supposed to happen. He stared out the large window at nothing in particular. If that stupid bitch had just kept her nose out of my business, everything would have been fine. But I couldn't take the chance she knew something.

My plans went up in smoke thirty years ago because of Bishop, and it's taken all this time to get back what he took away from me. If things had worked out the way I'd planned, I'd be living in a mansion somewhere instead of this small Podunk town.

"I should have just left her alone," he chided himself. But seeing Clay Bishop had brought all of his hatred back
~~~

in a rush, and he wanted payback. Was Sheriff Stevens so sick he wouldn't look really close at this murder? Having her charged with murder would be the ultimate revenge on her old man. He gave a bark of laughter, enjoying that thought.

CHAPTER TEN

Monday's were usually very productive with few interruptions, but not today. I couldn't keep my mind trained on what needed to be done. My thoughts kept going in circles. James Burke, Edward Simmons, Betty Richards. How did all of these fit together, or not at all? Why was Betty Richards killed? Why on my property? She hadn't said she knew who was attacking the wineries, or even that I was the main target.

Would Greg and the other investigators find anything at her home, or office that would lead to her murderer? She mentioned both the sheriff and mayor in her article. Did she really have something on either one, or both of them? Or was she just blowing smoke like always? It'd be a shame if she'd lost her life because of one of her little lies. By the end of the day I was exhausted, and just wanted to crash.

Greg was tied up with the murder investigation, and Joe was with Dora. Joe didn't want to leave me alone, and wanted me to go with him, but I declined. In my present mood, I wouldn't be good company. Instead, I decided to do some detecting of my own.

The internet is a wonderful invention where you can find out things about people they probably wish you couldn't. If I could find out something about James Burke, proving once and for all he isn't Edward Simmons, maybe I could forget him, and look elsewhere for my mystery caller. Greg keeps saying he's too young to be Edward Simmons, but I need to set the doubts in my mind to rest.

I was looking for background information on the James Burke here in New Haven. Just my luck, about a dozen people with that name popped up. I didn't know if some of these hits were duplicates, which seemed most likely. I can rule out those who are either too old, too young, or the wrong race. Three or four could qualify as being the James Burke here. Getting information wasn't as easy as I'd imagined. There were no pictures of any of the men. I finally decided to look at the bank's website to see what I could find there. The picture matched the man, but gave no background information that wasn't job related.

Maybe I should have gone over to Dora's with Joe, I thought. Frustrated, I stepped out on the front porch, the soft evening air and gentle breeze tickled my skin. When a Templeton Vineyards truck pulled into the lane, I groaned, slumping against the porch post. What is he going to blame me for now?

Chase looked more than a little sheepish as he stopped at the base of the steps. We hadn't spoken since the morning his winery was broken into. "I know you don't want me here, and I don't blame you." he spoke before I could say anything. "I came over to apologize. I know you didn't break into my tasting room." He drew a deep breath before continuing. "I finally looked at the tape from that night. There's no way that person is either you or Joe. I should've kept my mouth shut until someone looked at the video. I was just so mad about the break-in, I wasn't thinking straight. I was still smarting from your threat, so I jumped to the conclusion that you did it. What else was I supposed to think? I've never had any trouble before. And..." He faltered for just a heartbeat, looking embarrassed before continuing softly. "I was sort of jealous, too."

My chin almost hit the ground with that statement. My operation was much smaller than his, what did he have to be jealous of? Besides, he'd made it clear what he thought of fruit wines when I first started. I was so speechless I couldn't even pose the question, and he hurried on. "I've tried for five years to get you to go out with me, but you weren't interested. It didn't take Wilkinson more than a week, and he was a shoo-in. What's he got that I don't have?" He sounded like a petulant little boy. I started to say something, but he held up his hand to keep me from speaking. "Never mind, that's not why I'm here. I just wanted to apologize, and to see if you were all right after what happened to Betty Richards."

I didn't know what to say when he finally sputtered to a stop. I decided to ignore his comment about Greg. "I'm okay, I guess, just sorry for what happened to her. I don't understand why someone would kill her here, or use my bees to do it. Greg... and the rest of the sheriff's department," I added quickly when his face darkened at the mention of the man he perceived as his rival, "will figure it out. I accept your apology. Can we go back to being friends and neighbors?" Calling us friends was a stretch, but until recently there hadn't been any real animosity between us.

He eagerly agreed, and a few minutes later he left. I didn't know if I should believe he'd actually been jealous of Greg. I hadn't taken his advances seriously, thinking he was more interested in impressing Dad. I guess that was the problem.

Sitting there in the dark, I continued to consider all that had been happening. It's been more than thirty-six hours since the murder, and still nothing from Edward Simmons. Until now, he'd taken delight in calling me in the middle of the night to taunt or threaten me. Since the murder there has been only silence. I didn't know what to make of that.

Greg looked exhausted when he stepped out of his SUV several hours later. He'd been working almost around the clock trying to sort out what happened, and still doing his other duties. "Jim Stevens is in the hospital." He sounded defeated as well as tired. "It looks like he's going to have to resign in the near future."

Wrapping my arms around his waist, I offered him the only comfort I had to give. "I'm sorry, Greg. I know he's your friend. What happens now?" I didn't know if I was asking about the murder investigation or Jim's health. Maybe the truth lay somewhere in the middle.

Greg shrugged his broad shoulders. "Until the County Supervisors decide something, I guess we continue the way we are. Next in line is one of the detectives, but I'm not really sure he wants the job."

"Are you going to run for sheriff? You'd be great."

"Jim's been pushing me to run," he admitted. "That's sort of why I came down here, besides to help him out. I just didn't think it would be this soon. I haven't been in the county very long, and I wanted to get a better feel of things here before I did something like that. It's a small county and there hasn't been much crime in the past. Until now, the biggest problems have been drunk drivers between the wineries, and smugglers crossing the border. I'd like to see what the feds are going to do next on that score."

CHAPTER ELEVEN

For the remainder of the week, the silence from Edward Simmons continued to be deafening, and I still didn't know what to make of it. Had he decided to leave me alone? Why now? Betty's murder was putting our small town in a bad light. Did that make a difference to him? I studied everyone I met, trying to decide if they were Edward Simmons in disguise. There were plenty of men in town in the right age group, but they had either lived in New Haven their entire life, or had been here longer than me. Either way, that didn't fit my idea of who he is now. Why would he just now begin to harass me if he'd been here when I first moved to town? I had kept to myself until recently, but I hadn't been invisible. What happened to set him off now?

First thing Saturday morning, James Burke showed up in the tasting room. "Good morning. I told you I'd be back to taste more of your delicious wines."

I looked around the room to see who was talking because his mouth hadn't moved. His face was totally expressionless, while his eyes danced with mischief. I wanted someone else to see this phenomenon. Unfortunately, I was alone with him, and he was freaking me out. "G...good morning, Mr. Burke." I hated the quiver in my voice, but I couldn't help it.

"Oh, please, call me James. I hope we'll become good friends."

Not in this life, I thought, trying to maintain a friendly smile. At least I hoped it was a smile. I breathed a sigh of relief as more customers came in, Cody basking in the attention they were paying him. Sensing my discomfort, he came behind the bar, leaning up against my leg to give me comfort.

"Welcome to Sky Vineyards," I started my usual greeting, setting out lists of wines for everyone to choose from along, with my signature glasses.

"The last time I was here I didn't get to try your fruit wine," Mr. Burke stated through barely moving lips. "I've heard nothing but good things about them." The young woman standing next to him looked up when he first started speaking. Now she stared openly, before looking at me and her friends. I knew exactly what she was thinking. He sort of looked like a ventriloquist practicing without his dummy; just creepier.

"We just got the blackberry and raspberry wines bottled," I said. "They're among the sweets on the list." I pointed them out on the list in front of the young woman, trying to avoid getting any closer than necessary to James Burke.

I silently willed the small group to stick around as long as he was here. I didn't want to be left alone with him again. It was still early in the day, and no others came in. He finished his tasting quickly, and left with two more bottles. Maybe he sensed the discomfort from the rest of us. Or maybe he just got self-conscious of the fact that every time he said something, the others stared at him. At least he didn't promise to return, and I hoped he wouldn't.

As the door closed behind him, I sagged against the bar. I couldn't stop the sigh of relief that escaped my lips. Cody relaxed, too, heading for his bed by the front door. "Who is that guy?" the young woman whispered as if Mr. Burke could hear her. "What's wrong with him?"

I shrugged. "He's a local businessman. I'm not sure what's wrong with him." I didn't want to gossip, and I really didn't know what was wrong with him. If he is only in his forties, why is he having so many Botox injections? If he is Edwards Simmons in the guise of James Burke, why is he coming here pretending to make nice?

With more customers arriving, the day was in full swing leaving me little time to ponder the mystery of James Burke. If he realizes I work the tasting room by myself first thing each morning, I felt certain he'd be back. If for no other reason than to creep me out. Did he even realize how strange he looked when his facial muscled didn't move, when he talked?

~~~

Greg and I were becoming regulars at Manuel's on Friday or Saturday evening, sometimes both, when Greg wasn't working. While we waited for our meal, and munched on chips and salsa, I recounted James Burke's visit. "I'm not the only one who noticed how weird he looked," I said, unable to completely stop the shiver of revulsion passing through me. "He's never shown any interest in Sky Vineyards before. Why is he taking a sudden interest now?" In my mind, this confirmed he was somehow connected to what was going on with Edward Simmons.

Before Greg could answer, Mayor Brady stopped at our table, an expression of concern on his deeply tanned face. He nodded solemnly to both of us before addressing Greg. "I am sorry to hear about Sheriff Stevens. I know he was your friend." My stomach turned over. Had the sheriff passed away, and Greg hadn't said anything?

"He still is my friend," Greg stated coldly, the muscles in his jaw bunched as he clenched his teeth. "He's still alive."

"Of course, I misspoke. I didn't mean anything by that." Mayor Brady cleared his throat. "I went to see him this afternoon, and we had a nice talk. It looks like he is going to be in there for a while. We agreed it is time to appoint a new sheriff."

"I doubt Jim agreed to that. Besides, you aren't in charge of the sheriff's department. That's up to the County Supervisors; a special election will need to be held."

"Of course, of course," the mayor agreed quickly, his face turning red beneath his dark tan. I couldn't decide if it was from anger or embarrassment. "I will be working with the supervisors on this matter. Well, I will let you finish
~~~

your dinner." He turned to me. "It's nice to see you again, Skylar." With that, he stomped off. His slightly formal speech pattern was in sharp contrast to his down home, good old boy way of dressing. He always wore jeans, his shirt sleeves rolled up to his elbows. He seldom used contractions, causing me to wonder if English was his second language.

"What was that about?" I whispered, afraid he'd hear me.

"There's been a power struggle between Jim and Mayor Brady ever since he became mayor. With Jim sick, he sees it as his chance to grab some power that shouldn't be his. The man is so full of himself," Greg muttered the last words.

"How long has he been mayor?" I didn't keep up with local politics.

"Almost as long as he's lived here. He moved to New Haven seven or eight years ago. No one knows anything more about him than they did when he first moved here. He's tried to take control of everything in the area, and Jim told him to stay out of county business.

"If he manages to convince the supervisors to let him appoint an acting sheriff, you can be sure it will be someone who's nothing more than Brady's lap dog. He acts like this is his own little kingdom. He had some big plans when he first moved here, but hasn't been able to push them through yet."

"Will the supervisors go along with him?"

Greg shrugged. "I can't say for sure."

I took his hand, gripping it tightly. "Greg, you have to run for sheriff. You'd make a great one, and you know what you're doing. Do you really want to leave the county open to Mayor Brady's appointee? Think about what it'll be like working for someone like that."

He gave a slight shudder at the thought, then laughed at my enthusiasm. "You sound just like Jim. He even got the paperwork, and filled out most of it." He grew thoughtful, "All I have to do is sign it."

“So what are you waiting for?” Juanita brought our food, placing sizzling plates of steak fajitas and refried beans in front of us, preventing him from saying anything more. The spicy aroma made my stomach rumbled in spite of all the chips I’d eaten. Breakfast was just a distant memory. It was several minutes before either of us spoke again as we attacked the hot, spicy food.

Finally coming up for air, I repeated my question. “What are you waiting for? Sign the papers, and officially start running for sheriff. Isn’t that why you transferred here from Coconino County?” He’d never said as much, but I’d read between the lines. That’s why Jim Stevens wanted him here.

He slowly chewed the bite he’d just taken, giving himself time before answering. Finally he nodded. “I know that’s what Jim wanted when I came here, and I guess I want it, too. But there are other deputies who’ve worked for the department a lot longer than I have. I don’t want to step on any toes, or cause problems with any of them.”

“If they wanted the job, wouldn’t they have already started campaigning? Hasn’t everyone been aware that Jim is sick? Not everyone wants to be boss.”

He was quiet for several more minutes, giving what I said some thought. His next comment wasn’t what I expected though. “Not everyone is cut out to be married to a law enforcement officer either. Is it something you could live with?”

I nearly choked on my food, and I covered my mouth with a napkin until I got my breath back. Was he proposing to me? We haven’t known each other all that long.

He laughed. “I was just asking a question. Not something requiring an answer tonight, just food for thought.”

Food for thought, indeed! I’ll be chewing on that for a week. Make that a month.

Throughout the rest of our dinner we were both preoccupied with our own thoughts. Instead of going somewhere else when we left the restaurant, Greg drove back to the vineyard. I wasn't sure if he was going to drop me off, and leave, or stick around. In answer to my unasked question, he sat down on the porch swing, pulling me down beside him to enjoy the cool night air. Nights in southeastern Arizona are beautiful, and I never tire of sitting outside in the evenings.

After several minutes, the silence began to get uncomfortable when Greg cleared his throat. "Ah, I didn't mean to spook you at the restaurant, Sky. But I want you to know that being a cop is all I've ever wanted to be. Not some glorified version like the FBI, just a cop. Is that something you can live with?"

I smiled in the dark. "I know what you mean. All I've ever wanted to be is a vintner, and own my own small winery. So I understand your life-long dream. I have a question for you." I looked up at him in the dark, hoping my expression was very serious. "Does sheriff qualify as being just a cop? Or is that a glorified version? This county needs, and deserves someone who knows what they're doing. I think we need someone like you."

He gathered me up in a bear hug, burying his face in my neck for several long seconds before kissing me. It was a good thing we were sitting down because my legs never would've held me up by the time he lifted his head. Without knowing how it happened, I ended up on his lap, and that was fine by me.

It was a while before we got around to talking again, but I stayed cuddled up on his lap. "Being sheriff is more politician than cop," he finally said. "But in our small county I think I can live with that. I'd still be a cop most of the time. What happens when the voters decide they want a change though?"

"Then you go back to being just a cop, not a cop and a politician. You're going to be great at both." I assured him.

We spent the rest of the evening talking, among other things. I told him about being raised by a single father with the help of Joe, and any number of neighbor ladies who wanted to gain my dad's attention. "I didn't date much in high school or college," I admitted. "I was always more interested in learning all I could about the wine business. Dad wanted to send me to France to study under the masters, but I decided to go to UC Davis to their Winemaker's Certificate Program. I just want to be the best vintner possible."

"You've got a good leg up right here. Do you plan on going back to California at some point?" He seemed to be holding his breath, waiting for my answer.

"Of course," I waited a beat before I finished my statement, "I'll always go visit Dad." I poked him in the ribs forcing him to expel his breath in a whoosh. "This is my home now. I like what I'm doing, and I'm earning a few awards along the way." In the few hours we'd been talking, he knew more about me than anyone besides Dad and Joe. Some of the things we talked about even they didn't know.

When Joe came home several hours later we were still on the porch swing. He drove around back, and came through the tasting room to join us for a minute. "It's getting kind of late, kids. Morning will be here soon with another busy day."

"Yes, Daddy Joe. Did you have a nice evening? It's a little late for you to be out yourself."

He chuckled, and turned back inside. "See you in the morning. Don't make too much noise. Us old folks need our sleep."

It wasn't as late as Joe hinted, but late enough. Like he said, tomorrow would be busy, and Greg had to work, too. I watched his truck until it was out of sight then went inside. I'm not sure my feet even touched the floor as I floated off to bed.

~~~

Dora, Greg and Pattiann met us outside the church the next morning. Greg's open display of affection surprised me when he placed a light kiss on my lips. He was in
~~~

uniform since he had to go to work shortly after the service was over. Most men would forgo getting up early enough to go to church if they had to go in to work. Another sign of his good character, I told myself with a small smile.

Pastor Rick greeted us with his usual hug after the service. "Now here is a happy couple. Can we be expecting an announcement in the near future?" Before either of us could answer, he looked up at Dora and Joe. "And here's another happy couple right here. Maybe I should ask if there will be a double announcement." Joe turned every shade of red.

Turning to Pattiann then, Pastor Rick gave Joe a reprieve. "How about you, young lady? Is there any chance you'd be making it a triple announcement?"

She took a step back with a look of mock horror on her face, and holding up her hands as though to ward off an attack. "Not anytime in the near future, Pastor. I'm happy just as I am." We all laughed along with several of the others around us.

Outside, Greg placed another soft kiss on my lips. "I'll see you tonight." He kissed his mom and sister on the cheek, and hurried off so he wouldn't be late for work. Right up until the time we unlocked the door on the tasting room, I floated through my normal routine. Within minutes of the door being unlocked, James Burke walked in, my happy mood plummeting into the wine cellar.

"Good morning, Skylar." Again his mouth barely moved with his words. "It is alright if I call you Skylar, isn't it? Miss Bishop sounds so formal." His muscles still didn't work but his eyes danced merrily like he knew the exact reaction he provoked in people.

My stomach churned. Even if he isn't Edward Simmons, he makes my skin crawl. The only polite answer to his question was yes, but I nodded instead of speaking. I couldn't get the word past the lump in my throat.

"I'd like to talk to you about a business proposition," he stated. "National Bank is a statewide bank, giving extremely great service. We also have top of the line products. I'm certain we can top any rates you're getting at your current bank." The entire time he spoke, I watched his mouth to see if his lips moved. They did, but barely.

I'm sure my jaw dropped open for just a few seconds before I recovered my composure. "Mr. Burke."

"Oh please," he interrupted, "call me James."

That wasn't what I wanted to call him, but I didn't tell him that. Drawing a steadying breath, I said through gritted teeth, "James," not bothering to curb my annoyance, "the four days the tasting room is open I'm very busy with customers." He looked around at the empty room, and I pushed on. "Although we aren't busy at this particular moment, I still have things to do in anticipation of a busy day. Besides, I'm very satisfied with the bank that I do business with, and have no intention of changing."

Although his jaw muscles didn't even twitch, anger flashed in his pale eyes. It was gone just as quickly as it appeared. He managed to keep his tone even and friendly. "Since you're such good friends with one of my top employees and her family, I thought you'd like to help her out with her job."

Was he implying Dora's job might be in jeopardy if I didn't switch banks? "My father always told me not to mix business with pleasure. It can cause trouble on both fronts." I watched carefully for any reaction to the mention of my father, but there was nothing. "I don't think Dora would appreciate you trying to trade on our friendship." I was sure he was gritting his teeth, but his frozen muscles didn't even twitch. His eyes were a clear expression of just how angry he was though. They were now nearly black and flashing with fire.

Before either of us could say anything more, the door opened, admitting a laughing group with Cody enjoying the attention they were showering on him. Without another word, James Burke left. If the door hadn't had an automatic closer on it, I'm sure he would have slammed it on his way out.

Feigning a cheerful greeting, I smiled at the newcomers. "Welcome to Sky Vineyards." Now that he was gone, and any danger, real or imagined, was over, I tried to relax. It took several minutes before my hands stopped shaking. I drew several deep breaths, concentrating on my usual chatter. I had very little time to think about James Burke for the next several hours. By then Becky was helping out, and I took a breather, stepping outside for a minute.

"What's wrong, Kiddo?" Joe walked across the yard, a frown of concern creasing his forehead. "That psycho Simmons call you again?"

"No." Giving my head a shake, I told him about James Burke's visit. It took much less time to tell what happened than it felt like, as it was happening. He'd probably been in the tasting room only five minutes, but it felt more like five hours.

"We have to let Dora know what he tried to do," I said when I finished relaying our conversation. "I don't want to jeopardize her job."

"Honey, Dora can take care of herself. She'll be just as upset at what he tried to pull as you are. I'm sure she'll take him to task come tomorrow."

"She could lose her job! I don't want anything to happen to her."

Joe gave me a hug. "Don't worry about that. We take care of our own. We'll make sure nothing bad happens to her. Now you go back in there and help Becky. We'll work all this out tonight when Dora and Greg come over." Joe's calm, easy going nature helped ease some of my fears, and I managed to make it through the rest of the day.

As expected, Dora was furious with her boss when I told her what he'd tried to pull. "You were right to tell him I'd be upset. He's not going to get away with it either." She paced around Joe's kitchen for several minutes.

I looked expectantly at Greg, hoping he'd say something to calm his mother down. He just smiled at me. "Dora, please don't do anything that will get you fired," I said into the silence. "He didn't do anything really wrong."

She laughed, giving me a hug. "Now don't you worry yourself, Honey. He has no grounds to fire me. If anyone loses their job over this, it will be him." She laughed again. "I have connections much higher up than he does." I wasn't sure what she meant, but for now I let it go.

~~~

Dora looked disgruntled, and more than a little frustrated Monday evening when she came over. My stomach began to twist, which was becoming a normal state for me lately. "What happened? He didn't fire you, did he?" I wanted to grab her hands, but stayed rooted to my spot by the counter.

She released a frustrated sigh. "He didn't say anything; he didn't even bother to come in today. He called before I got there, and told his secretary he was sick. He's taking a few days off. I'm not sure what's wrong with him, but if he was still as bad as you say he was yesterday, his Botox treatments are probably backfiring. Mary said he sounded terrible."

I didn't know what to make of this development. Was he really sick? What were the side effects of Botox? Was he trying to avoid Dora? Or was something more sinister going on? I still had suspicions that James and Edward Simmons were one and the same. There was nothing I could do about it now though.
~~~

CHAPTER TWELVE

Edward Simmons ended his silence three days later at his usual inopportune time of two in the morning. When my cell phone went off, startling me out of a sound sleep, it took me several beats to wake up enough to find it. Sliding my finger across the screen to accept the call, I put the phone to my ear. "Good morning, Edward. It's been a while. I hope you haven't been sick." I had rehearsed this speech over and over while I waited for him to call again. My pleasant tone must have thrown him off his tirade because the silence continued for several beats. I could hear his harsh breathing so I knew he was still there.

"Edward Simmons is dead," he finally growled at me. "Your old man made sure of that."

I ignored his comment about Dad, keeping my voice calm, even while my heart tried to pound its way out of my chest. "I don't know what else to call you. Why don't you give me your current name so I don't make that mistake again?" I concentrated on his voice, his words, hoping to recognize the person behind them.

"Nice try." His laugh was as gravelly as his voice. Was that because he was sick, or his continued attempt to disguise his voice? Could Botox affect a person's vocal cords, making his voice sound that way? "I'm not stupid enough to fall for your tricks, Skylar."

"Well, then I'll just have to call you Edward. What can I do for you in the middle of the night?" I was determined to keep my voice level and pleasant.

"You've enjoyed the benefit of having a great many people watching out for you, but I want you to know all of that is about to end. You're going to lose everything you hold dear."

Ignoring his current threat, I asked him a question instead. "Why did you kill Betty Richards? What did she have to do with me or you for that matter?" My heart was pounding, but I managed to keep my voice calm.

"She got in my way. She was one of those watching your back when she had no right to do that. She had to pay."

"So you admit you murdered her?" My voice was incredulous. I couldn't believe he was that callous and cavalier about murder. By now I'd gotten smart; I was recording our conversation. I wasn't sure what good it'd do, but I wanted to have some proof.

He gave a nasty chuckle. "There is no harm in admitting to something you can't prove. You still don't know who I am. Enjoy what little time you have left with your little winery, and all your friends." With that, he hung up. My hands were shaking so bad I jabbed at the end button on my phone several times before managing to shut it off.

Sleep was out of the question now, but I needed to be doing something. I just didn't know what. I wanted to go outside, but I no longer felt safe even on my own front porch in the middle of the night. This maniac could be sitting at the end of the lane watching, waiting for a chance to do God only knew what.

I paced around the house, checking and rechecking the doors and windows to make sure everything was secure. Cody followed in my footsteps. Finally I sat down in my overstuffed rocker staring out the big window at my vineyard, and the orchard beyond. What's he going to do next? There was little doubt in my mind he had some diabolical plan up his sleeve. Replaying the conversation over and over in my mind, something tugged at my memory. He had managed to disguise his voice so I wouldn't be able to recognize it. Still there was something nagging at me, I just didn't know what.

He admitted he killed Betty Richards, feeling safe I'd never be able to identify him, or get any proof of his crimes. Greg said the cause of death had been "blunt force trauma," meaning someone had hit her over the head with a hard object. She was still alive, but just barely, when the bee hives were dumped on her. I don't know if she felt the hundreds of bee stings. I certainly hope not, knowing how painful that would've been.

Edward Simmons tried to make it look like I'd killed her, but he didn't do very good job. There was no evidence I'd been anywhere near the hives recently. I wasn't the one who collected the honey, or did whatever beekeepers had to do with the bees. So why had he put her on my property if he wasn't going to do a better job of placing the blame on me?

The thoughts swirled in my mind until eventually I fell asleep in the comfortable chair. It felt like only minutes later when Joe gave me a gentle shake to wake me up.

"What's going on, Kiddo? Why are you sleeping out here?" Concern furrowed his rugged face.

I uncurled myself from the chair, stretching out the kinks in my back and legs. "Our friend called again to let me know he's still lurking out there ready to cause more trouble." I rubbed my hands over my face. "He's so confident he won't get caught, he admitted killing Betty."

Joe shook his head. "Greg won't let him get away with it. There's no such thing as the perfect crime." He reached out his hand to pull me out of the chair. "Let's get something to eat. Then you can give Greg a call. He needs to know."

~~~

"Miss Bishop, this is Jake Henderson at the Bank of New Haven. We just got a wire transfer order to close your accounts, and wire the money to a bank in California."

"What?! No! Don't do it!"

"We didn't do it. Your father doesn't have that authority. I just wanted to call, and check if you had any knowledge of it." Jake Henderson is the manager of the bank where my accounts are. I'd met him at the time I opened the accounts, but since then hadn't had much contact with him.
~~~

"My father? He wouldn't do something like this. Is there something you can do so no one can try this again, and maybe succeed next time?"

Mr. Henderson assured me they'd make certain nothing happened to my accounts; Only Joe and I are authorized to withdraw money or move the accounts. "I suggest you run your credit report, Miss Bishop, both you and Mr. Barnes, to make sure whoever did this hasn't tried to take out credit in your name. We're also going to try, and trace the origin of the wire transfer order. I don't hold out much hope though. Whoever tried this was good."

"Thank you, Joe and I will run credit reports right away. And thank you for protecting our accounts." I put my phone back in my pocket. "This day just keeps getting better," I muttered, "and we haven't even opened yet." I paced across the room. There was only one person who would do this, Edward Simmons. Like he promised in the night, he wasn't through messing with me yet. To me this was more proof James Burke and Edward Simmons are one and the same. Who else would have the knowledge needed to pull a scam like this?

But he's too young, a little voice reminded me. Who else but a banker would know about something like this? I argued back. Wouldn't he know the bank would check before closing my accounts? I continued the argument with myself.

I knew Dad hadn't done this, but I needed to call and let him know. He had to protect his accounts as well.

As expected, Dad was furious about this latest attack. We were both grateful Mr. Henderson had stopped the wire transfer. At least no harm had been done, and we now have a warning that he's trying something else.

"Everything okay with Clay's accounts?" Joe spoke quietly, worry written on his face.

I nodded. "He's upset that Simmons is trying to use him to hurt us, of course. We have to figure out who this guy is before he does anything else. If it really isn't James Burke, who else can it be?" Both Greg and Joe had listened to the recording of the latest call, but didn't recognize the voice. Something still nagged at my memory, but continued to elude me. I needed to check with Dora when she came over to see if her boss was still out sick.

Taking Mr. Henderson's suggestion, Joe and I ran our credit reports. It'd take several hours before we got our answer, but deep down inside I already knew what it would show. I just hoped we were in time to prevent any damage to our credit rating.

We had a slow start on the morning, and I wondered if our sign was missing again. But if that was the case, we wouldn't have any customers at all. Maybe it was just a slow day. One of the area tour guides brought in a group just after noon. It was unusual to have tours during the week, but we welcomed them just the same. "Hey, Ted. How's it going?" I waved at the driver when he got a cold soda out of the small fridge by the door.

"I wasn't sure if you were open today, Skylar. You planning on heading back to California?" He leaned against the bar while his customers made their wine selections.

"We're always open on Thursday. What would make today different? The tourist season is heating up so I can't get away right now." I wasn't really paying attention to what he said.

"Why are you selling out then? I thought you liked it here."

That caught my attention, and I walked away from the group so they wouldn't hear. "What are you talking about? I'm not selling." My stomach was already churning, and my heart was lodged in my throat making it difficult to breath or talk.

He leaned close, following my example. "There's a for sale sign out by the road. You don't know anything about it?"

It took enormous control to stay where I was when I wanted to run outside to see what he was talking about. This couldn't be happening. I shook my head at his question. "Will you do me a favor? Go out and find Joe. Tell him about the sign. I'm definitely not selling the vineyard!"

He went outside like I asked, and within minutes Joe's truck roared down the lane. A few minutes later he stepped into the tasting room, giving me a thumb's up. My muscles relaxed, but my stomach was still churning. The sign was down, and no harm had been done. That was good, but I needed to find out who put it there and why.

Becky came in the back door a half hour later. God bless Joe. He knew just what to do. Becky could deal with the customers while I called the real estate agent in Tucson.

"Coleworth Realty, this is Jennifer. How may I help you?"

"I'm calling about the winery in New Haven you have listed."

"Oh, that's a very nice property."

"Have you seen it?"

"Ah, well no. But I have pictures, and all the statistics here. Would you like to see it?"

I ignored her question, asking one of my own. "Who listed it?"

"Well, the owner, of course."

"No, I'm the owner, and I didn't list it. I live here, and I operate the winery. What did this 'owner' look like?"

"Ah...Well, I've never actually met her. This was all handled by fax and mail."

"And you didn't think that was a little odd?"

"Well, no. It's done all the time when the owners live out of state."

"But you didn't actually check any of this out, did you?"

"Ah." She hesitated again. "Well, no, but I have all the documents signed and notarized. Everything is legal."

"Except it isn't legal, because I didn't sign any of those papers, and I can prove I'm the legal owner. Take that listing down immediately. I've already removed your sign. When did you put it up? It wasn't here last night."

"There wasn't supposed to be a sign. My client said she didn't want her neighbors or employees to know she was selling. It's all in the contract." Jennifer sputtered.

"Except it's a fraudulent contract, signed by someone other than myself. Either you remove the listing immediately, or you'll be talking to my lawyer. Didn't you think it rather odd that your supposed client didn't want a sign on the property? That sounds rather fishy to me." My hands were shaking so hard with anger I could barely hold the phone to my ear.

"No, sometimes commercial property owners don't want anyone knowing they're selling, especially their employees. That's what Miss Bishop said. She didn't want her employees to quit before her business was sold." This whole thing was getting more bizarre by the minute.

"I didn't say any such thing because I didn't list my property. Now take down the listing immediately!" Trying to remain calm wasn't working, I was almost screaming at this point.

"I can't do that," she objected. "I already have an offer. I'm waiting to hear from Miss Bishop if she will accept the offer."

"You're talking to Miss Bishop, the real Miss Bishop! If you do anything to move forward with this, you'll find yourself in more hot water than you know what to do with."

"I'm going to have to check with my client," she said stubbornly. "I can't just take your word that you're the rightful owner."

"But you took the word of someone you'd never met when you listed the property. Where is this person supposed to live? Did you even talk to her on the phone?"

"Ah..." She hesitated. "I'm sorry, but I can't give out that kind of information," she finally said. "It's confidential."

"Well, you enjoy your confidential information for now because it won't be for long. You'll be hearing from my lawyer. If you send anyone out to look at my winery, I will be sure to tell them that you took a fraudulent listing."

"You can't do that! You'll ruin my reputation!"

"Not my problem. You need to check out your clients a bit more carefully. Good day." I hit disconnect, wishing I had a land line so I could slam the phone down in her ear. That would have been much more satisfying.

I hadn't been off the phone five minutes when Chase Templeton came barreling around to the back of the winery, tires sending a cloud of dust into the air as he screeched to a halt. "Skylar, tell me you haven't signed the final papers yet." He gripped my arms so tight I would probably have bruises. "Why didn't you tell me you were going to sell? I would have saved you the realtor fees. Whatever the offer is, I'll up it by ten percent. You know I've always been interested in your vineyard." So much for his professed desire for me, and not my land. I should've known he wasn't really jealous of Greg.

I shook off his hands, and glared at him. "Slow down, Chase. I'm not selling the winery! That sign was just another attempt to harm me." Chase looked so disappointed I would have laughed if I wasn't so angry.

"It's just a joke?" he asked. "Who would do something like that?"

"No, it's not a joke! Someone is really trying to put me out of business. Someone else put the winery up for sale."

"They can't do that, it's illegal."

I wanted to say something totally inappropriate; I settled for sarcasm. "Really? Gee, I didn't know that. I thought you could sell something that doesn't belong to you." He had the grace to blush, but at this point I didn't care if he was embarrassed. "Yes, it's illegal," I snapped, "but someone tried it anyway. Now, if you'll excuse me, I need to contact my lawyer. It was nice of you to come over, and show your concern. I'm sorry I can't accommodate you, and sell you my winery." My sarcasm wasn't lost on him, and his face turned a brighter red. I let the door slam shut when I went inside.

I put my phone on speaker so Joe could hear both sides of the conversation when I called Max Baker, my attorney. He assured both of us he'd put a stop to the real estate listing immediately, and make certain no deed of trust was filed fraudulently, as well as seeing what could be done to trace the person responsible. "We'll get to the bottom of this," he promised. "You and Joe can both relax. I'll take care of this. Identity theft is a serious crime. Even the FBI is looking into it. When we find out who this person is, he'll have his hands full trying to cover his tracks."

I sagged against Joe's hard chest, resting my head on his shoulder. "This just keeps getting more and more complicated. How is Greg going to untangle all this mess, and still run a campaign for sheriff?"

"Greg isn't alone in this," Joe reminded me. "There are a lot of people working with him, including Jim Stevens. He might be sick and in the hospital, but I'm willing to bet he's still chewing on this mess."

"But Mayor Brady wants his own man put in place as sheriff. He'd be just as happy if they don't find the murderer so it will discredit the sheriff. What's up with that?"

"Politics and power plays. Neither is a very nice game to play. As for this mess here, we'll keep an eye on everything, and make sure there aren't any more for sale signs put up. Henderson at the bank will be watching our accounts, and so will we. We don't need to be too trustful of anyone right now."

~~~

"How the hell does she keep slipping out of everything I throw her way?" Again he was staring out the window. Right now it seemed like his life revolved around windows, and he got little else done, but stare out one or another. It really didn't matter where. Everything he'd been working for, everything he'd built for himself in the last thirty years was in danger of collapsing. He'd lost everything once
~~~

because he'd been careless, and Bishop had destroyed him. He couldn't let that happen again. If it did, he didn't have enough time left to rebuild; to get it all back again.

"I should have left her alone," he told himself one more time. "If I hadn't seen Bishop with her, this wouldn't have started all over again." He wasn't sure walking away was an option anymore. What would she do if he just faded away, and nothing else happened to her? Would she let it drop? Or would she keep digging until she uncovered the truth about him? "She's just as tenacious as her old man," he muttered to the empty room. Was he going to have to kill her to get her to drop this whole thing? Was that even an option?

He'd tried to reason with that stupid reporter, but she'd suddenly found some integrity, said she was going to print the truth. Not something she'd been concerned with all these years, why now all of a sudden?

If the realtor in Tucson had done as he'd instructed in his emails, Skylar wouldn't even have been aware her property was up for sale until the deal was recorded in the name of his blind corporation. There wasn't even supposed to be a sign on her property. Identity theft has ruined more than one upstanding citizen, putting them into bankruptcy before they were even aware there was something wrong. Why couldn't it happen to Skylar? How did she avoid it?

In his mind he went over every communication with the realtor to see if there was any way it could be traced back to him. He'd used fax machines at public places; driving miles so there was no way anyone would remember who had used the machine at any given time. His emails were also sent from public terminals making them impossible to trace back to him. He'd even used that stupid little man to do some of his errands. Was that enough to cover his tracks?

The account he'd set up in California to receive the funds from Skylar's accounts, was a blind account that wouldn't lead back to him. Within minutes of receiving the funds, they would have been transferred to another bank, and from there to several more banks before they went into an account in the Cayman Islands that couldn't be traced to him. How did she keep avoiding everything he threw at her? he asked himself again. Even the credit cards he'd set up in her name were now useless. What more could go wrong?

~~~

"Good afternoon, Skylar. How are things today?" I bristled at Roland Brady's familiarity as he walked into the winery where customers weren't welcome unless invited. And I hadn't invited him. He wasn't someone I particularly disliked, I just wasn't happy with all the interruptions. And I'm not necessarily fond of politicians.

"Good afternoon, Mayor Brady."

He held up his hand to interrupt me, "Roland, please. We don't have to be so formal."

Nodding assent without actually saying so, I walked outside, hoping he'd follow without any prompting from me. "Can I do something for you?"

"Of course not. In fact, I came to see if there was anything I can do for you and Joe. I know you have been having a hard time lately. I want to make sure you are doing okay. Nothing more has happened, am I correct?" He didn't wait for me to answer his question, and his frown of concern didn't fool me for a minute. He had to know Greg and I were... I'm not sure how to describe our relationship, but the mayor had to know about it, however it was described. "I like to check up on any of my, our citizens," he corrected himself quickly, "who are having troubles." His formal voice boomed across the yard.

"Thank you for your concern. Greg and the entire sheriff's department are working hard to figure out what happened to Betty Richards." His face tightened at the mention of Greg. This latest attempt to put me out of business was not any of his concern, and I wasn't going to enlighten him.
~~~

"Yes, of course. Still I wanted to check up on you. As I have said before, all of the citizens of the area are important to me." He was in full reelection mode.

I nodded, but I couldn't think of anything else to say so I remained silent. Apparently he couldn't think of anything to add so the silence stretched out for several uncomfortable minutes.

"Well, I will let you get back to work." He looked around. "Even after all these years, I have never taken time to tour your beautiful winery. I need to make the time to do that." He looked at me expectantly.

I didn't take the bait. "We give tours several times a year. You're welcome to join us then." That wasn't the response he was looking for, and red started creeping up his neck, coloring his face with an angry hue. Or was he embarrassed by his own pushy attempt to ingratiate himself with me.

"Yes, well, some other time. I must get back to town." He acted like he suddenly couldn't wait to get out of Dodge.

I watched until his big Town Car was out of sight before going back inside. Once again the man driving the car stayed behind the wheel when the mayor got out. He hadn't even bothered to shut off the engine. What's going on with the mayor? I wondered again. Why is he suddenly acting so concerned? Is it only because elections are coming up next year, or is he trying to undermine Greg and the sheriff's department? That seemed like a more likely scenario.

By the time Greg arrived after his shift, I'd all but forgotten about Mayor Brady's visit. With everything that had happened, the mayor was the least of my worries.

"Any news on the murder?" As always it was my first question. I wanted Betty's murderer found as much as I wanted Edward Simmons found. But of course, they're one and the same.

"Still working on it," was his standard reply. He couldn't tell me what was going on, and it was frustrating.

With no newspaper of any kind, gossip or otherwise, in town, and the state media more or less forgetting about the murder, there was no way to get information. Just because I was his girlfriend, or whatever, and Betty's body had been found on my property, didn't mean I had any right to confidential information.

"Babe, when I have something I can share with you, I will. Until then, you have to be patient. Unless the murderer comes forward with a confession, it's going to take time." He pulled me close, his kiss distracting me, as it was meant to.

Everything but work seemed to be at a standstill. James Burke was still out sick, the murder investigation seemed stalled, Edward Simmons was still wreaking havoc with my nerves, and I still didn't have a clue who he is.

"How's the campaign coming along? That's something you can talk about, right?" Gratefully, Greg acknowledged the touch of bitterness in my voice with just a raised eyebrow.

"Yes, I can talk about it, and it's coming along just fine. I think I have the backing of most of the other deputies, some of the county supervisors, and a large part of the county residences. Jim's out of the hospital, and returned to work today. He's put in his resignation effective after the election. At least the County Supervisors didn't appoint an acting sheriff to take his place like Roland Brady wanted. My only opponent is Gerald Williams, a friend of the mayor's. Actually, you've seen him."

I frowned, trying to recall the name. Finally I shook my head. "I don't think I know him. The name doesn't ring any bells. Who is he, besides a friend of the mayor's?"

Greg shook his head causing a lock of dark hair to fall over his forehead. My fingers itched to run through that thick mass, but I kept them in my lap for now. "The campaign bio he's put out says he's lived here for about ten years, working odd jobs, sort of a jack-of-all-trades master of none," he said. "Then he started driving the mayor around. Now he lives out of the mayor's hip pocket. That seems to be as close to any law enforcement experience the man has ever had. I don't know why Brady thinks he'd make a good sheriff." He sighed with frustration. "I don't understand why he's trying so hard to keep me from getting elected. I've never had a run in with him until now."

"You won't let him call all the shots," I said. "Like you suggested before, he wants to be in charge of the entire area, probably the entire county. He should run for some county office if being mayor isn't prestigious enough for him. Speaking of our wonderful mayor," I added, remembering his visit, "he paid me another visit today. He wanted to make sure nothing more had happened, and we're doing okay. Something about the man is a little off. He's always so formal yet he dresses like a cowboy or something. That glorious head of snowy white hair is never out of place no matter how windy it is. You don't suppose it's a wig, do you?" I added in an aside. Greg's deep laugh rumbled against my ear as he hugged me close to his hard chest. "I have no answers or explanations about or for our mayor. He's certainly different." He grew serious again. "I just wish I knew why he's suddenly taken such a strong dislike to me."

CHAPTER THIRTEEN

Pattiann confirmed James Burke was in the hospital, and had been for the better part of a week when Edward Simmons called. That didn't mean he couldn't call from his hospital bed, but how had he managed to set up the realtor and the transfer of my accounts from the hospital?

"I think I'm the only visitor he's had," Dora had told us at dinner on Sunday after she'd been to see him. "He's pretty sick. He seems like such a pathetic little man. I know he's not married, and I don't think he has any family in Arizona. It's too bad he didn't check out the side effects of Botox before he started taking the shots. They aren't pretty." She shook her head. "Not that he admitted that's what made him sick, of course. He wouldn't want anyone to know about that."

Max Baker, my lawyer, was still trying to trace the origins of the faxes and emails, but so far it was a dead end. "Every fax and email was sent from a different public location, usually a very busy location," he told Joe and me on Monday morning. "No one remembers who was using what machine when. The signatures that are supposed to be yours don't even come close. Whoever is behind this didn't have a sample of your handwriting, so they didn't try to get it right." He sighed with the same frustration I was feeling.

"What about the offer for my place? Was it legitimate?"

"I seriously doubt it. So far I haven't found out much. I do know it's a blind corporation buried so deep in other corporations I'm not sure we'll ever be able to find out who really owns it. I can't find a real person behind any of the corporate offices. Everything is phony. My guess is the same person who tried to sell your place is behind the offer. You're lucky the realtor screwed up, and put the for sale sign up when she wasn't supposed to. If you hadn't found out when you did, and the sale was recorded, it could have been months, maybe years, before you found out what happened. By that time, it could have been transferred into a dozen other names, and you never would have gotten to the end of it."

"Are you saying I could have lost my winery to this blind corporation, and there wouldn't have been anything I could have done about it?" I was incredulous. How could this happen?

"Unfortunately, that's exactly what I'm saying," Max answered softly. "The police in Tucson are looking into this along with the County Attorney's office. Someone will probably be down to talk to you. The realtor is in some hot water."

"As she should be," I stormed. "Not verifying who you're doing business with isn't very good business practice. She should lose her license."

After dinner, Greg and I sat on the porch while Dora and Joe went for a walk in the fading light. Evenings in southeastern Arizona cool off even when the daytime temperature reaches into the nineties. Giving the swing a push with the toe of his boot, setting us in motion, Greg pulled me close, nuzzling my hair. "Are you finally convinced Burke and Simmons aren't the same guy? He's been in the hospital while the last attacks were being set up."

"Okay," I sighed. "You're right. That leaves me with no one to look into." He could have an accomplice who sent the faxes and emails, but even I thought that was a little farfetched. I didn't want to turn into a conspiracy theorist. Some things just couldn't be, and I had to accept James Burke wasn't the person doing this to me.

"You don't have to look into anyone, Sky. That's my job."

I poked him in the ribs with my elbow. "Let's not start that again. In case you haven't noticed, I'm not one to sit on the sidelines while someone else does all the work or waits on me. It can't hurt anything for me to think about who could be doing this."

"Thinking is okay; actively looking into someone's background could backfire on you. There is such a thing as invading someone's privacy."

"You mean like Simmons has done to me?" I raised my eyebrows in question. "That doesn't seem to have stopped him at all."

Greg nodded, "That's right, and when we catch him, he's going to pay for everything he's done, including murdering Betty Richards. Identity theft and invasion of privacy are minor next to murder, so I don't think a few laws about those are going to cause him many sleepless nights. I don't want to lose you to this psycho." His lips captured mine in a mind blowing kiss. When we finally came up for air, I couldn't even remember what we'd been talking about. I was content to rest my head on his shoulder, enjoying the fragrant night air.

After Greg and Dora left, Joe handed me a glass of wine, and sat on the porch railing. As a rule, he didn't drink this late at night. I wondered what had brought it on now. Trying to pull the words out of him wouldn't work, so I sat silently, sipping my wine waiting for him to say what was on his mind.

After several minutes, he cleared his throat. "Ah, I want to ask you something, but you have to promise not to laugh."

I frowned at him in the dim porch light. "When have I ever laughed at you when you have something serious to say? Is something wrong?" Whatever was bothering him had to be serious if he needed a drink to work up the courage to tell me.

"Ah, well, I'm ah," he stammered. I wanted to help him, but I didn't know where he was going with this. "Would you think I'm being an old fool if I said I, ah, well," He cleared his throat again.

By now my stomach was beginning to churn. Was he going to tell me he wanted out of our winery, so he could go back to California? I thought he and Dora had something good going here, would he want to leave her? Again I wanted to help him along, but I didn't know how.

"I'm thinking of asking Dora to marry me," he finally blurted out the words. "Does that make me an old fool?"

I let out a shriek, jumping up, and wrapping my arms around his neck. "Oh that's wonderful!" I kissed his whisker rough cheek, happy tears running down my face. "You could never be a fool, old or otherwise. I'm so happy for you."

He hugged me back for several long seconds then held me away from him. "Careful there, Kiddo, I haven't even asked her yet. Don't go getting all sloppy and excited yet. We don't know what she's going to say."

"I know what she's going to say. I'm not blind. She's going to say a loud and resounding, 'Yes!' I've known that since the first time I saw the two of you together." Even in the dim light, I could see the high color on his face.

"You won't mind? It's just been you, your Dad, and me for a good many years. For the last five it's just been the two of us. I don't even know where we'd live, here or her place." Suddenly all the color drained from his face. "Things would change for Pattiann, too. I didn't think about that. She might not like giving up her mom to a craggy old man like me."

"Stop that right now!" I scolded him. "Pattiann isn't selfish, she wants what's best for her mom, and that's you. She's going to be just as happy as I am for both of you. When are you going to ask her?"

Nervous energy propelled him down the length of the porch and back. "I thought I'd go with you to Tucson the next time you go in, and I'd look for a ring. What do you think?" This was all new territory for him, and he didn't know exactly what to do. We spent the next hour discussing all the different options and choices. By the time we finally went to bed, it was late, but my heart was happy. Did Dora have any idea he was about to propose? I fell asleep with a giddy smile plastered on my face.

~~~

"Let's keep this just between us," Joe said at breakfast the next morning. "I don't want anyone else to know until I've asked her. When are you planning on going to Tucson next?" Buying something as monumental as an engagement ring in New Haven, expecting it to remain a secret was out of the question. It'd be all over town before Joe even made it back home.

"Do you think she might want to pick out her own ring?" I asked. "Some women prefer it that way."

Joe put down his coffee cup, and began pacing across the kitchen. "This is more complicated than I thought it'd be. What do I do now? Should I ask her first, and then get a ring, or buy the ring first then ask her? I never thought I'd be doing this, especially at my age." He was muttering to himself and stomping around. Cody watched from his corner of the room, his big head tilted to one side as though wondering what was going on. "Maybe I should just forget it, and keep things the way they are."

"Oh, no you don't!" I stepped in front of him to stop his pacing, my hands resting on my hips. "Do you love Dora?" His face turned beet red, and he looked down at the floor, shuffling his big feet. "Well, do you?" I pressed.

"Yes," he whispered. "I really do."

"Then don't back out now. Whatever you pick out for her, I know she'll love it because she loves you."

The color in his face ramped up even more now, and he dipped his head, but not before I saw his broad smile. "Yeah, she does. She told me." He looked up at me, his eyes shimmering with happiness. "I feel like a kid for the first time in...in well, a long time. How soon are we going to Tucson?" We usually make the thirty or forty mile drive once a month. This time we'd make a special trip.

I was almost as nervous as Joe at dinner that evening. Greg and Pattiann were both there with Dora. Greg kept looking at me, a curious frown drawing his dark brows together. "Did something happen that you're not telling me about?" he whispered before we sat down to eat.
~~~

I tried to act like I didn't know what he was talking about, but I wondered if I'd somehow given away Joe's secret. "No, nothing unusual." I couldn't quite meet his steely eyed gaze though.

"Simmons didn't call again, did he?"

I relaxed. His question was so far off the mark I couldn't stop my nervous laugh. "Of course not, I would have called you immediately."

His look clearly stated he wasn't convinced in light of my assertion that I didn't need someone to protect me. But he didn't press the issue.

Joe said grace, and started passing the food around. I wasn't sure how he was going to go about proposing, or if he'd wait until he and Dora were alone. I think I was more nervous than he was now that he'd made his decision. He'd been more nervous when he asked me if I'd object than he was throughout dinner. By the time we finished eating and Joe still hadn't said or done anything, I figured he was going to wait until they were alone. I chased everyone outside, and cleaned up the kitchen by myself. Maybe I was making him nervous with my own case of jitters. I needed to relax, and let him pick the right time.

"James is still in the hospital," Dora was saying when I came outside a few minutes later. "He called in today to say he'd be getting out tomorrow." She turned to Pattiann. "Is he really well enough to get out? What does the doctor say?"

Pattiann didn't say anything for a long moment, weighing what she could share, and what was confidential patient information. "He was doing much better today, so he probably will be released tomorrow. I'm not sure he's ready to go back to work though. He's still pretty, um," She didn't finish her sentence, fearing she was getting into confidential territory.

"Swollen?" Dora filled in. "Covered in a bright red rash? Facial muscles still pretty much immobile?" She laughed at her daughter. "I saw him yesterday, remember? I can't believe all that went away overnight, so you aren't giving away any secret medical information."

"Um, no, none of that's gone away, just not as bad. Except for his muscles. I'm not sure how long it will take to repair those. If ever," she whispered the last.

Dora stared at her daughter. "You mean it could be permanent? I thought the effects of the Botox wear off after a while. That's why you have to keep having more injections, so you don't have wrinkles." Pattiann nodded, but didn't comment. Now they were getting into information she couldn't give out.

Dora released a frustrated sigh. "What did that fool man do to himself? I suppose he wasn't even going to a certified doctor. I thought only women were so vain they risked their lives to stay young looking." We were all quiet for several moments considering the stupidity of some people.

"Anyone care for a glass of wine?" Joe asked, breaking the silence. He stood up, and went inside without waiting for us to answer. He came back a few minutes later with an open bottle and five glasses threaded through his fingers. Ceremoniously, he poured each of us a glass then remained standing. "I'd like to say something." I'd never seen him so formal. He turned to Dora, and to everyone's surprise; he dropped to one knee producing the velvet ring box.

"Dora, would you do me the honor of being my wife?" He opened the box with the ring he'd picked out earlier in the day.

She stared at the ring for a long moment; all the breath seemed to have escaped her, tears shimmered in her eyes. "Oh, Joe," she whispered. "It's beautiful. Yes, yes, yes." She flew off the wicker chair, wrapping her arms around his neck, nearly sending both of them in a heap on the porch. When they finally untangled, Joe carefully placed the ring on her finger, kissing it when he was finished.

"I hope you don't mind that it's not the traditional white diamond," Joe said. "I wanted something as unique as you are. It's called a blue diamond." Something told me Dora didn't mind at all. Pattiann, Dora and I had tears streaming down our faces. Greg was grinning like a fool. Who would have guessed the stoic man I'd known all my life would turn out to be such a romantic.

When Pattiann could finally get Joe away from her mom, she wrapped her arms around his neck, placing a kiss on each cheek. "Thank you, Joe," she whispered. "You've made my mom very happy."

Greg slapped him on the back, "Congratulations, Joe. I'm happy for you both."

I couldn't stop grinning. We had all forgotten the wine for a few minutes. Now I picked up my glass. "To Joe and Dora, best wishes always, and many happy years together."

When we finally settled down, Dora stepped over to me, a small worried frown creasing her forehead. "You don't mind, do you, Honey? I really do love him."

I gave her a hug. "I don't mind at all," I said. "You're the best thing that's ever happened to him, and your family is the best thing that's happened to both of us. Thank you."

When I finally went to bed, thoughts of Edward Simmons were far from my mind for once, and I slept the sleep of a baby.

The next day Joe called Dad to ask him to be his best man. I thought someone on his end was going to have to call 9-1-1. He was speechless for the better part of a minute, and Joe looked at the phone to make sure they were still connected. When Dad finally found his voice he let out a loud whooping cheer. "You even need to ask such a thing?" he wanted to know. "Of course I'll be your best man. I can't believe you're finally going to take the leap."

Joe's face turned red at the gentle teasing, but he managed to turn it back on Dad. "When are you going to get up the nerve to ask Molly? You've known her a lot longer than I've known Dora. What are you waiting for?"

"Ah, well, we're both busy at our wineries," Dad hedged. "I'll get around to it."

The teasing was so typical of these two important men in my life. It was the way they'd always dealt with each other. My heart was filled with love for both of them.

CHAPTER FOURTEEN

Over the next few weeks life returned to pre-Edward Simmons normal, but I felt like I had a bulls eye on my back just waiting for the next arrow to be fired. I couldn't believe he'd done all this only to give up, like he'd taken his best shot at me and lost. When he couldn't send me running, he just quit? That didn't fit the picture I had in my mind of the man.

James Burke was back at work, but just barely. "Anyone who uses Botox needs to make sure they go to a reputable doctor," Dora said after he was back at the bank. "He's never said, but I don't think what the guy was using was all Botox. I'm not sure his facial muscles will ever work the way they should." I was at least ninety-nine percent convinced he wasn't my tormentor. But I still harbored a small doubt.

With a wedding to plan, Greg's campaign in full swing, and the summer tourist season only half over, we were all busy. "Are you sure Joe doesn't want a big formal wedding?" Dora asked for the third time as we were shopping for her dress.

"Oh, Mom," Pattiann sighed dramatically. "He's told you, Skylar's told you, and I've told you, Joe will be happy with whatever you decide."

"Since this is his first wedding, I keep thinking he should want something big and flashy. Just because I've done this twice, he shouldn't have to down size his plans." This was a recurring lament of hers.

"A big flashy wedding, or any occasion for that matter, isn't Joe. He's more the smaller the better type." I laughed, giving her hand a squeeze of reassurance. "With him, what you see is what you get. If it's big and flashy, you might scare him off. A lot of pomp and ceremony would freak him out." I laughed at the image of Joe in front of the church with hundreds of people watching him.

"Okay, if you're sure." She didn't sound convinced. There would probably be more questions along this same line before we got them married in the fall after the grape harvest. Winter being the slowest time for the vineyard, they would be able to go somewhere for a honeymoon without worrying about leaving us shorthanded at home.

~~~

When Greg wasn't working at the sheriff's department, he was campaigning all over the county. Good thing we're a small county, I kept thinking. Otherwise he wouldn't have time to do his job, and I'd never see him. Things were heating up between him and Gerald Williams. The man was even putting ads on the local television stations that ranged from Tucson to the border with Mexico. Most of the people seeing the ads couldn't even vote for him. I wasn't sure where he was getting the money for all this, but my guess was Mayor Brady. I didn't know how he could convince the voters he'd make a good sheriff when he had no law enforcement experience.

Greg had Jim Stevens' endorsement along with most of the people he worked with which was a good sign, but Mayor Brady seemed to have a lot of pull with the people of the town. I was learning that he'd done a lot for the town during his tenure as mayor, and some people were willing to listen to anything he had to say.

I was also learning people tended to be a little lazy when it came to their politicians. They're willing to keep re-electing the same people over and over so they didn't have to spend time learning about a new candidate. That's how Congress has so many people making politics their life long careers while nothing really meaningful gets done in Washington, D.C.

~~~

Staring out the window was becoming a habit lately, but he didn't see the people walking past. All he saw was his whole life going up in smoke; again. He'd lost everything once because of her old man. He wasn't going to let her get the best of him too. Breaking her wasn't as easy as he thought it would be though. She had more backbone than he expected. Somehow he had to discredit her, or make her give up and leave.

The murder should have done the trick, but that deputy wasn't as stupid as he'd hoped. How does she always come out on top? he wondered. She has more people watching her back than the military. If that stupid realtor hadn't screwed up by putting up the sign when he'd instructed not to, it might all be over by now. Once the place was sold, she couldn't have done anything about it. She could have fought, but it would have cost her a fortune. Someone is always conspiring against him. If that deputy gets elected sheriff, he'll never stop until he unravels everything I've built here. "I can't let that happen," he whispered. "I won't let it happen!"

What he needed was someone not afraid to get their hands dirty. Or someone he could squeeze just enough to do his bidding. Templeton wanted her land, but he was too chicken to force her out. He also has the hots for her. Stupid man! He's letting her run the game just because he wants in her pants. There has to be someone who will do what I want, he thought again. An evil smile curved his full lips. "And I know just who that is," he said into the empty room. When he's no longer valuable to me, or if he begins to question my orders, it won't be hard to get rid of him either. His nasty laugh filled the room with a sound that would send shivers down the spine of anyone listening. But he was alone in his den, his man cave, his lair, whatever he wanted it to be. The only place he felt comfortable and safe.

~~~

In my "spare" time I was still trying to find out more about anyone I thought could be Edward Simmons. I kept that little project to myself though. Neither Greg nor Joe would approve, but especially Greg. Investigating was his job, he'd pointed out more than once; also pointing out that
~~~

what I was doing could be construed as invasion of privacy. Yet someone had done the same thing to me, and no one seemed to mind, except me.

Okay, "turnabout's fair play" isn't something the Bible teaches, and I'm certain Pastor Rick would frown on what I was doing. But I couldn't sit back, and let that maniac continue to take potshots at me. Just because nothing had happened for several weeks didn't mean he wasn't out there dreaming up his next move. I had to be ready.

The internet offers a wealth of information about anything you can imagine, but I was having a hard time finding background information on the people I was checking out. Most of what I found was recent history, nothing as far back as thirty years ago. Either the internet information didn't go back that far, or there were a lot of people in New Haven with no long-term background. I didn't know what to make of it. Was our little town a hot bed of intrigue, a resting place for people in witness protection? Even for me, that was a little far-fetched.

I know skip tracers use the internet looking for people who were missing, or had skipped out on debts. I wasn't interested in that. Looking for the Edward Simmons of thirty years ago led me to articles of his early life, his death, and even his death certificate. There was mention of the embezzlement, and failure of the bank he'd started. That was a dead end since he remade himself into someone else. I just can't find out who he is now. The genealogy sites went far back in a person's history looking for ancestors. That didn't help me either. I didn't know where else to look.

Whoever he is now, he's still in New Haven; a fact that made me a little jumpy whenever I went into town. "What's wrong, Babe? Why are you so nervous all the time?" Greg touched my hand across the table causing me to jump in my seat.

I shrugged, trying to shake off the feeling of being watched, and concentrate on him instead of the other people in the restaurant. "I just have a feeling someone is watching me all the time." We were at Manuel's on Friday evening, and I was trying hard to relax. I wasn't doing a very good job of it though.

He surveyed the other diners sitting around us. "No one's paying any attention to us, Babe. You need to let this go. Whoever Simmons is today, he's probably laying low because of the murder. That was his big mistake, and it will be his downfall. When his latest attempts to attack you failed, he's probably given up. He isn't going to want to call attention to himself." The prickles on the back of my neck told me otherwise. Did this mean Greg and the sheriff's department was giving up looking for him? I certainly hope not.

The next morning I had just opened the door of the tasting room, and gone back inside when it opened again. Turning around, I came face to face with James Burke. My heart dropped to my toes. Even though there wasn't much expression on his face, he seemed indecisive, like he didn't know if he should come all the way in, or turn around, and high tail it out of there.

I could sympathize with him because I wasn't sure if I wanted to stay in the same room with him. Was he going to press me to move my accounts to his bank again? Or did he have something more sinister in mind? Cody was curled up in his bed by the door, his big head moving between Mr. Burke and me probably wondering the same thing I was.

For several long seconds we stood paralyzed; neither of us saying anything. The rash Dora said had covered his face was gone leaving his skin more pink than red. His face was still puffy from the swelling, but not grotesquely so. Finally he broke the strained silence. "Miss Bishop, I want to apologize for the way I acted the last time I was here. I've been in the hospital, or I would have come sooner." His lips moved more than they had previously, but still not in a normal manner.

"I'm sorry you were sick." I said the only thing I could think of.

"My own doing," he said, brushing away my sympathy. "Anyway, I didn't come here to talk about that. I just wanted you to know how sorry I am for the way I acted. I can only think my actions were caused by my..." He searched for the right words, settling on a medical condition. "I wasn't acting, or thinking right. I hope you can forgive me sometime."

There was only one thing I could say to that. "Ah, yes, of course. I hope you're feeling more yourself now."

"Thank you." He nodded his head in acceptance. "I won't bother you anymore. Good day." Just as quickly as he appeared, he was out the door again.

I sagged against the tasting bar. Before I gathered my wits, Joe rushed into the room. "Was that Burke? What did he want? He didn't try anything, did he?" My face must have been pale, because he gripped my arms, examining me with a critical eye.

"I'm fine." I patted his hand. "He came to apologize. He's still creepy, but I sort of feel sorry for him."

He released a pent up sigh, leaning against the bar next to me, his own relief evident. His hands shook slightly as he raked his fingers through his thick gray hair. "I agree he is creepy. I wish Dora didn't work for the guy. Maybe he isn't dangerous though."

I gave a nervous laugh. "He's probably not dangerous, just creepy." A thought occurred to me, and I looked up at him. "Did you see his car out front? When I unlocked the door, I didn't see any cars. He just appeared as soon as I opened the door."

He shook his head. "There weren't any cars out front. How did he get here? I saw him walking down the lane to the road." His bushy brows drew together as he considered the possibilities. "We're too far from town to walk. I don't know where he lives, but I'm going to find out." He stomped out through the store room as customers came in the front door. Suddenly, I wasn't feeling sorry for Mr. Burke anymore.

CHAPTER FIFTEEN

The big day finally arrived. Dora was a beautiful bride in a street length pale pink dress; a small veil covered her blond hair. Joe was more handsome than I'd ever seen him in a charcoal gray suit and tie. Dad was his best man, and Molly sat with me, holding my hand. Pattiann was Dora's maid of honor and Greg walked her down the aisle. "Joe looks so happy," Molly whispered as Dora stopped beside him in front of Pastor Rick. Happy tears blurred my vision, and I could only nod. He really was happy. Next it was Dad and Molly's turn.

The church was full. What had started out as a small, intimate affair had turned out much larger, with half the town in attendance. Even Mayor Brady sans his faithful chauffeur was there. I'm not certain how he managed to get an invitation, but I'd worry about that later. I'm not sure Joe was even aware of how many people were there. His eyes never wavered from Dora's face as they spoke their vows.

At the reception, I circulated through the crowd, thanking everyone for coming. The mayor had disappeared after congratulating Joe and Dora so I didn't need to speak with him. I'd almost forgotten the feeling of being watched until the hairs on the back of my neck seemed to vibrate. Turning in a full circle, I tried to see if someone was paying particular attention to me. The only one showing any interest was Greg. He walked across the big hall, his dark eyes trained on me, an intense expression on his handsome face.

Taking my hand when he reached my side, he briefly pulled me against him then turned, leading me outside. Away from the throng of people, he dipped his head, placing a light kiss on my lips that quickly deepened into something much more heart stopping. "Are we going to be doing this anytime soon?" he asked quietly. "Have you thought about being married to a part-time politician, and a full-time sheriff?"

My heart was pounding so hard, I'm sure he could feel it as he held me against his chest. "I've thought about it a lot." My voice wouldn't work above a whisper.

"And?" He prompted his face anxious.

"Whenever you're ready to do the asking, I'm ready to say 'yes'." For several long moments, neither of us said anything, we were otherwise occupied.

"This might not be as romantic as Joe's proposal to Mom, but," he pulled a small velvet box out of his jacket pocket before dropping to one knee. "Skylar Bishop, will you do me the honor of becoming my wife, and spending the rest of our lives together?" He opened the box where a beautiful, old-fashioned ring was nestled. "It is the ring my Dad gave Mom when he asked her to marry him. I hope you like it."

"Oh, yes, I like it very much, and I'll gladly be your wife." I pulled him to his feet, wrapping my arms around his neck before he could even place the ring on my finger.

A half hour later, Dad came outside looking for us. We hadn't moved any farther than the garden in back of the church where Greg had proposed. "I was wondering where you two had disappeared to. Joe and Dora are getting ready to cut the cake. Come on inside."

"Um, just a moment, sir. I'd like to ask you something. I kind of got this backwards, asking Skylar first, but I want to marry your daughter, and I'd like your blessing."

Dad beamed at both of us, slapping Greg on the shoulder. "Son, if you make her as happy as she is right now, I'll never have any complaints." He placed a soft kiss on my cheek. "Now let's get back in there for some of that good looking cake."

~~~

"That bastard! I should have been prepared for him to show up for the wedding of the century." The words were
~~~

sarcastic, muttered low, so no one else would hear. "I suppose I'll have to get used to having him show up all the time now that his precious little girl is going to marry that damn deputy. Why couldn't she just leave?"

He watched as they went back in the church hall completely unaware he'd been watching them. What would happen if I walked up, and introduced myself? he wondered. Would he realize who I am? Or would he be clueless, and accept me for who I am now? That would be priceless! Toying with them for a while could be fun. When the right moment comes along, I can give him the payback he so richly deserves.

For now though, he had to stay away. He didn't trust himself to face the man who had ruined him once, and would do it again if given the chance. He walked out of the garden without a backward glance. Tomorrow is another day, he decided.

~~~

Dad and Molly stayed in Joe's end of our house. I didn't ask their sleeping arrangement, and didn't want to know. There were two bedrooms in each apartment so I could tell myself that everything was above board. Laughing at myself, I crawled into bed. It was past midnight, and I still had to get up early for church in the morning. The tasting room was open as usual. Joe didn't want me to close because of him. He and Dora would be gone for a week on their honeymoon to Hawaii.

Now that the harvest was behind us and, this year's crush was in full swing, we had a different set of duties keeping us busy. Bottling was done throughout the year as the wine was ready, and several were ready now. We'd keep busy through the winter making the wine for the coming year. After church, Dad worked outside doing what Joe would normally be doing while the tasting room was open. It was like old times.

Molly worked with Becky and me inside, and we got a chance to get reacquainted. She's great for Dad and I'm
~~~

happy for them both. She hadn't changed much since I'd last seen her. Just a few inches shorter than Dad, she was still whip thin. I knew that was a deceptive image though. I'd seen her lift weights some men would stagger under. She'd always worked beside her husband, and since his death; she'd taken up the slack his absence had brought. Her dark hair was now more salt and pepper, but she kept it stylishly cut in a short bob that was flattering to her heart-shaped face.

Sitting in Manuel's that evening felt a little strange without the rest of the 'family,' but Greg and Pattiann were both working the late shifts, and Joe and Dora were in Hawaii by now. The feeling of being watched was back, and every few minutes I looked over the other diners. "What's wrong, Kitten?" Dad touched my hand in the same way Greg had a few weeks earlier when we were here. Again, I jumped at the contact. "Why are you so jumpy?"

"Just looking at the people," I tried for an offhand answer that didn't quite work. Both Dad and Molly looked skeptical. "Really," I pressed. "I just like to see who all is here. I still don't know all that many people in town. I've kept to myself for too long." I thought that explanation sounded pretty good.

"Hmmm. Is that so?" Dad raised one eyebrow like he always does when he knows I'm not telling him the whole story. This time he didn't push me for a further explanation, and I was grateful.

Instead he changed the topic of conversation. "What are you and Greg planning for Christmas? Have you set a date for your wedding yet?"

I had to laugh at him. "Come on. He just asked me last night, and we haven't had a lot of time to talk since. I guess it will depend a lot on his work, and the campaign. If he can't get away for Christmas, why don't both of you come over here? We're closed that day, and so are you. You can let someone else run your places for a few days."

The look Dad and Molly shared had excitement bubbling up in my stomach. "Okay, what's going on with you two?"

"Well, we sort of thought if you could all get away for a week, maybe we'd ah," Dad hesitated, looking at Molly again. She gave a nod of encouragement, and he continued. "We thought we could have a small wedding, maybe just our combined families." For a minute I thought he was talking about me and Greg, but he knew I wanted something here, and more flashy than just the family.

"Are you trying to tell me something without coming right out, and saying it?" It was my turn to raise an eyebrow.

"I've asked Molly to marry me, and she said yes. I asked Joe to be my best man. I hope you don't mind that I didn't say anything to you first. We thought we'd get married between Christmas and New Year's."

I didn't let him finish his sentence before I let out a happy squeal, jumping up from my chair, and running around the table to give them both a hug. "Why would I mind?" I finally asked when I sat back down. By now, several other people were watching us, but I didn't feel the creepiness this time. "What have Barbara and Donna said?" I asked Molly the question, hoping they didn't object. I felt bad now that we'd lost touch over the years. It was mostly my fault. I don't even know what they're doing now.

Molly's contented smile eased any fears that they might object to their mother getting married after all these years. "They're both happy I've found someone to share my life with now that they're so busy with their own lives. Donna is expecting my first grandchild in the spring." Her smile told me how happy that made her. "She married Jim Hensen, maybe you remember him? They live about ten miles away. Barbara will be getting married sometime next year. They haven't been as involved in the winery as you always were, but they help out, and both men have joined the family business." It was fun catching up on the people

I'd grown up with. The wine community is small and close-knit no matter where it takes place. It's also rather solitary or exclusive. I'm glad her daughters were close by, and they approved of Dad.

By the time we left the restaurant, I'd forgotten about someone watching us, but walking to the car I suddenly felt exposed, the prickly feeling was back. For a Sunday evening there were a fair amount of cars parked on the street, and in the parking lot. I couldn't see if anyone was sitting in one, but I was willing to bet my last dollar someone was, and paying close attention to us.

Dad waited until we were sitting on the front porch before he questioned me. "What's going on, Skylar? And don't give me that malarkey about checking out the people because you don't know that many people in town."

I coughed, postponing my answer for several seconds trying to come up with a plausible explanation, but nothing came to mind. Finally I settled on the truth. "It feels like someone is watching me every time I go anywhere, sometimes even here at home. I never see anyone paying any attention to me so I guess it's just an overactive imagination." At least that's what I was hoping.

"What's Greg say?" Molly asked the question.

I shrugged. "He thinks I'm imagining it, or being paranoid."

"Then he's not the man I thought he was," Dad groused. "Being in law enforcement, he should understand intuition, and pay attention. Just because you're not a law officer doesn't mean you can't get gut feelings about things. Especially when so much has happened around here. Has he found out who murdered that reporter yet?"

"He can't talk about an ongoing investigation, but they're still working on it. So far, they haven't arrested anyone. These things don't get solved in one hour like they do on television cop shows." Dad was frustrated, but no more so than me. I wanted to know who was doing this. I wanted it all to stop.

Tears prickled my eyes the next morning when Dad and Molly left for the airport in Tucson. I missed them already, and I missed Joe and Dora. Joe had been with me every day for the last five years here, and all my life in California. Now they were all somewhere else. I felt truly alone for the first time in my life.

I didn't feel sorry for myself for long. Greg's big truck came to a stop in front of the tasting room a few minutes later. "What are you doing here? I thought you'd be ready to get some sleep." He pulled me close for a long, hot kiss before answering my question.

"I can't sleep right after I get off work. Thought I'd put in a little time here, and then grab a few hours' sleep. You doing okay here alone?"

I snuggled closer to him, trailing kisses along his neck. "I'm doing fine now. How about some breakfast?" Arm in arm, we went inside where there was still some bacon and eggs in the warming oven. "I can make some pancakes if you want me to." By noon, his energy was beginning to lag. "Hon, you need to go home, and get some sleep. You look like you could fall asleep standing up." Between working his shift and campaigning, he'd probably been up close to twenty-four hours.

"I thought I'd lie down on the couch, and grab a nap."

"What you need is a solid eight hours, not a nap. Go home." I gave him a push towards his truck, but he didn't budge.

"I can sleep here. You've been so uneasy lately; I don't want to leave you alone."

I placed my hand on his bristly cheek, touched by his concern. Maybe he'd been downplaying my eerie feelings so as not to worry me. "I'm not alone. Juan is here along with a couple other workers. Nothing will happen. Get some rest. As much as I think this county needs you for sheriff, I'm not sure it's worth the hours you're putting in to get there."

He gathered me close to his hard chest again, his turn to nibble on my neck. “I’ve done with less. Don’t worry about me.”

I nodded solemnly. “Okay, as long as you stop worrying about me. Deal?”

He laughed. “Like that’s going to happen. I’ll go home if you promise not to get too far away from the others. I asked Juan to keep an eye out for anyone who shouldn’t be here.”

Bristling, I pulled away from his embrace. “I don’t need a man to watch out for me. I can take care of myself.”

“I know you can, but humor me for a little while. I just got my very first and last fiancé, I think that gives me the right to be a little possessive, and over protective until I get used to her. Don’t you?”

The anger drained out like someone had pulled the plug in a sink. “Okay, but don’t make a habit of it. I’m really very self-sufficient.”

We walked to his truck, leaning against the side as we spent a few more minutes cuddling there. “Would it compromise your self-sufficiency if Pattiann spends the night here after she gets off work? She isn’t thrilled about staying alone while Mom and Joe are gone. She wouldn’t admit it, but I think she was a little uneasy last night alone in the house. I think she’d appreciate the company.” Put like that, how could I refuse? That would make me insensitive to her paranoia. I suppose he’d use the same tactic when he asked her to stay with me.

Watching him leave, I scanned the road and fields. His was the only vehicle in sight at noon on a week day. Our back roads didn’t get a lot of traffic until the tourists descended on the weekends. A shiver traveled up my spine, and I hurried into the winery where Juan was working.

When Greg stopped by on his way in to work, he looked more tired than he had when he left. “Didn’t you get any sleep? What did you do?” Dark circles bruised his eyes, and he couldn’t seem to stop yawning.

“I slept some. But I tried to get out, and do a little campaigning.” He gave a humorless chuckle. “I don’t know how Jim did it all those years. Running for office isn’t for sissies. My opposition has even asked when I had my last physical, and a whole lot of other personal questions.” He shook his head, wondering if it was all worth it.

On a quick change of subjects, he added, “Pattiann will be getting off work in about an hour. Will you be okay until then? She said to tell you thanks for the offer. Even when she was in college, she had roommates, or stayed with Mom. She’s never been completely alone at home for several days.”

I shook off the unease I’d been feeling since my employees left for the day, putting on a brave face. “I’ll be fine. For your information, I have stayed by myself before.” I tried for a superior tone, but was afraid it fell way short of the mark. Besides, I wasn’t being completely truthful. Joe had always been in the other end of our house here, and at home with Dad, there were always people around the property, if not in the house with me.

“Have you seen anyone around who doesn’t belong? No one has bothered you?” Concern drew his dark brows together. “Simmons hasn’t called?”

I wasn’t positive he’d believed me when I said it felt like someone was watching me, but maybe that had just been for show. Just the mention of Simmons brought on a sense of dread. He was still out there, and he had to know I was alone. Would he try something? “I haven’t heard from him for a while,” I answered. “I’m hoping he’s decided to give up on me. I still don’t know what he thought he would accomplish by harassing me. You’d better go, so you aren’t late.” I needed to change the subject before I completely freaked out. Leaning up on tiptoe, I placed a soft kiss on his lips. Before I could pull away, he deepened the kiss. When he lifted his head, his eyes were clouded with worry, and something else. “Make sure the doors are all locked, and don’t go out, and sit on the porch even after Pattiann gets here." Instead of making me feel better, his warning added to my unease.

When he left, I checked and rechecked all the doors and windows. Cody followed me through the house then went to the door leading to the tasting room, and Joe's end of the house. He wasn't used to having Joe gone either, and didn't understand why he wasn't here. On impulse, I let Cody into Joe's apartment, following close behind him, checking all the doors and windows there. I didn't want someone to get in, and have easy access to my place through the tasting room.

With everything safely locked up tight, I waited for Pattiann to come over. It wasn't quite eleven yet. In the stillness of the night, every little sound was intensified, and had me jumping. Until now I never noticed all the night sounds the countryside held.

The crunch of tires on the gravel drive outside my door had my heart pounding. Cody gave a low woof at the sound, but didn't get excited about visitors. With all the strangers he welcomed every day in the tasting room, he didn't get upset when one appeared at our door. "Skylar, it's me." Pattiann's soft voice carried through the solid door, and I released the breath I was holding. At the sound of her voice, Cody seemed to release a sigh of his own. They still hadn't made up. Before I opened the door to let her in, Cody went in search of a place to stay out of her way.

She looked tired, but wasn't ready for bed yet. I'd never worked a late shift like this, but I figured it was like any other shift. You can't go to sleep the instant you get home. We sat around for a while talking, and sipping a glass of wine to help both of us relax. "Where's Cody?" she asked, looking around the room. "I thought he'd be here with you."

"He knows you're afraid of him," I laughed. "He took off when he heard your voice."

She buried her face in her hands. "Oh, that makes me feel terrible! Everyone says he's just a big cuddly teddy bear." She drew a steadying breath. "When I was little, a dog knocked me over, and bit me. I've been afraid of dogs ever since. I need to grow up, and get over it." The last was said forcefully as if to admonish herself.

"It's okay." I took her hand. "You don't have to do something that makes you uncomfortable."

She stiffened her spine, sitting up straight. "It's time I got over it. I want to like him." In a small voice, she asked, "If you call him out, will he come while I'm here?"

Cody crawled out on his belly, like he was going to his death when I called to him, and I burst out laughing. But Pattiann felt even worse. "Oh, I'm so sorry, Cody," she crooned. "I know you're a nice dog." At her soft voice, he crawled over to her, his tail giving a tentative thump on the floor. She put her hand down for him to sniff, and within minutes he was giving her a bath with his big wet tongue. "Oh! I hope this means he likes me," she laughed. She moved down to the floor, so she could hug him.

When we went to bed a few minutes later, Cody laid on the hall floor between the two bedrooms. He'd made a new friend, and he was going to protect us both.

CHAPTER SIXTEEN

It felt like minutes after I shut my eyes that my phone sounded off with the loud train whistle. "Go away, Edward," I groaned. Without turning on the light or checking the display, I hit the dismiss button. I wasn't in the mood to listen to him rant, or threaten me. Immediately, it rang again. From past experience I knew he wouldn't give up until I answered.

Heaving myself up in bed, I finally answered the noisy thing. "What is it now, Edward? Can't you call at a decent hour?"

"What? Skylar? Who's Edward?" This wasn't Edward Simmons. Who else would call me in the middle of the night?

"Who is this?" I snapped, suddenly angry enough to spit nails. I'd had it with middle of the night callers.

"It's Chase." His voice was urgent. "Your vineyard's on fire! I've called the fire department, and sent a couple of the guys over with hoses."

I was out of bed, running for the window. Through the closed curtains I could see orange flames taking hold. Cody was barking in the hall. "Thanks Chase. I'm on my way outside."

As I started to close my phone, I heard him tell me to stay inside. "When pigs fly," I muttered. "This is my place, and no one is going to burn me out." Pulling on a pair of jeans over my pajamas, I dialed Greg's cell phone, but it went straight to voice mail. Pattiann met me in the hall, her phone to her ear.

"Greg, someone set Skylar's vineyard on fire!" She'd beat me to the punch. She was pulling on a pair of jeans as well.

The fire wasn't as big as it had looked from my bedroom window, but it was bad enough. Several rows of vines were destroyed. Thanks to Chase's employees it hadn't spread further than that. By the time the fire department arrived from town, they had the fire almost out. Greg arrived as they were laying out the big hoses.

As soon as the fire department got set up, Chase rushed across the field to me, gripping my hands in his. "Are you all right, Sky? Nothing happened at the house?" His grip was so tight the engagement ring I wasn't accustomed to wearing was cutting into my other fingers.

"I'm fine, physically, but I'm mad as hell! He's still trying to ruin me." I pulled my hands free, flexing my fingers to make sure they still worked. We hadn't had time to announce our engagement, and Chase didn't know. I wasn't sure how he was going to take it after he declared being jealous of Greg not so long ago.

Greg worked with the firemen, and when he could break free, he came over to Pattiann and me. "Are you both okay? Did you see anything?" He pulled me into a tight embrace ignoring the fact that others were watching.

We both shook our heads. So much had been happening recently that when we finally fell asleep, nothing disturbed us until my phone rang. I turned to Chase. "How did you notice the fire? I'm glad you did, but it's the middle of the night."

He looked a little sheepish, ducking his head. "Since the break-in at my place, and Betty's murder here, I've hired some men to keep an eye on things at night. They just walk around the boundary of my vineyard." He looked at Greg, with a defensive glare. "They aren't armed with anything but a cell phone. When they saw the fire, they called it in then called me."

"I'm going to need to talk to those men," Greg said. "Maybe they saw someone. Even if they can't identify them, it would help." The fact that Betty Richards had been attacked somewhere else, and brought here to make it look like she died from bee stings wasn't public knowledge. Hopefully, it would help convict the real killer later.

I listened while Greg interviewed the three men Chase had patrolling his vineyard. They seemed nervous, and were probably illegals. Greg made it clear he wasn't interested in their status. He wanted to know about the fire. One of the men stayed close to the buildings, and hadn't seen anything until the alarm had been raised. The other two men walked around the boundary, looking for anyone who might be out and about doing mischief.

"When I see the man I think ett is Senor Joe making sure things all okay like he do before. Then I remember Senor Chase say Senor Joe on his...his," he looked around, hoping someone would supply the right word.

"Honeymoon," Greg prompted.

"Si, honeymoon! Senor Joe on his honeymoon, so he not out here tonight. I not go on your land, Senorita, so I not know who was there. He not doing anything so I think everything okay. A few minutes later I see the fire! It small, but getting big. I call 9-1-1 like Senor Chase say, and then call him. He tell me to get water to put out fire. I had to go on your land then, Senorita. I sorry." I guess Chase had told the men to say off my property, or I'd call the sheriff and have them arrested for trespassing.

"It's all right. Thank you for helping put out the fire." I looked at the other men thanking them also. If it weren't for them being there, I could have lost a lot more than a few vines. I could have lost my entire vineyard.

Greg asked more questions, but Jorge was the only one who saw the man. Distance and the dark night prevented him from being able to describe the man. I thanked him again before they went to stand beside Chase.

Once the fire was completely out, I was surprised by the crowd that had gathered. Most surprising were Mayor Brady and his candidate of choice standing off to one side. Gerald Williams sauntered up to Greg, nodding his head in my direction otherwise ignoring my presence. "This isn't going to look too good for your campaign, Wilkinson," he said, sneering at Greg. "If you can't even keep your girlfriend safe, how can the people of the county think you're going to protect them? Maybe it's time for a change of guard."

"Someone like yourself?" Greg asked, as one eyebrow rose questioningly. "Someone with no law enforcement experience under his belt? Just what would you have done differently, Williams? Would you hire enough deputies to have someone sitting on every property in the county? Good luck with that. I don't think the County Supervisors will agree with that idea. Then again, maybe Mayor Brady will help you hire a few of your friends." Greg was baiting the older man.

This was the first time I'd gotten a look at Gerald Williams outside the mayor's car, and it wasn't a favorable impression he was putting forward. I judged him to be in his mid-fifties, about the same height and build as his buddy the mayor, but that's where the similarity ended. The extra weight he carried was beginning to hang over his belt buckle while Mayor Brady had no paunch. His salt and pepper hair was thinning on top, and he had a very ugly comb-over to hide the bald spot. I've never understood why men did that. It only draws attention to the very thing they're trying to hide. He was dressed in jeans and long sleeved sports shirt, the sleeves rolled up to the elbow. He was copying to the letter the way the mayor was dressed. I wanted to snicker at him.

Muscles bunched in Gerald Williams' jaw. For a minute I thought he might take a swing at Greg. Before that could happen, Mayor Brady joined us, his tone conciliatory. "I am sorry to see you are having more trouble, Skylar. This has been a very bad year for you, but we will get to the bottom of your troubles." He turned to Greg with only a slight nod, then ushered Gerald Williams back to the edge of the field.

"I wonder who he's going to try to pin this on," Greg muttered. "It would look really good for his candidate if he could bring in a suspect before I do."

I couldn't imagine how Mayor Brady would profit by having Gerald Williams as sheriff instead of Greg; or Jim Stevens, for that matter. As an unincorporated town, New Haven didn't have a police department of its own. They depended on the sheriff's department for law enforcement. Did Roland Brady have something going that he needed to control the law in town? Maybe I needed to check out these two men, and see what the internet could find.

~~~

According to the official town web site, Mayor Roland Brady was born, and raised in Arizona. His speech pattern says otherwise, I thought, but kept reading the mayor's bio. The only child of a wealthy Arizona land developer and his wife, he attended Arizona State University for a year, but didn't graduate. He dropped out during his sophomore year. Unfortunately, I couldn't discover why he didn't continue his education. After dropping out of college, there was little information on our illustrious mayor until he showed up in New Haven seven years ago. What brought him to southern Arizona? What had he been doing in the intervening years? His parents still lived in Paradise Valley, a posh part of Phoenix with million dollar homes. He's never been married, and has no children; at least none that he acknowledges in his official bio. He's the right age to be Edward Simmons, but that doesn't mean he is.

"Hmmm, I wonder if he's ever dated any of the women in New Haven," I muttered to the computer. No one has ever mentioned anything about him dating someone. Nothing was said about him needing to have a driver for health reasons either. That little fact was an oddity that didn't sit well with me.

Why would a small town mayor need or want a chauffeur? The town is small enough you can walk up and down the main street in less than an hour, taking in most of the sights as well. The official population of the town and surrounding area, which includes all the vineyards, ranches and outlying businesses, is less than ten thousand people. Only those actually living within the town limits can vote
~~~

for anyone holding town office. The rest of us can only vote for county, state and federal positions. So why has Mayor Brady taken such an interest in what's been happening at Sky Vineyards? And why is he trying to undermine Greg's campaign for sheriff? What did he have to gain?

Without actually "friending" him, the only information I could get on Facebook was a repeat of what there was on the town web site. Almost word for word. What a coincidence! Any personal information on either site was almost non-existent. Why? Is our mayor trying to hide something in his past? If so, what is it?

Frustrated, I decided to see what I could find out about Gerald Williams. Since he isn't an official employee of the town, there was no information about him on the town web site. Where does Brady get the money to pay Gerald Williams from his own pocket? I wondered. I couldn't imagine the town pays well enough for him to afford a chauffeur on his own. Public employees' salary should be listed somewhere online, but so far, that piece of information was missing.

There were several Gerald Williams on Facebook, but none seemed to match the man living in New Haven, and driving the mayor around. He isn't in the town phone book either. Another dead end, I thought. I needed to have more information about the man before I could learn anything about him; sort of a Catch 22.

I didn't want to "Friend" any of the men listed, including Mayor Brady. If one of them turned out to be the Gerald Williams I was looking for, he would know I was checking up on him. Not a good thing even if everything was above board. I didn't think that was necessarily the case here though.

~~~

How did I get myself into this mess? He asked himself as he paced around the small room away from prying eyes. She's made of gold, solid gold, nothing sticks to her. Or
~~~

maybe I should say Teflon. He chuckled at his own joke, but quickly grew serious again. The mess he was in was no laughing matter. In fact it was serious, deadly serious.

Maybe a better question would be how do I get out of this mess? I know exactly how I got into it. It always boils down to that damn Bishop. But I can't dwell on that now, he told himself. He had to figure out a way to extricate himself from this situation because it was rapidly spiraling out of control, and Wilkinson was proving to be very tenacious. He was going to figure everything out sooner rather than later.

CHAPTER SEVENTEEN

By the time Joe and Dora returned from their honeymoon, most of the cleanup in the vineyard was finished, but the blackened vines stood out like skeletons against the green vines growing nearby. "Why didn't you call me?" Joe demanded. "You knew I had my cell phone." His rugged face was dark with anger.

"There was nothing you could do from five thousand miles away. Besides, you were on your honeymoon. I wasn't going to interrupt that. Did you have a good time? Tell me all about the island." I tried to change to subject, but I should have known better.

"And if it had been you over there, and me here, wouldn't you have expected a call?"

I hung my head. "Good point. I'm sorry. I just didn't want to worry you when there was nothing you could do from Hawaii. It could have been a lot worse if Chase didn't have men posted around his place." I kept trying to calm him down, but I wasn't doing a very good job of it.

"Is it because this is your vineyard, and not mine that you didn't think you needed to call me?" he asked sharply.

"Joe, no!" Dora reached out to touch his arm.

I could only gasp and step back, my mouth gaping open. I could feel the color drain from my face. In a flash, Joe gathered me to him, holding me close. "I'm sorry Kiddo," he whispered against my ear. "I didn't mean that."

"I guess we both have something to apologize for," I said. "I really didn't want to ruin your honeymoon. This place is as much yours as it is mine." I frowned up at him. "If it wasn't for you, this place wouldn't even exist. Your name is on everything here."

"I know, Kiddo. I just let my temper get the best of me, and I took it out on you when everything should be laid at

Edward Simmons' feet. If I ever get my hands on him, I can't promise he'll come out of the meeting whole. I just don't know how to find out who he is now." He ran his big hands through his bushy hair in frustration.

Taking a deep breath in an attempt to calm himself, he sat down on the top step of the porch where we'd been talking. "What's this about Templeton having men posted around his property?"

I filled him in on how Chase had men keeping an eye on things at night since Betty Richards was murdered. "It's a good thing they were there," I finished. "If the fire hadn't been detected as fast as it was, we could've lost all the vines, trees, and possibly the house. By the time the fire department got here, they had the fire almost out. There's little doubt the fire was deliberately set. But without any physical evidence, or a confession, Greg doesn't hold out much hope of finding the culprit or getting a conviction."

Until now, I'd forgotten what Jorge said about seeing Joe in the vineyard at night. "Do you check the vineyard during the night?"

He shook his head. "After I was attacked, and the attempt to start a fire, I checked the fields before I went to bed, and first thing in the morning, but I didn't go out in the middle of the night. I didn't think it was necessary when nothing more was done."

I filled him in on what Jorge said about seeing someone he had assumed was Joe wandering among the vines in the middle of the night. "Dag nab it," he slammed his fist down on the porch. "I should have figured that low life would be skulking around in the dark. That's when he does his best work. I guess we need to take a page out of Templeton's play book, and hire some men to patrol the fields at night. I don't want to take any more chances."

He had a few more questions, but I had very little information to add. Finally he let me change the subject. "Tell me about Hawaii. What did you see?" I didn't want to get too nosey, and delve into the personal side of their trip.

“That place is amazing,” Dora spoke up first. “It rains a little every day, but not enough to put a damper on the sightseeing. You’ll never guess where Joe wanted to go.”

His face turned red, and I was almost afraid to ask. “No, I guess not,” I said cautiously. “Where did you want to go?” I looked at him now.

“They have wineries over there. I just wanted to see if things were different because they’re on an island.” His tone was a little defensive until Dora and I laughed. “Call it a bus driver’s holiday,” he chuckled. “Their pineapple wine wasn’t half bad but not as good as your peach and raspberry.”

~~~

For the next few months we’d be playing musical houses. It had been decided before Dora and Joe left they would stay in the little rental Dora and Pattiann shared until the lease ran out in a few months. Then they’d move back into Joe’s side of the winery. Until then, Pattiann would live there with me. When Greg and I got married, he’d move in with me, and Pattiann could take over his apartment lease. We would all have our own space. Until everything could be moved, Pattiann would continue to stay in my spare bedroom and Joe, of course, would be with Dora.

“You’re sure you’re okay with that arrangement, Honey?” Dora turned to Pattiann, still concerned. “What about Cody? Will you be okay with him?”

Pattiann laughed, “We’ve come to an understanding. He doesn’t knock me over, and I let him sleep outside my bedroom. We’re best friends now. It’ll be fine. Besides, I’ll be on the other end of the house, and I’m at work at lot.” As though he knew we were talking about him, Cody came around the corner of the house. Seeing Joe, he loped across the yard, bounding into Joe’s lap like he was a small puppy. The two fell backwards on the porch. Joe roughed up his ears, and got a face washing for his efforts.
~~~

Joe was anxious to get back into the daily routine. In all the years he and Dad worked together, I remembered him taking a vacation only once or twice. Whenever Dad urged him to take time off, his response was always the same. "Don't have anywhere I want to go. If I did, that's probably where I'd be now." He spent the rest of the day checking things out to make sure I hadn't screwed anything up, and it was all up to his standards. When Greg came over, Joe spent more time grilling him on what happened, and what was being done. They stayed outside, and it was my guess he was getting more information out of Greg than I ever did.

Dad kept us posted on the plans for his wedding, and we kept him up to date on what was happening since the fire. The five of us were making arrangements for our trip to California the day before Christmas. I wasn't totally comfortable leaving the vineyard because of Edward Simmons' latest attack on us, but I wouldn't miss Dad's wedding for anything in the world.

Becky would look after the tasting room. I knew she would do a good job, and not let anything happen. Juan would work as he always did, but while we were gone, he had agreed to spend the night in Joe's end of the house. True to his word, Joe hired three of Juan's friends to patrol the vineyard and orchard every night. He wasn't taking any chances with someone starting another fire.

For the next month Joe cleared out the burned vines, and preparing the soil for new ones. It'd be another three to five years before we harvested anything from them for wine. The first year vines are planted is for root growth, the second year is foliage growth and finally the third year is for fruit. You can't get good wine from bad vines, so you need to care for the vines from day one. I hated cutting down on our case production, but there was nothing I could do about it now. "Do you think we should try another varietal, or replace the burnt vines with what we lost?" I asked Joe while we were working outside.

As usual he took his time answering, chewing over the options. "You already have a good variety of grapes.

Adding more could be confusing down the line. You've been talking about going into production of your mead. Maybe this would be a good time."

"Seriously?" I was excited by the challenge, and the fact that he was encouraging me. Every step of the way I have waited for him to give me the go ahead. He innately knows when it's the right time to try something new and different. That ability as much as any other reason is why he moved to Arizona with me instead of staying with Dad. It had been time for something new and different for him, too.

I'd need more bee hives if I was going to do it right. George Davidson was first on my list to help me there. Since putting in my first hives he'd proven his knowledge, and I'd trust him now. So much was happening in such a short space of time, but I was anxious to begin producing the mead.

Right after Thanksgiving Pattiann helped put up the tree in the tasting room. In the past it was the only tree Joe and I had. We put our packages there, opening them Christmas morning, having dinner together in either my kitchen or Joe's. Dad had made a habit of coming over to spend Christmas with us, even if for only one day. This year everything was different. Pattiann was now living where Joe had lived for the last five years. Even though we wouldn't be spending Christmas day, or the following week at home she wanted to have a tree of her own. Greg spends most of his time with me at the vineyard, and he wanted a tree. So this year we decorated three trees.

~~~

Since the fire, Edward Simmons had been silent. Again. I didn't know whether to be grateful or nervous. Did this mean he'd finally given up harassing me, or was he thinking up some new and diabolical torment? The feeling of being watched wasn't as strong as before, and only part of the time now. I didn't know what that meant either.
~~~

Whatever the cause, I knew I still needed to keep a watchful eye out.

Greg's campaign was in full swing, and our wedding plans were beginning to shape up. We'd chosen early April for our wedding. Spring pruning and early bud would be almost over. Peach harvest wouldn't be started yet. We'd debated about waiting until after the election to get married, but we didn't want to wait close to a year. The first Saturday in April would be our special day. Pastor Rick and Beverly were helping out with both the wedding plans and Greg's campaign. Gerald Williams was proving to be less of a threat every day. Few people wanted a sheriff with no law enforcement experience.

The week before Christmas the charred remains of Gerald Williams were found in the burned out trailer where he lived. There was no evidence of foul play, and the arson investigator listed the cause as a combination of faulty electrical wiring and smoking in bed. The trailer was over thirty years old, and not in the best shape. Because the trailer was sitting in the middle of a field, and the nearest neighbor, Mayor Brady of course, was more than five miles away; there had been little hope of anyone calling the fire department in time to save the man. I was surprised to learn Roland Brady owned so much property in the county. Again I didn't know where he came up with the money. Was his father still a land developer, and working on something in our small county? Was this why Mayor Brady needed to control law enforcement? I kept asking myself that question.

"What does this do to your campaign?" I asked Greg that evening. "Will there still need to be an election if you don't have an opponent?" I'm sorry to admit I'm so uninformed about politics of any kind, especially county politics.

He shrugged his broad shoulders, causing the material of his shirt to pull against his muscled chest and forearms, temporarily drawing my attention from the subject at hand. When he answered, I had to drag my mind back to what he was saying. "Unless someone else decides to run in his place, the election goes forward with only me on the ballot, I guess." He didn't sound completely happy with that. If he didn't have an opponent, he couldn't be certain the people really wanted him for sheriff. They just didn't have a choice.

~~~

"I hated doing that, but it was necessary," he muttered in the empty room; he was talking to himself again. "He was becoming a liability," he continued out loud, "beginning to think he could call the shots." Giving a snort, he shook his head, "Not likely. No one is going to have that kind of power over me again. Too bad I couldn't leave more evidence to indicate he was behind everything that's been going on. But it was too risky. That deputy is no dummy. He could see through any attempts at that. I need to call a halt to this, so he doesn't keep digging. At least I made sure they couldn't do any tests on the remains. There's nothing for Wilkinson to find," he assured himself. "Without any evidence, he can't pin anything on me." Satisfied with himself, he stared out the window at the street. Christmas lights twinkled in the dark night. Christmas was just days away. At times like this, he wished he had someone to share his life with. But the feeling would pass soon enough. He was better off alone.

~~~

Dad's house hadn't changed much in the five years since I moved out. Twin love seats still flanked the large stone fireplace, now sitting at an angle to accommodate viewing the large screen television against the far wall. A comfortable leather sofa sat across the large room. The familiarity of the rooms was comforting. It was home.

My old room had changed though; it was no longer the frilly teenage girl's room. It now had heavier pieces that I liked very much. Dad always had good taste but I wondered if maybe Molly had helped him pick things out.

Greg was staying in the spare room, while Joe, Dora and Pattiann were in Joe's little house that sat about a hundred yards from Dad's.

Dad hadn't said whether he and Molly would be living here, or at her winery about five miles away. Selfishly, I hoped they'd stay here. I didn't want the house to be deserted, but it wasn't my choice. I'd keep my opinions to myself.

Christmas morning I was barely out of bed when I heard a soft knock on the door. "You awake, Kitten?" Dad's voice came through the door panels. If I'd been sleeping, I wouldn't have even heard him or his knock, and that was probably on purpose. He wouldn't want to wake me if I was sleeping in.

I pulled on my robe before opening the door. "Merry Christmas." I kissed his cheek, enjoying the bear hug he gave me in return.

"Merry Christmas to you too, Kitten. It's good to see you here in your old room. I've missed having you around." He looked a little misty eyed.

I hugged him again before climbing back on the tall bed, pushing the pillows against the headboard and leaning back. "If I'd stuck around, you might not have noticed Molly when you did. You ever think of that?" I raised an eyebrow.

He sat down in the overstuffed chair, propping one foot on top of the other knee. "I'd like to think I wasn't that blind all these years. Things happen at the right time, in the right order. If it's right, things always work out. Now tell me all about your wedding plans."

I felt a little sad that he wasn't with me as I planned my wedding, but he couldn't be in two places at once. His place was here with Molly working his own winery the same as mine was now in Arizona with Greg.

By the time we made it to the kitchen, Greg was already there lounging against the counter, his dark hair still damp from his shower, a cup of coffee in his hand. I don't know which was more delectable, him or the steaming cup of coffee. I wasn't aware I was staring (and maybe drooling just a little), until Dad cleared his throat. "Would you kids like me to go to my room so you can have a proper good morning?" he teased. I could feel my face heating up. "It's a good thing you decided not to wait until October to get married."

My face got even hotter. To cover my embarrassment, I opened the cupboard, pulling out two cups. "Want some coffee, Dad?"

He laughed at me, but let the subject drop. "Sure, Kitten. Thanks."

Unfortunately, Greg didn't. He straightened away from the cupboard, facing Dad. "Um, Sir. We aren't living together, and haven't done anything wrong. That's part of the reason we decided to get married in April instead of waiting until after the election."

Now I wanted to find a hole to crawl into. Dad and I have always had a very open relationship. We could discuss almost anything, but this was getting a little out of hand.

"Son, I know my daughter," Dad answered. "All I'm saying is temptation is out there for everyone, sometimes it's pretty hard to resist. Especially if you wait longer than you should." He clapped Greg on the shoulder. "You're a good man, and I'm proud to be calling you my son-in-law."

"Okay, if we're through with the touchy-feely, can we have some breakfast? It's time to open presents as soon as Joe and family get here." It felt great to say Joe's family. To my great relief, he opened the door for Dora and Pattiann just then, letting in a breath of cool air.

"Did we interrupt something?" Dora looked at each of us questioningly.

"Nothing at all. We were just discussing whether we were going to eat first, or open presents first." No one believed my prevarication, but didn't push it either. We decided on food first and Dad, Joe and I went to work, falling into the routine we'd established years ago while I was growing up; working around and with each other.

Christmas dinner with Molly and her family was fun. I hadn't seen Donna and Barbara in five years, and we had a lot of catching up to do. I remembered Donna's husband, Jim Hensen, from high school. He was three years ahead of me, but had been part of any group activity. He'd always been sweet on Donna and that hasn't changed one bit; the love they shared was clear each time they looked at each other. Barbara's fiancé, Bob Jackson, had moved to the area after I moved to Arizona, but he was friendly and obviously in love with her. It was a Christmas dinner that would last long in my memory, and warm my heart forever.

~~~

I didn't think I'd ever see the day when my dad, who was usually the calming influence in any situation, would become so nervous he couldn't sit still. Perspiration dotted his forehead, and he kept wiping it away. "What's the hold up? Let's get this show on the road."

My chuckle turned into a cough when he scowled at me. "The ceremony isn't supposed to start for another fifteen minutes. Give Molly the time she needs to get dressed."

"She could be wearing a gunny sack, and I wouldn't care," he grumbled. "Maybe we should have just gone to Las Vegas instead of going to all this hoopla."

A shocked expression settled on my face. "You're kidding, right? You'd deny Molly and her family the pleasure of being with her at this time, not to mention Joe and me being here for you?" My hands were braced on my hips, and tears prickle behind my eyes. "You would really want to be married in one of those crummy 'chapels' without the benefit of a pastor?"

Before I could dissolve into a puddle of tears, he gathered me close. "I'm sorry, Kitten. I'm just...I don't know what I am. I don't remember being this nervous when I married your mother, and I loved her beyond distraction."

"Are you having second thoughts?" I looked into his face. This wasn't a good time for that.

He laughed at himself. "No second thoughts, Honey. I'm just anxious to have it done." Turning serious, he added,
~~~

"I've been alone for so long I'm not sure I know how to be a husband anymore. What if I screw it up, and Molly ends up hating me?"

I'd never seen him so unsure of himself. Placing both hands on his face, forcing him to look at me, I asked softly. "Do you love her, Dad? Do you want to make her and yourself happy?" He nodded, but couldn't force any words out. "Then everything will be fine. You might fumble around each other for a while, but I know it will work out. You know God is right there beside you all the way."

He visibly relaxed then. "When you're right, you're right. Long before I asked Molly to marry me, I talked it over with God. I don't know why I'm so worried now."

The strains of music coming from the church changed, and Joe opened the door. "You about ready to do this, Clay? Your bride is waiting for you." Calm now, Dad walked out beside Joe, and I slipped into the front row beside Greg, Dora and Pattiann.

"It's our turn next," Greg whispered against my ear, sending trickles of excitement through me. I hope I'm not as nervous as Dad just was, but I probably will be.

Molly was a picture perfect bride, wearing a yellow cocktail dress setting off the tan she acquired from working in the vineyard all these years. Donna and Barbara walked ahead of their mom, Donna's round tummy filling out the front of her teal blue dress. Both girls looked as happy for their mom as I am for Dad. This was going to be wonderful for everyone.

During the reception, Pastor Don Clark gave me a hug. "Your dad said you'll be getting married soon. Will you be coming here for that?"

This was the first opportunity I'd had to introduce him to Greg, Dora and Pattiann. "No, we're getting married in New Haven."

"In church I hope." He gave me the fish-eyed look I remembered so well from my childhood whenever he wanted to admonish one of the "wee ones" as he called all of the kids in his congregation.

"Pastor Rick Bennett is doing us the honor," Greg answered for me. "I've only been going to the small church since the three of us moved to New Haven about a year ago. But Skylar's known him for the past five years."

Pastor Don smiled broadly. "I know Rick Bennett! We've met several times at different meetings. He's a good man. I didn't know he was pastor at your church. Be sure to tell him I said hi." He stayed to visit for several minutes before moving on to greet others in his congregation.

Dad and Molly left the following morning for their honeymoon in Hawaii. After Joe told Dad about the wineries there, and Dora told Molly about the real tourist attractions, they'd decided to following their example and go to Hawaii. The Arizona contingent of the family left at the same time for home. I was anxious to see if there'd been any trouble while we were gone.

CHAPTER EIGHTEEN

Mayor Brady must have been watching for us to return because Greg had just deposited our bags in the house when the big Town Car pulled up behind Greg's Ford F250. "I'm sorry to intrude when you just arrived, Deputy," he nodded at Pattiann and me without saying anything. "I know you are still on vacation until tomorrow, but I thought you would want this information as soon as possible." He held out a small laptop computer for Greg to see.

Without taking the computer, Greg tipped his head to one side. "What's this?"

The look Mayor Brady shot Greg said plenty. "A computer," he stated, like he had to explain what a laptop was.

Well, Duh, I wanted to say, but Greg kept his voice level despite the frustration he had to be feeling. "I know that. Why are you bringing it to me?" I knew he was wary of anything the mayor had to say or do, after trying so hard to keep him from being elected sheriff.

"As you are aware, Gerald Williams had been my friend and driver for the past few years. He lived on my property until..." He let the rest of his sentence die on his lips. His attempt to look sad at what had happened to his friend almost worked, but not entirely. Greg waited without saying anything; a technique I recognized from television cop shows to get people to fill the uncomfortable silence. "Um, well, Mr. Williams, Gerald," he corrected himself, "had no family, and I was about his only friend. He always had free access to my home and vehicles. I was going through the trunk of my car, and found this buried in the tire well under the spare tire." Greg waited again for the mayor to continue. He was clearly uncomfortable now.

"Anyway, this isn't mine. I thought, since it had probably belonged to Gerald, you would want to see it. I didn't know the man even knew how to turn on a computer let alone owned one." He seemed a little unsure of himself now.

"Why would I want his personal computer?" Greg remained unflappable.

The mayor stiffened his spine, looking down his nose like Greg was beneath him; he also seemed to think Greg was dumber than dirt. "He was obviously trying to hide it. There might be something on it you should see. After all, you are trying to solve several crimes, are you not?"

"Why didn't you take it to Sheriff Stevens? He is still sheriff for a few more months. Unless something happened to him while I was away?" He phrased it as a question. My stomach churned at the possibility, and I could see Greg felt the same.

"No, of course not." The mayor was quick to reassure Greg. "I am sorry if I gave you that impression. I just thought I should give it to you since you are the one heading up the investigation."

"Did you turn it on to see what's on it?" Greg still hadn't taken the laptop.

Mayor Brady recoiled. "Certainly not!" He was getting impatient. He wanted Greg to take the laptop. "I didn't want to compromise any evidence that might be on it. Are you going to check this out or not?" Again he thrust the small laptop towards Greg.

"Why would you even think it has anything to do with the cases? What makes you think it belonged to Williams? Do you think Williams was involved with what's been going on around here?" Greg still didn't take what the mayor was offering.

"I simply know it isn't mine, and the only other person who had access to my vehicle was Gerald, so I can only assume it belonged to him. You don't hide something unless you have something you don't want others to know about. With the things that have been happening lately, I am guessing there might be something on it."

Greg went to his truck, and took out a large plastic evidence bag, finally letting Mayor Brady slide the laptop inside. He sealed the bag, writing his initials across the seal along with the time and date. "I'll have the state lab guys take a look at it. If there isn't anything useful on it, I'll let you know. Thank you for bringing it to me." The meeting was over as far as he was concerned.

The mayor had obviously been hoping Greg would check out the computer right here, and was disappointed. "Yes, well, I thought you should see it." He turned to nod again to Pattiann and me. Without another word, he got back in his car and drove off. Apparently he didn't need a driver any longer.

"What was that about?" Pattiann voiced what we were all thinking.

Greg shrugged. "No telling. I don't know if he thinks his good buddy had something to do with the trouble going on here or not. Like I said, the crime lab will have to take a look at it. I'm no computer expert."

Granted, I hadn't known Gerald Williams, and had only seen him up close and personal once, but he didn't strike me as a tech savvy kind of guy. Since we hadn't opened the laptop there was no way to know what might be on it. Whatever it was, why would Gerald Williams, or anyone, put a laptop in the trunk of someone else's car under the spare tire? Obviously he was trying to hide something incriminating.

My stomach fluttered at the thought. Had he been my mystery caller? Was there a chance he was Edward Simmons? I'd heard nothing more from him since the fire at my place and Williams' death after that. But that didn't mean he was behind everything. Or that he was the man who embezzled from Dad thirty years ago. That would tie everything up into a neat little package; maybe too neat.

~~~

As a small county with limited resources, crime scenes and lab work had to be farmed out to the Pima County lab
~~~

in Tucson. This wasn't a high priority for them, and it took more than two weeks for Greg to hear back. "Am I the only one who thinks this is too much of a coincidence?" he groused as he paced around the tasting room just after we closed for the day. "There's no such thing as coincidence in law enforcement, but the lab techs don't agree. They're ready to mark these cases closed."

"It does seem a little too neat," I agreed. "What was on it?"

"The phone calls, Betty Richards' murder, the break-in at Templeton's, the fire here. Details of everything that's been going on around here. Even the real estate scam is detailed on there. Like I said the lab techs think this wraps it all up. They want to turn everything over to the Pima County Attorney to tie up their end of the case, and think I should do the same here. I just don't buy it. It's too neat."

"But how did the laptop get into the trunk of the mayor's car if Williams didn't put it there?"

"I'm thinking the mayor put it there. If it was ever in the trunk."

I stared at him, my mouth hanging open. I didn't particularly like the mayor, but that didn't make him a murderer. "Why would he do that?"

Greg pulled me to him giving me a soft kiss before continuing. "Sweetheart, if he's Edward Simmons, he's going to want to point the blame in another direction. Maybe he can't think of another way to get out of the mess he's created for himself. I don't think he'd want to walk away, and start over again like he did in California." He released me, pacing around the room again.

"Maybe I'm just grasping at straws. I want to wrap this up, but I don't want to do it if it isn't the truth. Whoever this guy is, he's making the entire department look incompetent. Other than the laptop, there's very little evidence pointing to anyone in particular. I only have the mayor's word it belonged to Williams. I've tried to find out background information on anyone who could possibly be behind this, and I've come up empty. Neither the mayor nor

Williams have a criminal history." He ran his fingers through his dark hair causing a stray lock to fall over his forehead. My hands itched to comb it back into place.

Dragging my thoughts back, I remembered my own useless internet search for information on Roland Brady, Gerald Williams, and James Burke. I knew the frustration he was feeling. He hadn't fared any better than I had. We'd been hoping the lab would find something on the laptop. But if the information they found led them down the garden path, and they considered the cases closed, they weren't going to look any further. Was that what this was all about? Is this a red herring?

Greg pulled his cell phone off his belt when it started chirping, but he didn't stop pacing. "Wilkinson," he barked. "Yes, what can I do for you?" For several minutes he listened without interrupting. "What difference does it make if it's refurbished?" Again he listened, impatience written all over his face. "I know what refurbished means. I'm asking what difference that makes. A lot of people buy used computers and laptops. They're cheaper." It was hard to follow the one-sided conversation. "If you think you'll find anything more, or where the thing came from, do whatever you need to do. Thanks." He replaced the phone on his belt, staring off into space for several moments, digesting what the person had said.

When he finally came back to earth, he gave me a lopsided grin. "I guess we aren't the only ones who think something is a little fishy with that laptop."

"Who was that? What did he say?" I was hoping he wouldn't give me his standard reply that he can't comment on an ongoing investigation.

"At least one of the computer techs thinks there are some inconsistencies on the dates in the files. He also found pieces of files that had been erased. Whoever did it didn't do a very good job of erasing the files. He's going to do some more digging, and see what he can find. He'll let me know."

"What will it prove even if the computer originally belonged to the mayor? He'll say he gave it to his friend when he got a new one."

"It all depends on what's in the erased files. But if the mayor gave the laptop to Williams, why didn't he tell me when he brought it to me?"

"As careful as Edward Simmons has been all these years, even going so far as to fake his own death, I can't believe he'd suddenly be so careless, leaving something behind pointing to himself now. How many people has he killed to get away with his first crime? Do you really believe Mayor Brady is capable of cold blooded murder?"

Greg began pacing again. "I don't know what to believe anymore. Some of my evidence pointed in his direction, but it could also point to Williams. It's just too neat of a package. The only thing missing is the ribbon."

~~~

Everyone acted like the cases were solved, but Greg and I still had serious doubts. The tech in Tucson was working on the laptop in his spare time, and we were still waiting to hear from him. "Do you think Gerald Williams could be Edward Simmons?" I asked Greg. We were sitting on the porch swing enjoying the last few rays of the winter sun.

He sighed in frustration, giving a fatalistic shrug. "If I'm to believe the lab guys in Tucson and the Pima County Sheriff, everything has been wrapped up in a nice neat package for me. All the cases solved. Williams was a master criminal, carrying all this out by himself. But if they're wrong, he was someone's patsy, a scapegoat." He gave the swing a shove with the toe of his boot.

"But what do you think?" I pressed.

He was silent for several long minutes weighing the pros and cons of both sides of the argument. Finally he looked up, rubbing the palms of his hands over his tired face. "My vote goes to scapegoat. Master criminal just doesn't fit what I knew about Williams, and what I've learned about him since he died. Someone was pulling his
~~~

strings. Edward Simmons is still out there. I feel it in my gut I just can't prove it."

This wasn't exactly what I wanted to hear, but I knew in my heart he was right. Was Simmons going to come after me again? It's been two months since Gerald Williams died. There have been no more threats, no more phone calls, nothing. What was I supposed to think?

~~~

"There wasn't anything incriminating in the deleted files," Greg sighed with frustration. The Tucson tech finally called with his report. "There were bits and pieces of files, maybe the originals of what's on there now. There was nothing indicating who wrote them. I thought for sure it was going to point me to the smoking gun in this mess. He did say there's something 'funky,' his word not mine, regarding the dates the files were created. I don't know what that means. But what really caught my attention was the fact that someone, either Gerald Williams or the previous owner of the laptop, was checking you out on the internet."

"What?! How do they know that?"

"I can't give you details on how he figured it out because I didn't know what he was talking about most of the time. He just said someone had been doing some internet research on you and your dad. It'd help if we knew when Williams got the laptop and from whom. Of course, if the mayor gave it to him, he wouldn't give me the correct timeline if he's the one who did the checking."

"But why would Gerald Williams or Mayor Brady check me out unless one of them is Edward Simmons?" My heart was pounding so fast I thought it was going to jump out of my chest. "How do we prove it?"

Greg shook his head, "If Williams really was Simmons, there's nothing we can do to him now. I wish there'd been some way to run tests on his remains to see if his death really had been the result of the fire, or if there was some other cause. There wasn't any way to tell if he died from
~~~

smoke inhalation, if he burned to death, or if there were drugs in his system. The fire burned undetected so long there was nothing left of the trailer or Williams but rubble, ashes, and bones." He was thinking out loud now as much as he was talking to me. "If Brady, or whoever gave Williams the laptop, is Simmons, proving it isn't going to be easy. At least for now, he's faded into the wallpaper again. Only difference is this time he didn't have to disappear in order to stay under the radar." This fact as much as any other frustrated both of us.

CHAPTER NINETEEN

Since October, I'd been working on a limited line of Mead, even experimenting by adding some raspberries for a different flavor. George Davidson had installed two more bee hives to increase the honey production. I'd lost a lot when the hives were dumped onto Betty Richards. I could buy honey from other producers, but honey from different areas might give the mead a different flavor. I didn't want to do that while I was still learning. For now, I'd only have enough for a reserve label until I had more of my own honey available. It takes four parts of honey to one part water when making mead so I would need a lot more than I currently had.

Greg was still campaigning for sheriff even though he didn't have an opponent. The voters still needed to know him, and know he was running. The final findings on the laptop from the Pima County lab were inconclusive as far as Greg and I were concerned. Unfortunately, there was no concrete evidence anyone other than Gerald Williams had used it. "The way it looks now, I'm going to have to close all of the cases with Gerald Williams as the suspect. It's very convenient for someone that he's dead." Greg told me.

"You don't think it could have been Gerald Williams?" We were at our usual table at Manuel's on Friday night. Our wedding was three months away; I really wanted to put all this behind us before then. I know he felt the same urgency, and was still looking into anyone who could be responsible.

He thought about my question before answering; finally shaking his head. "No, I don't think he was smart enough to pull off this kind of thing. From start to finish this was a very in-depth plan. Just look at the way someone tried to sell your winery right out from under you and Joe. That was a very complex deal. The Pima County Attorney is as frustrated as I am, but without any evidence, I'm afraid he's going to have to stop digging to uncover who is behind all the faxes and emails, not to mention the numerous corporations involved. If Williams had been behind it, where is the rest of the evidence? There has to be more than just the laptop. Did it get burned up in his trailer?

"Another question I'd like answered is why was he living on the mayor's property in a dumpy little trailer if he was this master criminal? Where's all the money he made from his scams?" He shook his head. "Someone else was pulling the strings. I just don't know how to prove it."

"So you're going to close the cases?" I asked again.

"Officially, I have to," he stated flatly. He didn't say anything else for several long minutes, and I wondered what he was thinking. Giving a slight nod like he'd made a decision, he looked at me. "This all started when your dad came to visit last spring. Right?" I nodded, but didn't say anything. If he was ready to tell me what was on his mind, I wasn't going to interrupt. "You said he usually came straight out to the winery, but this time you met him here in town." Again I nodded. "If that's what set Simmons off," he continued thoughtfully, "maybe we could do it again. That is, if Williams wasn't Simmons like I believe." He stopped, waiting for me to comment.

"You mean recreate that day, hoping Simmons will see Dad again and start over?"

Greg nodded, "I know it sounds crazy, and maybe a little risky, but it's the only way I can figure out how to draw him out if he's still here." Even though it was noisy in the restaurant making it difficult to eavesdrop on the next table, he kept his voice low, leaning closed to me.

My heart started pounding with excitement. I was ready to do anything, but would Dad agree if he thought it might put me in danger?

~~~

Seeing them across the room with their heads together, he knew they were plotting against him. Why can't they
~~~

accept what's right in front of them? he thought. I had all the evidence laid out for him on the laptop, but that damn deputy just keeps on digging. What do I have to do, spoon feed him? If he digs deep enough, he might just hit on something that will lead him right back to me. No matter how deep I bury myself in corporations, there's always a way to unravel things. I can't let that happen. Panic welled up inside him. He couldn't lose everything again. I had the perfect patsy, he told himself; everything was going along fine until he decided he should be the boss. I'm going to have to do something to stop them. Leaving her alone hasn't worked. I'm going to have to do something drastic, and do it soon.

~~~

When we got back to the house, I called Dad. I wasn't sure he would agree it was a good idea to bait Edward Simmons, if in fact he was still alive. Greg laid out his plan, and I held my breath waiting for Dad to either agree, or come unglued at the idea. When he finished talking, Dad was quiet for so long I thought he'd hung up on us.

"Are you agreeing to this, Kitten?" he finally spoke, his voice hesitant. "If Williams wasn't Edward Simmons, and he's still there, this could be very dangerous. Nothing more has happened to make either of you think he's still around, has it?"

"No, but if he's still here, what's to keep him from coming after me next month, or next year when we let down our guard? I don't want to spend the rest of my life waiting for the next shoe to drop on my head."

"I'm going to do everything in my power to make sure she's safe. I don't want anything happening to her either. I have big plans, and they all need her to be here for a long, long time." He reached out, taking my hand in his, and bringing it to his lips.

Dad cleared his throat. "That's a little too much information, Son. Remember it's my one and only daughter you plan on doing those things with." He chuckled, and I
~~~

could feel my face turning red. He'd put a different spin on Greg's words.

"Are you sure this is going to work, and you can keep her safe?" Dad asked growing serious again. "What do you say about this, Joe?"

"I'm no crazier about this than you are." Joe and Dora were with us when we called Dad. "But I can't think of a way to be certain Simmons is gone for good either." His voice was gruff with pent up emotions.

"Sir," Greg started to say something when Dad interrupted him.

"Do you think you could call me something besides sir?" Dad chuckled, trying to break the tension. "You make me feel as old as Methuselah in the Bible. Think you could call me Clay or Dad?"

"I can certainly do that," Greg paused before adding, "Dad."

"Okay, so how do we go about setting this up? When do you want me to come over?"

A week later I met Dad in front of the bank like I had last spring. He wrapped me in a bear hug, whispering in my ear. "Are you sure you're okay with this?"

"I'm fine, Dad." I pulled away, trying to act as normal as possible. He turned, staring at the bank just like he had last spring. "Do you feel like we're being watched?" I whispered, looking at the mirrored windows of the bank.

"No, but this is what I did before. I want everything to be just like it was then. If Edward Simmons is still alive, I want him to think he's reliving one of the worst days of his life." We walked along the street towards Manuel's, the whole while his gaze never wavered from the bank building. We reenacted Dad's entire trip, coming back to town the next day, standing in front of the building as we had then. If Edward Simmons was still alive and watching us he had to be freaked out right now.

Two days after Dad's visit, Roland Brady came striding confidently across the yard just as I came out of the winery. I thought my heart was going to jump out of my chest.

Greg had suspected him all along. Had Dad's visit forced his hand like we'd hoped? What was he going to do? It was broad daylight. Surely he wouldn't try something here with people around. My paranoia ran rampant. "Hello, Skylar," his big voice boomed. "I was hoping I could impose on you to give me a tour of your winery. I've heard so many good things about your wines, and now you're making something new. Have I come at an inconvenient time?"

I wanted to send him packing, but wasn't this what we'd wanted; to draw him out? I have to admit I was more than a little afraid. All of the evidence Greg had pointed at Gerald Williams, but it could also point to the mayor since Williams worked for him. Roland Brady waited patiently for me to answer. I looked around, hoping to find an excuse, any excuse, to say no I was too busy. Nothing came to mind. Joe and Juan were working in the vineyard behind me, and Joe was aware of the mayor's presence. If he tried something, they'd be right here to stop him. Making my decision, I gave him a tentative smile. "Of course not, I'll be glad to show you around." If he was Edward Simmons, and he was going to try to hurt me, I'd rather he do it with people around.

As I explained the different processes the grapes, and eventually the wine went through, I saw Joe come into the building. He didn't have any work inside right now, but the mayor didn't know that. He seemed engrossed in what I was saying. I could expect a lecture once the mayor was gone; and another one from Greg when he found out what I was doing. We really hadn't expected Edward Simmons to try something in broad daylight.

I kept the tour short and the explanations simple. Roland appeared to be interested in every process, asking intelligent questions at the appropriate time. "Thank you very much, Skylar." He smiled at me when we stepped outside again. "That was very interesting. I can see why you're business is doing so well."

Before he walked away, I got up my courage to ask a question of my own. "You've never shown any interest in Sky Vineyards before, Roland." I emphasized his name. "I was wondering why now? What brought on this sudden interest?" If I baited him, would he make a mistake, and say something about Dad? I was emboldened by the fact that Joe was right inside the winery. He would be there to defend me if the need arose.

Roland cleared his throat before answering. "I've been trying for some time to put our small county on the map, and have failed in my efforts so far. When you started having trouble I knew I needed to do more. Ignoring the small businesses outside of town was my mistake. I know that now."

"New Haven isn't the only town in the county." I frowned at him. "What exactly are you trying to do?"

"I'd rather not get into the specifics at this time. Suffice it to say that bringing in more tourists, would benefit everyone." He sounded more stilted than ever.

"Does this have something to do with the land where Gerald Williams kept his trailer?" Curiosity overrode fear, and I forgot to be afraid of him.

"Like I said, I don't want to get into specifics; details are still pending." He paused, and then smiled at me. "Thank you for the very informative tour. I enjoyed my time with you, and I will make a point of coming back when your tasting room is open to sample your wines. All of our wineries are a big boon to the county." Before I could react to this speech, he was in his Town Car with the door firmly shut.

Joe stepped up beside me, and I looked up at him as the big car disappeared. "Do you know anything about these plans of his?"

He shook his head. "I don't go into town all that often, but no one has said anything to me. Maybe Dora's heard something at the bank." He frowned down at me. "What were you thinking, inviting him in like that? What would you have done if I hadn't seen him, and he tried something?"

The lecture begins, I thought ruefully. "I knew you saw him when he first got here. You also saw us walk inside. I left the door open giving myself an exit in case he tried something. Weren't we hoping Dad's visit would bring Edward Simmons out of the shadows? If he's still alive, that is. I thought this might be it."

Joe grumbled, but didn't say anything. "I wish I knew what Brady was doing thirty years ago," I went on. "I couldn't find anything on the internet about the years after he left ASU until he arrived in New Haven."

Joe raised an eyebrow questioningly. "You think he might have been in California?"

"I have no idea, but it would be interesting to find out where he was."

To say Greg was unhappy when he learned I gave Mayor Brady a tour is an understatement. "What were you thinking?" He paced around the living room like an angry bull, snorting and stomping. "You couldn't be certain he wouldn't try something just because Joe was right there. Until we know for certain Edward Simmons is dead, you need to avoid Brady. He's still my prime suspect." This conversation was almost word for word what Joe had said earlier.

I was trying hard to remain calm. I'm not used to having anyone tell me what I can and can't do. "Recreating Dad's visit last spring was your idea, Greg. Weren't we hoping it would draw Edward Simmons out? What did you think would happen?" My voice was tight, but there wasn't anything I could do about it. "I made sure Joe was close by." My hands were braced on my hips, and I glared at him.

"I just didn't expect him to come after you during the day," he said unhappily. "That's why we have men posted around at night."

"Well, he didn't try anything." I recounted the mayor's story about 'putting our little county on the map.'

"What does that even mean?" Greg frowned. "What's he got up his sleeve? Maybe that was just another red herring to throw us off his scent." He drew a deep breath, blowing it out slowly. Putting his hands gently on my shoulders, he began to massage the tight muscles there. "Babe, I'm sorry I got upset. Fear is a very powerful emotion. When you said Brady was here today, I was scared to death," he admitted. "For the first time in my life I have something more precious to me than life itself. I don't want to lose you."

How could I stay mad after that statement? I let him draw me close, resting my head against his muscled chest. His heart beat loudly against my ear. "Okay, this is going to take a little getting used to," I admitted. "I don't usually have to explain why I do something, even to Dad and Joe. I'll try to remember I'm part of a couple now, and I need to think before I do something stupid."

"Not stupid, Babe, just potentially dangerous. We don't know who to trust right now." It was a while later before we headed to the kitchen to find something to eat.

CHAPTER TWENTY

"I never should have called her the first time. That was a mistake. I should have just sold that stupid vineyard right out from under her. She wouldn't have found out until it was too late to do anything. It's worked so many times before. Why did she have to find out? She could have continued making her dumb little fruity wines for years before learning she didn't own the place anymore." A high pitched giggle escaped his full lips at the thought. "But I wanted to taunt her, to taunt him with what I was going to do to his little angel. They were both going to pay for what her old man did to me."

He was talking to himself more and more, but it didn't matter. There was never anyone around, just him, and all that belonged to him. That's the way he liked it, the way it should be. He didn't need anyone. He was building his own empire right here. He couldn't let her take it away from him.

"Where does this leave me now?" he asked the empty room. "I have to figure out a way to make them forget all about me. He stared out the big window. "Why did she have to choose this town to move to? Her old man is going to keep showing up just like he did the other day. I can't stand having him so close." Why can't they let Edward Simmons die? What do I have to do to make it end?

~~~

"Nothing more's happened since I was there? That didn't bring him out?" Dad's frustration was obvious. "You're watching your accounts, right? How about you, Joe?" He wanted this over as bad as we did, and called daily to make sure nothing more had happened.

"All of our accounts are as protected as we can get them. Mr. Henderson at the bank is keeping a close watch
~~~

on everything, and we're doing all we can to protect ourselves from having the vineyard sold out from under us." We were sitting around the speaker phone in my kitchen. "When Mayor Brady showed up last week, I thought he was going to slip up, and reveal he was behind all this mess. But I guess he's not Edward Simmons either."

Dad huffed and puffed for several seconds. "So it's over? Do you think he's really gone?"

Greg sighed heavily. "The way it stands right now, unless we come up with some evidence we haven't found so far, or he makes another run at Skylar, he's home free. If he's still alive, that is. We've found nothing to tie anyone else to what happened. We don't even know if there are other victims out there waiting to find out their property has been transferred out of their names the way he tried with Sky."

"But you still think he's around; Williams wasn't behind it all?" Dad asked pointedly.

Greg waited a beat before answering; then his voice was soft. "Yes, I think he's still out there, and no, I don't think Williams was the mastermind behind what happened. He just didn't have the background, or knowledge to do it."

No one spoke for several long seconds, finally Dad spoke, "Okay, if he's still alive, and my presence brought him out the first time; maybe he just needs a little more prodding. I'm going to be coming over once or twice a month, making myself known around town. We'll see what happens then."

For the next two weeks Dad came over for a day or two at a time. We spent as much time as possible in town hoping to draw Edward Simmons out of hiding. This was taking a lot of time away from both wineries. I just hoped it didn't take too long. I wanted this resolved before the wedding, and time was growing short.

Standing in front of the bank like we always did for several minutes before walking to the restaurant, a shiver traveled up my spine. "You cold, Honey?" Dad asked, slipping off his jacket, draping it over my shoulders. Late

February can still be cool in southeastern Arizona, especially when the wind was blowing. Today though, the winds were calm, and the sun was shining brightly.

Grateful for the warmth of his jacket, I looked around at the buildings surrounding us. The big bank building was the only one with mirrored windows, even on the second and third floors. Someone was standing at one of them watching us. I just couldn't tell which one. "He's still here, Dad, watching us right now. I just can't tell where he is. If I knew which window he was hiding behind, I'd know who he is." Frustration made my voice sharp.

"What's in the building besides the bank?"

I shrugged. "I guess just offices, but I'm not really sure. I've never paid attention. Dora would know. Should we go in and ask? She's at work now." Walking across the street, I continued to watch the windows hoping to see something.

There were only a few customers in the bank when we walked in. Chase was leaving the teller window when he saw us. He flew across the tile floor of the lobby, sliding to a stop in front of us. Or I should say, in front of Dad. He barely noticed I was standing there. His actions drew the attention of everyone in the lobby. Now, they were staring at us. "Hello, Mr. Bishop, it's nice to see you." For a minute I thought he was going to reach for Dad's hand to kiss his ring.

"Ah...Nice to see you too, Mr. Templeton." Dad didn't know what to make of Chase. Since my engagement, he has made himself scarce, not that I saw much of him before.

"Oh, please, call me Chase. Skylar and I have been friends for five years, and I feel like I know you as well."

His words were so syrupy sweet, I wanted to gag. Somehow I managed to cough instead. Before Chase could make more of a fool of himself, Dora came to the rescue. "Clay, Skylar, it's nice to see you." She knew Dad was coming to town, but didn't expect us to turn up at her work. "How are you doing?" She stepped between Chase and Dad, linking her arm through his, leading us to her office.

Looking over my shoulder at Chase, I wanted to laugh at the crestfallen expression on his face. He really wanted to suck up to Dad. Fortunately, Dora had managed to save us all the embarrassment.

James Burke's office door was closed, so I assumed he had a customer, or he was busy with something else. For that I was grateful. I wasn't sure what he would make of us being here. I didn't want him to think I was here to do business with him.

Safely away from prying eyes and ears, Dora asked, "What's up?"

"What businesses are on the second and third floor here?" I asked. "I've never paid attention before. I guess it's time I became more involved in town."

Dora shrugged, "There are a couple of law offices, an accountant, a doctor and dentist on the second floor. The third floor is all city offices. The town is small enough there isn't an official town hall, much to the mayor's dismay. I've heard people say he's been trying to get the town council to pass a resolution to build a separate town hall with room for a police department and jail, but so far he's had no luck."

I remembered the mayor's comment about putting our little county on the map. So much had been happening; I forgot to ask if she knew anything about his plans. She shook her head when I asked her now. "Joe asked me about that, but I haven't heard anything. I do know he always has some big plan he's trying to push on either the council, or the county supervisors. Maybe that's what he was talking about."

Any grandiose plans the mayor had would fit with what we knew about Edward Simmons, I thought. He was the right age, and his office looked out on the street where Dad and I stood that day last spring. He could have been watching us, and decided it was time for a little revenge.

My mind continued to spin with these thoughts as we left Dora's office, walking across the lobby. Mr. Burke's office door opened, and he met us in the middle of the room. "Good morning, Mr. Bishop." He stopped right in front of Dad, acknowledging me with a nod.

Dad looked at me questioningly before frowning at him. "Good morning. Do I know you?"

"Of course not," Mr. Burke answered with his creepy half smile. "But I know Skylar, so I assumed you were her father. Right?"

The two men were roughly the same height and Dad stared at Mr. Burke for several long moments without saying anything. When he finally spoke, his words sent a shiver up my spine. "Hello, Edward. It's been a long time, but you haven't changed all that much." Mr. Burke's still mostly frozen features seemed to sag slightly, but he pulled himself to his full height.

"The name is James Burke. I don't know who you confused me with." He glared at Dad, pretending not to know what Dad was talking about.

"You can change how you look, but you're the same Edward Simmons inside, and that's what's shining out of your eyes. You're still a greedy little man."

"I don't know what you're talking about."

"Sure you do, Edward. You didn't think I'd recognize you, or you wouldn't have come out of your office. You were testing your new persona. It didn't work." Dad was baiting him, hoping to force his hand.

"Be careful what you say, Bishop," Burke's voice was a low snarled that I recognized from his calls. "You aren't in your safe little town where you reign as king. You're in my town now."

"Does your town condone murder, embezzlement, land fraud, and identity theft?" Dad didn't bother to keep his voice low.

"I said to be careful what you say here," Burke snapped in return. He looked around quickly, lowering his voice again. "I haven't done anything wrong, and you can't prove I have." He was acting very superior now.

I was aware of Dora watching the unfolding scene in the doorway of her office as well as the other employees, but I couldn't take my eyes off Dad and Mr. Burke. Did anyone realize what was happening? Would Burke get violent if Dad kept pushing him?

"There's no evidence I've done any of the things you're suggesting." His crooked smile was so smug, I wanted to smack it right off his face.

"You forget there's a dead man who's supposed to be you resting in a grave in California. I'm sure the authorities would love to have a discussion with you about that. There's no statute of limitations on murder." Dad sounded as sure of himself as Burke.

Burke's assurance eroded slightly, but he quickly recovered. "There's no proof there either." Now he was taunting Dad.

"You make sure of that every time, don't you, Simmons? Well, you're not going to get away with your scams any longer."

"The name's James Burke." For the first time, he took notice of his employees staring at us. Turning around, he smiled at them. "Get back to work, folks. Show's over. Just a slight disagreement over something long forgotten." Turning to Dad and me, his lopsided smile turned even creepier. "Why don't we continue this in my office? I do so enjoy a disagreement I can't lose."

"Don't do it, Dad." I gripped his arm. "He can't be trusted."

"I have no intention of going anywhere with him. I'm fully aware he can't be trusted." Dad's voice was loud enough now for everyone in the bank to hear him.

"Shut up," Burke snapped. "Keep your voice down. I'm not going to let you ruin my life again."

Dad chuckled, "I didn't ruin your life. You did that all by yourself when you thought you could get away with embezzling."

This time Burke didn't bother telling Dad to keep his voice down. He simply pulled a small gun out of his pocket.

Gasps could be heard throughout the bank along with a few screams. Dad pushed me behind him, keeping himself between me and the gun.

Burke turned to his employees with a smile. “Take it easy, folks. I have this problem well in hand. This man and his daughter came in here to extort money by telling vicious lies about me. I’m just protecting myself. Go back to work. Dora, will you come over here please? And bring your cell phone.” He held out his hand to her as she walked up, waiting for her to place her cell phone in his hand. Reluctantly she complied. He dropped her phone in his pocket, giving her a little shove to stand beside Dad and me.

Chase was leaning against his truck when we stepped out of the bank, and he leaped up, hurrying towards us. “Mr. Bishop...”

“Stay back, Templeton,” James Burke warned. “These are dangerous people, and I’ve made a citizen’s arrest. I’m taking them in.”

“Dangerous?” Chase stared at us. “Skylar and her father aren’t dangerous. Skylar has a winery right here, and her father is from California.” They both ignored Dora. She took a side step, hoping to get away for help.

“That’s just who they want you to think they are,” Burke continued. “Now please stay back.” His hand lashed out, gripping Dora’s arm so tightly she let out a yelp. “Don’t think I forgot about how you’ve been helping these two criminals,” he snarled at her.

“Skylar?” Chase looked at me, in dumbfounded astonishment.

“Do as he says, or you’ll get hurt,” I tried to keep my voice calm but failed. It was shaking as bad as the rest of me. “He has a gun.”

“A gun?” Chase squeaked. “Are you crazy?”

Before anyone could respond, Mayor Brady came out a small doorway I’d never noticed before. “Good morning, everyone.” His voice was as booming as ever. “What’s going on, James?” Was the mayor working with Burke?

"Glad you're here, Mayor Brady. These are the people behind all the trouble our little town has been having. I wouldn't be surprised to find out one of our very own deputies is also involved."

Dora whirled around, but was unable to move very far since he still had an iron grip on her arm. "Greg is no more a criminal than we are." Burke poked his gun in her ribs forcing her to stand still. Dad tried to move her behind him, wanting to protect us both.

"Oh my," Mayor Brady answered calmly. "We'd better call for some help." He pulled his cell phone off his belt, pushing a speed dial number before Burke could stop him.

"What are you doing? Put that thing away. I'm going to handle this myself. Once they're out of the way, we can talk. I'm sure you'll see things my way."

Ignoring him, Mayor Brady put the phone to his ear. "Yes, we have an incident going on in front..." Burke knocked the phone from his hand stomping on it before he could say anything more.

"I said I'd handle this. Now go back inside, or I'll have to take you with us."

"Yes, I see your point, James. I do have pressing business in my office." He turned to leave. My stomach went to my toes. Either the mayor was in cahoots with Burke, or he was a coward, and wanted no part of what was happening.

"Don't bother calling for help when you get back to your office," Burke snarled. "I cut the phone lines before I captured these three." I don't know how many people work in the city offices, or who they are. My only hope now was someone had a cell phone, and would call the sheriff's department. The mayor disappeared through the small door, and we watched him climb the narrow stairs. Why couldn't this window be mirrored like the rest of them in the building, so he could watch what was happening, and Burke couldn't see him?

Once Burke felt certain the mayor had obeyed his orders, he turned back to us. "Okay, now let's go for a little ride, just the four of us. Start walking to her truck over there." He nodded at my big truck across the street. My feet felt rooted to the sidewalk; I couldn't move. Neither did Dad or Dora. "I said move!" He gave Dad a shove hard enough to knock him in to me. I landed on the ground knocking the wind out of me. Dad started to leap at Burke, but the gun was shoved in his face, stopping him from moving.

Out of nowhere, Chase and Mayor Brady both tackled Burke, the three of them landing in a heap beside me. The gun was still in his hand, but not for long. Dad stomped on his wrist, and Dora managed to drive the spike from her high-heeled shoe into the back of his hand. Burke screamed, dropping the gun. I kicked it out of his reach. Somehow, each of us helped to take him out of commission.

We could hear sirens wail in the distance. I hoped this was finally over. I didn't think Burke would be able to wiggle his way out of trouble this time.

CHAPTER TWENTY-ONE

Two weeks later, Burke was still in jail. Even with evidence mounting up against him, he continued to proclaim his innocence. "I'm not sure we'll find out about everything he's done over the years," Greg told the family as we sat around the table in our kitchen. "He demands we call him James Burke, not Edward Simmons. He says he has no idea who that is, or why you say that's his name. Since no charges were filed against him all those years ago, his fingerprints aren't in the system. As it stands right now, we're only going to be able to tie him to the crimes here." To simplify things we chose to call him Burke instead of trying to decide between Burke and Simmons.

"I thought by giving him a break, he'd turn his life around onto the straight and narrow. Instead he just learned how to pull off his crimes without getting caught." Dad sighed in frustration. We had the phone on speaker like we did every night, so we could all participate in the conversation. He wasn't going to relax until Simmons was behind bars for good.

"Has he said anything you can use against him?" Joe asked.

Greg shook his head. "The only thing he'll say is he's innocent; Skylar and Clay are framing him. Says they came into the bank trying to extort money from him," he chuckled. "He has one little problem with that statement. Everyone in the bank that day has given statements. They all agree you didn't even speak to Burke until he came out of his office, and he approached you. Of course, he says they're all lying." He shook his head. "I don't know if he's trying for an insanity plea or what, but it's not going to work."

My stomach churned at the thought. If he got off with an insanity plea, he was smart enough to convince the doctors he was well in just a few years. Then he'd start his schemes all over again. He'd have even more reason to come after Dad and me.

"Have the feds told you what was in the bank safe deposit boxes?" Dora asked. When Greg and his team searched Burke's house they found three safe deposit keys. The boxes were "rented" to nonexistent customers. They matched accounts in the same names, accounts with pretty hefty balances. This brought in bank auditors and federal examiners.

"Yeah," Greg answered. "He had several phony passports, Articles of Incorporation for a lot of dummy corporations, probably the same ones he tried to bury himself behind when he tried to steal your winery." He leaned over, placing a light kiss on my lips before continuing. "There were also a lot of land deeds for properties all over Arizona, New Mexico and California. He's been working his scams for a lot of years, reselling the property to himself before the rightful owners discover what happened to them."

"What about Mayor Brady and Gerald Williams? Were they involved?" I asked. "Everything pointed to them at first, and the mayor was so against you taking over as sheriff. What was that all about?"

Greg shook his head. "Yeah, he wanted to be able to control whoever got in as sheriff. That wasn't Jim Stevens, and it's not me; but the mayor didn't have anything to do with Burke and his scams. His old man is a big time land developer in Phoenix, but Brady didn't want to work. He was more into the playboy life style. After dropping out of college he bummed around Europe until he ran out of money. His dad wouldn't bail him out; for the first time in his life he had to work for a living."

He chuckled. "Even then he didn't get his wake up call. After he moved back to the states, his dad still wouldn't give him any money. The man's fifty some years old, and he's still trying to win his dad's approval."

"We all want our parent's approval, Son, no matter how old we are. Especially when it's been withheld most of our lives," Dad said.

Greg nodded understanding before going on. "He finally decided being a small town mayor would give him the prestige he's always wanted while giving him the opportunity to make his own land deals. He's been buying up land in these parts since he moved here. He even wanted this place, but you beat him to it, Dad. He wants to build a fancy resort, make New Haven the next big vacation spot in Arizona. The wineries are a good draw for the tourists; he figured we needed someplace big and splashy for them to stay. He didn't want anything getting out until he had it all sown up, afraid the other land owners, or the county supervisors wouldn't go along with him. He wanted it to be a fait accompli before anyone found out."

So that was what he meant by putting our little county on the map, I thought, but didn't say anything. There was still a lot we didn't know, and as long as Greg was willing to fill us in, I needed to listen.

"As for Williams," Greg was saying, "we know now he'd been doing some of Burke's dirty work for a long time. Burke didn't want a strong sheriff who might find out what he was doing. Using Brady's own desire for secrecy against him, Williams fed the mayor a bunch of lies about Jim, and me after I moved here. Brady didn't bother checking out anything the man told him. He confessed all this to the town council, and offered his resignation. They convinced him to stay on. He'll probably be more careful in the future, as will most of the people in town."

"I can't believe how we were all taken in by Burke." Dora said, shaking her head. "I even felt sorry for the little weasel when he was in the hospital. He didn't fake that, did he?" She turned to Pattiann. "Was he really sick?"

She chuckled. "Yeah, he really messed up with those Botox treatments; he nearly died."

"That was another reason I didn't think he was Edward Simmons," Greg picked up the conversation. "He was in the hospital when the scam on Skylar went down."

"So who sent the emails and faxes while he was in the hospital?" Joe asked.

"Probably Williams. Since this all broke, we've discovered Williams visited him in the hospital at least once. Nurses now tell us Burke had a laptop while he was in there, and spent a lot of time on it. I suspect it was the one the mayor found in his trunk. Burke had a key to the mayor's Town Car locked in his desk at the bank. He probably planted the laptop to implicate Williams, and maybe even the mayor. Right now it's all guess work." Greg ran his fingers through his dark hair in frustration. "I can't believe how close I came to arresting the mayor. Burke is truly diabolical in his convoluted thinking."

"That's what I'm afraid of," Dad said. "Is he going to be able to talk his way out of this? Or claim insanity. A couple of years in a mental health facility, and he'll be out. He'll disappear the minute that happens. I don't want him to come after Skylar if they let him out." He voiced my own fears.

"No chance of that," Greg assured him. "Like I said, the Feds are all over him. Interstate racketeering is what they're looking at. He won't get away."

CHAPTER TWENTY-TWO

It was finally our turn; our big day was here! The time had gone by so fast while at the same time, so slow. So much had been happening in our small community and our lives, there'd been little time to think of much else, I'd wondered if this day would ever arrive.

"You're a beautiful bride," Dad smiled at me. "I'm so proud of you. I wish only happiness for you and Greg." He kissed my cheek. "You ready?"

I took a deep breath, releasing it slowly. "I feel like I've been waiting for this moment for a very long time. We haven't known each other as long as you and Molly, but I know it's right. Let's get this done."

Joe was waiting for us as we stepped out of the room set up for brides and their attendants to dress. For my entire life, Joe has been there for me, helping me grow as much as Dad has. It was only right to have both of them walk me down the aisle. Pattiann and Dora were waiting for us at the sanctuary door. Jim Stevens' health had improved enough so he could stand as Greg's best man along with another deputy.

The three men stood straight and tall at the front of the church waiting for us as first Pattiann then Dora preceded Dad, Joe, and me down the aisle. I was barely aware of anyone else there; I couldn't take my eyes off Greg. My heart was trying to beat its way out of my chest. In his dark suit and sparkling white shirt, he was the most handsome man in the universe. I'm not even sure how many people were in the small church, I only saw Greg. Only later did I realize every winery owner, vintner, and every person I had ever met in town had shown up. Somehow our wedding had become the social event of the year.

Weather in southeastern Arizona in April can be iffy sometimes, but God was smiling on us. The temperature was in the mid-seventies at three o'clock allowing us to spread out onto the pavilion between the church sanctuary and the meeting hall. The gentle breeze was welcome, instead of the sometimes fierce wind that can blow across the soft rolling hills. A DJ had set up a table, and was playing requests from the guests. Some people were dancing on the wooden plank flooring installed over the grass.

"You're the most beautiful bride in the world," Greg whispered as we swayed to the music. "Thank you for making me so happy." He kissed me, and I didn't care if the entire world was watching.

"You're welcome, sir. You've made me pretty darn happy, too." I smiled up at him. I felt like I was floating on air.

Instead of going to Hawaii like Joe and Dora and Dad and Molly, we chose something closer to home. Greg still had a campaign to finish. We left our guests to finish dancing and eating, and headed for the beautiful Lowes Resort and Spa in Tucson for three days in our own little paradise. I couldn't wait to start married life with Greg.

ACKNOWLEDGEMENT

I thank God for all He's given me and the ability to write this book. Without Him I could do nothing. I also want to thank Karyl Wilhelm of Wilhelm Family Vineyard for all her help with everything vineyard and winery related. Any mistakes or exaggerations are mine and not any fault of Karyl's.

I also want to thank Diane Scott, Irene Morris and Gerry Beamon for all their editing skills. Ladies your help and encouragement is greatly appreciated.

OTHER BOOKS BY SUZANNE FLOYD

Revenge Served Cold
Rosie's Revenge
A Game of Cat and Mouse
Man on the Run
Trapped in a Whirlwind
Smoke & Mirrors
Plenty of Guilt
Lost Memories
Something Shady
Rosie's Secret
Killer Instincts
Never Con A Con Man
The Games People Play

More Books Coming Soon

All of my books are available at Amazon.com in either e-book or paperback.

Dear Reader:

Thank you for reading my book. I hope you enjoyed reading it as much as I enjoyed writing it. If you enjoyed Killer Instincts, I would appreciate it if you would tell your friends and family. As an independently published author, I hope you will consider leaving a review on Amazon and Goodreads. I also appreciate any feedback you choose to give me. Thank you. Check out my other books at:

Like me on Facebook at Suzanne Floyd Author, or check out my website at SuzanneFloyd.com.

Thank you,
Suzanne Floyd

P.S. If you find any errors, please let me know at: Suzanne.sfloyd@gmail.com. Before publishing, many people have read this book, but minds can play tricks by supplying words that are missing and correcting typos. I would enjoy hearing from my readers, and you can follow me on Facebook at Suzanne Floyd Author.

Thanks again for reading my book.

ABOUT THE AUTHOR

Suzanne is an internationally known author. She was born in Iowa, and moved to Arizona with her family when she was nine years old. She still lives in Phoenix with her husband Paul. They have two wonderful daughters, two great sons-in-law and five of the best grandchildren around. Of course, she is just a little prejudiced.

Growing up and traveling with her parents, she entertained herself by making up stories. As an adult she tried writing, but family came first. After retiring in 2008, she decided it was her time. She still enjoys making up stories, and thanks to the internet she's able to put them online for others to enjoy.

When Suzanne isn't writing, she and her husband enjoy traveling around on their 2010 Honda Goldwing trike. She's always looking for new places to write about. There's always a new mystery and a new romance lurking out there to capture her attention.